the convenience store by the sea

sonoko machida

the convenience store by the sea

sonoko machida

Translated by Bruno Navasky

ORION

First published in Japanese as *Konbini Kyodai: Tenderness Moji-ko Koganemura-ten* in 2020 by SHINCHOSHA Publishing Co., Ltd. English translation rights arranged with SHINCHOSA Publishing Co., Ltd., Tokyo in care of Tuttle-Mori Agency, Inc., Tokyo.

An Orion Paperback
First published in Great Britain in 2024 by Orion Fiction, an imprint of The Orion Publishing Group Ltd. Carmelite House, 50 Victoria Embankment London EC4Y 0DZ

An Hachette UK Company

1 3 5 7 9 10 8 6 4 2

A CIP catalogue record for this book is available from the British Library.

ISBN (Mass Market Paperback) 9781 3987 2277 4
ISBN (Ebook) 9781 3987 2278 1
ISBN (Audio) 9781 3987 2279 8

Typeset by Born Group
Printed and bound in Great Britain by Clays Ltd, Elcograf S.p.A.

MIX
Paper | Supporting
responsible forestry
FSC
www.fsc.org
FSC® C104740

Prologue

'Hey, I'm here! Over here!'

'No, me! Look at me!'

A wave of screams washed over me, as if I were standing in the front row at a pop star's concert, and I recoiled automatically. The plastic bottle I was holding slipped from my grasp, but I couldn't move to pick it up. A crowd of women pressed forward, dressed to kill, fluttering like butterflies around a beautiful flower. Um, wasn't this supposed to be a plain old convenience store?

I looked around. As I did, I rewound my mental tape and thought back on how I had come to be here.

It all started when I got my driving licence and bought a second-hand compact car. It was a boxy black microvan – I called it 'Pipienne'. Pipienne was a pet name I had been holding on to, a special something that I knew I'd call my car once I finally had it. I had been dying for a car of my own, and dreaming forever about taking myself for a drive, which you could probably guess from the fact that I had a name for my car ready and waiting.

On the first holiday after I bought the car – a perfect sunny day right in the middle of the Golden Week holidays – I left my house in high spirits, ready to make my dreams come true.

I decided that for my first drive, I'd go solo. I'd play my own tunes, go where I wanted, free as a bird without worrying about anyone. I headed out of Kumamoto and promptly decided to hop on the expressway heading north towards Fukuoka.

I thought I'd go shopping in Hakata, and then swing by Dazaifu Tenmangu Shrine on the way home. They have fresh plum-blossom cakes there, and I could get some. I was happy as a clam and getting close to Hakata when I pulled into the Kiyama parking area for a rest stop. Then, before I knew it, everything changed, and I was ready to explode. I had texted a friend before heading out, and the reply had arrived:

'So you're probably going to Hakata, right? Kyūshū people all head to Hakata at the drop of a hat! It's such a joke.' All I had written was that I was going to have fun driving today, but he was obviously mocking me. If it hadn't been my own phone I would have smashed it on the ground.

'You're just jealous because you're still stuck with your learner's permit . . .' I began to tap an angry reply, sputtering and cursing, but then I stopped. It was true I had been heading to Hakata, but now it was the last place in the world I could go. He'd make twice as much fun of me. Damn, I shouldn't have been in such a rush to send that text.

Now I had to pick a new destination. Groaning, I pored over the map on my phone. As I was searching the map and racking my brain about where to go, my fingertip grazed a location.

'Mojikō . . .'

It was a place I'd heard of. I thought it was a fairly well-known tourist destination, but I'd never been there. It had an area called the Retro District, and the streets were supposed to be lovely. What else . . .? I couldn't remember, but after thinking about it a little, I decided it was my new destination. At times like these, you have to follow your heart.

Two hours later I was giving my heart a nice round of applause, having arrived in Mojikō without incident. Adorable retro buildings by the glittering sea, the sound of rickshaws rolling by – I heard a lively voice, and as I turned, a man hawking bananas called out to me. The bananas, a perfect bright yellow, shone as if they had absorbed all the sunlight streaming down on them.

It's awesome here, I thought. *I'd love to take a walk with a boyfriend here someday, if I ever have one. Or maybe even just a lame friend who's still stuck with his learner's permit.* Everywhere I turned I found something fun, so I just wandered around, totally absorbed.

May had barely begun, but it felt like a perfect summer day. I had another local speciality for dinner – baked curry *au gratin* – and afterwards I felt like having some tea. I noticed a convenience store nearby, so I went in.

Whenever I go somewhere new, I can't help thinking what strange places convenience stores are. No matter the town, you just have to step inside and the space transforms into something nostalgic, full of familiar comforts. Even if it was just the same products lined up in the same aisles of the same interior, somehow it gave you a sense of security.

3

My high spirits calming just a little bit, I pulled a plastic bottle of my favourite brand of green tea from the beverage section. I headed towards the register, and there, set out before me, was a sight that I've never seen before at any convenience store.

A group of women were crowded around the checkout counter, decked out in such nice clothes that I wondered if they were on their way to a dance. There was a man at the counter and they all seemed crazy about him. Maybe he was the clerk? He was wearing that kind of uniform, in pastel pink and light brown, so I was pretty sure. But he was so ridiculously attractive it was hard to believe he was a clerk, and he was radiating what could only be called 'sex appeal'. Were they shooting a movie or something? I had heard Kitakyūshū was famous for its great film locations. I looked around, but there was nothing resembling a film crew.

The male clerk smiled softly.

'Thank you as always,' he said to one customer. 'Ah, there's something different about you today, isn't there?'

'Oh, Mr Shiba, you noticed, didn't you! I changed my lipstick.'

'Yes, of course. You look cuter than ever thanks to those cherry-coloured lips, I have to say.'

'Mr Shiba, look at me too! I changed my nails today. Look, look! What do you think?'

'Ah, Miss Yūko. It's true, they look like jellybeans. Good enough to eat!'

He smiled sweetly. The clamour echoing through the store was loud enough that I wanted to cover my ears. Were they mobbing a pop star? What had I stumbled into, and why?

4

All I remembered was stepping into a regular convenience store. I was starting to wonder if my mind was playing tricks on me.

'Uh, Miss? I can help you over here.'

I heard a flat voice and came to my senses. Was the alien abduction over, then? I picked up the plastic bottle, which was lying by my feet, and when I looked up, there was a man at the other register looking my way. It must have been him calling me. He looked around the same age as me, so he was probably a college student, working part time. I don't want to be rude, but compared to the other man, his face was dull and ordinary. If he were in a TV show, he'd be an extra.

In a sort of trance, I stepped up to the register so the clerk – his name tag read 'Hirose' – could ring me up my purchase. But all the while, this wild scene was playing out right next to us. It was insane. I had to know what was going on. I turned to Hirose, who was working his register expressionlessly, and asked in a low voice, 'Um, is that a photoshoot or something?' He started to laugh. Then his face got sort of philosophical, as if he had resigned himself to something.

'Nope, it's nothing like that. It happens every day here.'

'Every day . . .?'

Hirose gave a small nod, put a 'paid' sticker on the bottle, and handed me my change. Bottle in hand, I took another look at the scene next to us. The women had seemed friendly enough at first, but now the atmosphere had started to turn hostile. The woman with the jellybean fingernails had held them to the manager's mouth, saying, 'Go ahead, taste them!' and someone else had told her – sharply – that she was behaving shamelessly.

'Please, don't fight! I want to see you all smiling.'

The man looked troubled, and the women tried to smile. But the more they tried to compose themselves and out-smile each other, the stiffer they looked. Of course, I'd seen this kind of stand-off between classmates, but was this the norm here? I looked at Hirose, questioningly, and he silently nodded. Seriously?

I felt like I wanted to hang out a little longer as a spectator, but it was getting late. If I didn't head for Kumamoto soon, it would be midnight by the time I got home. Reluctantly, I pulled myself away from the checkout, towards the automatic doors at the front of the shop.

'Thank you for coming!'

As I stepped outside, a voice that wasn't Hirose's came floating from behind after me, and I glanced back. That male clerk was looking my way and smiling. His gaze seemed to caress nerves hidden deep under the skin of my back, and a shiver ran down my spine. I dropped the plastic bottle again, and it started to roll. Flustered, I chased it to the middle of the car park and hurriedly gathered it up. When I looked up, he was still watching me, his full lips curving in a gentle arc. My heart skipped a beat.

'Please come again!'

Just as the quiet but assured voice reached me, the automatic door closed again, as if to separate us.

I stood motionless in the middle of the car park. Should I go back inside? Somehow I had the feeling that to enter again would be like falling into a bottomless pit. What should I do?

The automatic door slid open again, startling me.

'Hey now, if you're going to fight, it's time to go home!'

Exiting the shop were the same ladies from before, shooed along by a fierce, muscular old man who looked sort of like a Daruma doll. He was dressed strangely, in a white tank top and bright red overalls. All in all, it was a pretty bizarre look.

'Buy what you're buying, then it's time to go! Got it?' said the old man loudly. He looked at the women menacingly, as if he might just gobble each of them up, and they screamed, scattered and ran off. He snickered as he watched them go, and then our eyes met. 'And you?' he said, eyebrows raised, apparently thinking I was one of the ladies. 'Go home!' he growled.

'I—I'm going!'

What sort of place was this convenience store?! First I was lured in by a gorgeous clerk, then chased away by that demon of an old man – I was totally lost. I turned tail and ran for it with all my might, towards where I had left Pipienne in the car park. But as I ran, I found myself already thinking about when I would come back.

'Please come again!' he had said. I wanted to see that smiling face again. I wanted to get to the bottom of that smile.

As I sped through Mojikō Port, I worried about the sea of love that seemed to have washed over me.

Chapter One

My Convenience is Your Convenience

Mitsuri Nakao was living a full life. She'd married her college sweetheart seventeen years ago, and with her son, a high-school student, they were a family of three. She worried a little about her son – he was in a rebellious phase – but otherwise she hadn't a care in the world. She got along with her husband, her in-laws lived in the neighbouring prefecture, close but not too close, and her own parents were in good health as well. She and her husband had purchased a single-family home eleven years ago, which was modest but comfortable, and they were regular with the mortgage payments. A few years ago, she'd taken on a part-time job at a local convenience store to supplement their income, and it was all going well there. Actually, it had been going much better than well: the benefits there far outstripped the salary.

Anyway, for now, let's just say that Mitsuri Nakao was living a full life.

★

'I see the line-up is changing next month,' announced Nomiya, Mitsuri's part-time colleague, as he peered at the digital tablet in her hand. She was busy restocking. 'Cold soba noodles and chilled Chinese ramen. Oh, I get it. These are the summer items.'

'It's almost July,' she replied. 'Came on fast, didn't it?'

'Tenderness has the best ramen of all the convenience stores,' said Nomiya. 'It's got a fantastic balance of flavours and textures. Although the portions are on the delicate side, so I have to have two.'

Nomiya was a first-year student at Kyūshū Kyōritsu University. He'd started part-time at Tenderness when he enrolled. He used to be on the wrestling team, so his body was bulging with muscles, and though the store issued him an oversized uniform, his chest and shoulders always seemed about to burst through it. Apparently he had won no end of tournaments during high school.

Kyūshū Kyōritsu's team was a real powerhouse, but Nomiya gave it up when he left high school and wouldn't say why. Mitsuri, for her part, didn't feel the need to bother him about it.

She turned to Nomiya. 'I'm surprised! I'd have thought your regular go-to would be the beef bowl with summer vegetables.'

For young men, the beef bowl was the big winner on the summer menu. The charcoal-grilled beef and colourful array of vegetables were appealing to the eye, and it had more rice than the regular bento box lunches, so it was very satisfying.

'Nope, that one's special. But yeah, the rice at Tenderness is also really good. The white rice.'

'Well, that's because we take a lot of care with it. Bento, desserts – all the food, really.'

Mitsuri tapped confidently at the numbers on her hand-held screen as she replied. She had been working at the Golden Villa Tenderness branch in Mojikō for four years now, and had a good sense for how every product there would sell.

Tenderness was a convenience-store chain that operated only in Kyūshū. Their motto was 'Caring for People, Caring for You', and as far as convenience chains went, they were second to none. The Golden Villa Tenderness branch was about halfway down Ōsakamachi Avenue in Mojikō, the harbour district of the city of Kitakyūshū, on the ground floor of the Golden Villa apartment building. It was located in a quiet neighbourhood, slightly removed from the Station House and former Mitsui Social Club in the sightseeing area of the old port town, famous for its retro architecture. Patrons tended to be locals more often than tourists.

A gentle music-box melody drifted through the store when the automatic doors slid open and shut, signalling the arrival of a customer. The two of them turned their heads towards the door, just as an old man in a white tank top and bright red overalls came in. It would still be a while before the rainy season was officially over, but the man was dressed for high summer. He sported a beard that obscured half his face, had a bald head, and there was a sharp glint in his eye. The arms jutting out of his tank top were broad and muscular. He was tall, and his eyes swept the shop interior with an intimidating glare. But when he spotted Mitsuri and her colleague, his fierce demeanour brightened, and he patted each one gently on the head.

'Hallo, hallo!' he said. 'You're looking sweet as always, Mitsuri.'

'Good morning, Shōhei!' she replied. 'How are things in town?'

'Hmm, looked to me like a lot of tour groups in from China today. They said they're visiting the area around the station and then off to Karato via the Kanmon Ferry.'

Shōhei Umeda was a local celebrity. He pedalled all over town with a stack of homemade sightseeing maps of Mojikō in the rack of his bright red cargo bike. He looked intimidating, even scary, but because of his unconventional appearance and unexpectedly friendly demeanour, the local children were all fond of him, and called him 'Old Red'.

'They asked me if I was an actor!' he said with pride. 'Well now, I've been mistaken for a movie star more than once in my life. I can't help that.'

If Mitsuri had to say, she actually thought that with his bald head, beard and fierce gaze, he looked more like Bodhidharma, the famously cranky ancient Zen priest. So much so, in fact, that one could be forgiven for thinking the historic character had been reincarnated right here in Mojikō.

'They all wanted to take a picture with me. I was mobbed, and I ran out of maps. Now I've got to go home and print some more.' Shōhei chortled like a movie villain, which was just everyday behaviour for him. 'So that's it for today's patrol,' he said apologetically.

Shōhei was the self-proclaimed tourism ambassador for Mojikō. And a self-appointed guardian angel as well, maintaining peace in the neighbourhood. While he was pedalling around, handing out his tourist maps, he often stopped by the store when he needed a break.

SONOKO MACHIDA

'Nothing to worry about here, Shōhei,' Mitsuri said, laughing, 'the store manager is off today.'

'Oh, is he?' Shōhei replied, his face brightening. 'It's quiet when he's away.'

'Exactly. So we're okay.'

'In that case, I'll head home with no worries. Well, see you.' With a nod of satisfaction, Shōhei hopped on his cargo bike and off he rode.

'Take care, Shōhei!' Nomiya called after him with feeling. Shōhei was a dynamo, always bursting with energy, perhaps because he rode his cargo bike day in, day out, no matter the weather. People said he was well over eighty, but his skin had a radiant glow to it, and when he pedalled past on his cargo bike there was not a hint of weakness in those leg muscles. *When I grow old, I'd like to be rugged like that*, she thought.

The door melody played again, and when she looked over, another older man had come into the shop, this one very thin, and leaning on a cane. The man mopped the sweat from his temples with a towel and, spotting Mitsuri and Nomiya, made a curt grunt of recognition.

'Good day, Mr Urata! It's hotter than usual, isn't it?' Nomiya raised his voice in greeting, but Urata's face puckered into a frown. Urata lived alone in the neighbourhood, and unlike Shōhei, he had a difficult disposition. Perhaps Nomiya's bright and cheerful demeanour bothered him, but he never failed to find fault with him.

'No need for you to shout, young man, my hearing is just fine. If you have so much extra energy, why don't you go get some exercise instead of grubbing for spare change here?' He spoke sternly, shaking the tip of his cane at Nomiya. 'Look sharp, now. I came to eat. Hop to it and get my lunch ready.'

Nomiya pursed his lips for a moment in annoyance, then quickly covered it over with a smile.

'Right. One lunch special, coming right up!'

Nomiya dashed to the fridge in the stockroom to retrieve a bento, while Mitsuri called out to Urata, 'Please wait over here.' Without waiting for his reply, she walked over to the dine-in area, which was separated from the store by a doorway.

It wasn't particularly roomy behind the register. Nomiya returned holding a bento and a bottle of tea, wedged his expansive physique into the narrow space to heat the food in the microwave, recorded the entry on a checksheet, and then headed to the dining area, where Urata was waiting.

'Well, it should be getting pretty busy soon,' Mitsuri murmured softly, checking the clock. Urata always led the charge, then around the time he was about to finish, the rest of the seniors would trickle in one by one.

The Tenderness offered a service called 'Yellow Flag Lunch'. For a flat fee, participants received a bento lunch special each day. The service was particularly popular with older customers. The store changed the ingredients daily, of course, to keep it interesting, but the primary selling point for the seniors was that they got to tell everyone how they were feeling that day.

The apartments on floors two to seven of the Golden Villa building were reserved for senior citizens. Originally the lunch service focused on these building residents. It spared them the trouble of preparing lunch and gave them a place to socialise when they took their meals in the private lounge next to Tenderness, now open to the public as a dine-in area. Also, it served as an early-warning system if the unexpected should befall any of the residents. That was the original idea, but slowly and steadily, the number of participants had increased to include area residents from outside the building. Urata was one of these.

'I'm back.' Nomiya returned with an unhappy look on his face. It wasn't hard to imagine that Urata must have had something to do with it. Before Mitsuri could ask, he muttered, 'Am I annoying? He yelled at me. He said having a useless muscle-bound fool standing next to him made the food taste bad. He told me to get lost.'

Nomiya had a delicate, sensitive nature that existed in inverse proportion to his massive frame. The slightest word from a customer would wound him and cause him to brood. Mitsuri tried to help, telling him to lighten up and take it easy, but it seemed he was unable to take her advice.

'Mr Urata is rough on everyone. Don't beat yourself up about it.'

'Yeah, but it's hard when people speak to a person that way! Does he have to act superior to everyone just because he's older?' Nomiya balled up his fists, biceps swelling as they tensed. 'I don't like talking like this, but that old—'

'Okay, okay. Enough.'

Nomiya paused. Fortunately the store was empty, but they couldn't get in the habit of voicing their grievances so lightly. Nomiya made an unhappy face, but kept his mouth shut. 'Sorry,' he said, and bowed his head, 'I went too far.'

'I understand how you feel, but try to keep your cool, okay?' She gave him a sweet smile, and Nomiya returned the smile, stiffly. One of the nice things about Nomiya was his straightforward, unaffected manner.

The door melody rang out, and a flashy young man entered the shop. He was an employee of a hair salon about a five-minute walk away. He grabbed a ham, cheese and lettuce sandwich and a couple of energy drinks and placed them on the counter in front of Nomiya. Even from a distance, they could see his hands were painfully red and cracked. He had only joined the salon as an apprentice four months ago, so he must be spending all his days shampooing, Mitsuri thought.

'Oh, may I also have a box of fried chicken, please?'

'Got it, one fried chicken box.'

Nomiya briskly punched it up on the cash register. As he took a fried chicken box from the fryer shelf next to him, Mitsuri thought to herself, *I'd really like to toss in an extra piece for him!*

Maybe it was because she was getting older, but lately when she saw hard-working young people, she always wanted to give them a leg up. Particularly this young man, with his pretty face and gaudy dyed hair, so common among the new crop of hairdressers, but which suited him well. He looked a little like a character in a manga comic book that she was currently obsessed with. Actually, she thought, she'd like to give him two extra pieces of chicken.

She was watching his slim figure from behind as he paid his bill and turned to leave the store, when the young man suddenly stopped in his tracks.

'Oh! Mr Shiba!' A figure entered through the dine-in area, and recognising him, the young hairdresser called out to him gaily. The man, dressed in street clothes instead of his uniform, was none other than Mitsuhiko Shiba, the store manager.

The manager was tall, with the slender proportions of a model. And his style, well, even though he was just wearing a commonplace white shirt, chinos and sandals, he somehow managed to make it look fashionable.

'Hey there, Ayumu. Taking your break?'

'Yes, exactly!'

The young man – Ayumu, apparently – ran over, radiating happiness. Watching Shiba smiling gently at him, Mitsuri murmured quietly to herself: 'Hm. An unexpected turn of events.'

'Mr Shiba, please come to the salon soon! They tell me my shampoo technique has got really good, but you never come to see me.'

'Ah, I'm so sorry! – it's been difficult to get away. But I can tell from looking at your hands, Ayumu, that you've been giving it your all.'

Shiba took Ayumu's hand in his own. As he gently traced the fissures with his fingertips, Ayumu's cheeks blushed a deep red.

'You've already got the hands of a hairdresser,' said Shiba. 'I'll come visit soon.'

'Oh good. I'm looking forward to it so much! I'll be waiting.'

Ayumu gazed at Shiba adoringly. Shiba accepted the loving gaze as if it were the most natural thing in the world and replied, 'I hope work goes well this afternoon,' his white teeth gleaming as he smiled. Nodding repeatedly in response, Ayumu left the store, holding the hand that Shiba had touched elevated in front of him as if it were a great treasure.

Mitsuri, who had been carefully watching the entire sequence of events, was at a loss for words, and let out a deep sigh. The Phero-Manager had stolen this young man's heart and didn't even know it.

'Phero-Manager' was Mitsuri's private nickname for Shiba. He had a sort of mysterious magnetism that made him intensely attractive, so much so that she imagined invisible pheromones – love hormones – pouring out of him like water from a fountain. She didn't know for sure if it was flowing in his blood or baked into his soul, but one thing was certain: he was completely different from ordinary people. Mitsuri sometimes imagined there was a special pump inside of him, spraying out doses of pheromones on a regular basis.

Shiba's face wasn't perfect. His double-lidded eyes were of slightly different sizes and his full lips, perhaps a tad too sensual, left an unbalanced impression. But their exquisite incongruity, together with his tender shifts of expression, gave off an uncanny sort of sex appeal, like a female impersonator dancing in the Kabuki theatre. The scent of flower nectar seemed to follow him around, and his voice was strangely sweet as well and made her ears hum. Mitsuri was no expert in shiatsu massage, but she was pretty sure that if she squeezed him, pheromones would start to drip out of him, like water from a sponge.

When Mitsuri sat with Shiba in his office for her job interview four years back, she worried that she had come to the wrong store. It was hard to believe that the man in front of her was a convenience-store manager. But their conversation was normal, and there was nothing strange about the job description. She definitely recalled feeling confused, trying to process all the different signals coming into her brain.

As it turned out, Shiba was a typical hired manager, no more, no less. She wondered for a while if there could be something going on between him and the owner, due to his exceptional personal appeal, but the Golden Villa building was owned by a man in his seventies with a loving wife, which seemed to rule that out. Shiba could come across as a bit of a smooth operator, but he took his work seriously. In fact, one could say he worked too hard.

Mitsuri once asked Shiba why he took the job. After all, there must have been plenty of work where he could profit from his special hold on people's feelings. She wasn't knocking convenience stores, but it did seem like a waste of his charm, which some might call a special skill. With a telling smile, Shiba responded simply: 'I like convenience stores.' Clearly there was something he wasn't saying. She glared at him, thinking there had to be another reason, but she hadn't yet managed to uncover it.

After seeing Ayumu off, Shiba slowly turned and smiled. 'Good work today, Nomiya, Nakao.' But in contrast to Ayumu, Mitsuri and Nomiya's expressions didn't shift. 'Thanks. You too,' they replied. The one essential condition for working at Tenderness was some degree of resistance to Shiba's allure.

'Mr Shiba, you're here on your day off?' Mitsuri asked.

The owner let Shiba rent a studio apartment on the fourth floor of the building. With work just downstairs it was an easy commute, but Mitsuri always thought it seemed too close for comfort.

'It's almost time for lunch. I was thinking I might join everyone.' Shiba gestured towards the room next door.

'Huh?' Nomiya cried out in disbelief. 'Sir, don't you want any privacy? You're there all the time. Now even on your days off?'

'At this point we're the only ones that offer the Yellow Flag lunch service. So I got curious about how it's going.'

'Oh right. It was someone's suggestion, wasn't it?' asked Nomiya. 'Um, what was the name? Itako? Sasebo? It was one of the commenters, I remember that much.'

'Niseko. It was Niseko.'

The founder and chairman of the Tenderness chain, a man named Horinouchi, had set up a PO box for suggestions, and the idea for the lunch service had come from a letter to the suggestion box.

The chairman promised the customers their voices would be heard, and actually read every letter that came in. Among these, one 'Niseko' was a regular. Niseko's opinions were spelled out carefully, down to the most remote details, each time. Things like 'Branch X in Fukuoka is next to a boys' school, so they should stock more sports drinks and oversize bento', or 'Branch Y in Saga offers a lot of toys and penny candy, so the neighbourhood elementary-school students are happy', and so on. Whoever Niseko was, it seemed that he or she must travel all over Kyūshū for work, since their local knowledge was so extensive. This Niseko had written a letter asking if we knew of a movement called the 'Yellow Flag Campaign'.

The original Yellow Flag Campaign was a programme for seniors, in which people who lived alone hung a yellow flag from morning to evening on their balconies or rooftops – somewhere easy to see from outside – so their neighbours would know they were okay. If a flag wasn't raised or lowered at the appointed time, someone who noticed the irregularity could visit the home and make sure its occupant was safe.

'Of course hanging a yellow flag is all well and good,' wrote Niseko, 'but it also creates a risk: a person of ill intent may see the flag, and learn that the house is home to an older person on their own. If a person picked up a box lunch every day instead of hanging a flag, the risk would be reduced, plus they would have an additional benefit as well: deeper social interaction.'

The chairman was quite taken with this idea, and the Mojikō branch was selected for the trial programme. On his orders, Shiba quickly made the rounds of the building's residential floors, knocking at every door. Naturally, he signed up quite a few participants, far exceeding the minimum specified by headquarters, and they began to plan. The trial launched smoothly, with no major issues, and had grown to the point where it was slated to expand to other locations at the end of the year.

Mitsuri figured that since he'd put so much effort into getting everything up and running smoothly, he'd be ready for a break, but Shiba still hung out with the seniors and acted as a conversation partner, even during his free time.

Nomiya was put out by the attention the letters received from the chairman. 'Doesn't it bug you that he calls Niseko his *counsellor*?' he asked Shiba, looking annoyed. 'You do all the real work.' But Shiba just smiled.

The women gathered around Shiba, blushing like young girls. He smiled at each one in turn, and said, 'Shall we go next door? If we stay here we'll bother the other customers.'

'Yes, yes!' said the ladies, in their sweetest voices. 'Mrs Nakao, may we have the ladies' bento lunches, please?'

'Yes, of course.'

Mitsuri took the checksheet and gave a quick scan of the ladies' faces. As she checked them off the list, she listened to their chatter as they filed into the adjoining room. – *Will reservations be open soon for summer eel? I'm going to order two. – Really? I'm getting five, myself. I'll give a few to my daughter and her husband. – Oh, Mrs Kimoto, is it okay to order that many? – Well, we're getting eight, I think. – Dearie, you'll eat with us, won't you?*

'That's our Phero-Manager,' Mitsuri said under her breath. It looked like sales would be good again, if things kept on like this. She giggled as the door melody rang out once more, and glanced over as a man lumbered slowly in.

Oh, the Whatever Guy, Mitsuri thought to herself. The man was one of the store's regulars. He had shaggy hair, and a beard like Shōhei's fully covering the bottom half of his face. He always wore a light green coverall – it was possibly his only outfit – with white bubble letters on the back reading, 'Whatever Guy'. His customary ride was a white mini-truck, now sitting in the store's car park. On the tailgate was written: 'Junk Removal – Leave Your Problems to the Whatever Guy!' The truck was always loaded with old fridges and broken-limbed mannequins, so he must have been a junkman. She wasn't sure about the 'problems' part.

The man always spent a long time in the store. He worked his way through the aisles, looking at everything from the book corner to the beverage section to the house-hold items. She kept a close eye on him at first, but it seemed he just liked to browse.

'He's here again. That customer. What's his deal?' Nomiya said in a low voice. He had quietly drawn near to Mitsuri, never letting his suspicious gaze drop from the man. 'Shōhei says he doesn't know much about him, so he must be really shady.'

'Really? That's amazing,' replied Mitsuri. To make his tourist maps, Shōhei was always running around town collecting the latest news. He boasted that he was Mojikō's top informant. In fact, there wasn't much that Shōhei didn't know, if you asked him. Had he finally met his match?

The man had been coming in since Mitsuri started at the store. She'd had several chances to address him, but he never offered more than a syllable in reply: 'Oh', 'Yes', or 'Well . . .' A former colleague of hers at the store had surmised that he had some particularly severe form of social anxiety disorder, but if that were the case, he'd have difficulty working in the junk collection business, wouldn't he? It seemed as if he kept a deliberate distance around him somehow. She had the sense that he liked his privacy.

'Also, he could be trouble,' Nomiya whispered, dropping his voice another notch. 'Actually, I saw him together with the store manager at the Joyfull Restaurant in Mojikō – just the two of them.'

'Really?' she exclaimed loudly, without thinking, then hurriedly covered her mouth. Did Shiba's wiles extend even to the Whatever Guy? But a lover's tryst at a family restaurant, the two of them feeding each other cheeseburgers? Would the manager do that? It seemed impossible to imagine, but she couldn't resist trying . . .

'He handed the manager a package!' Nomiya continued, 'or it looked like that, anyway. Was it some kind of payoff?'

'Whaa . . .?' Mitsuri's jaw dropped and a meaningless gasp escaped her. Together with the Ayumu business, today was a day of too many surprises. Mitsuri was speechless, but then with a start she pulled herself together.

'Okay, this won't do at all. I'm going to the stockroom for a minute. You keep an eye on things here.'

Mitsuri emerged from the back, arms full of bento lunches for the people waiting in the dine-in space. As she was carrying them over, she noticed the man happily perusing the shelves, basket in hand. He was still standing there when she returned. In his basket she saw an assortment of sausages and a large spaghetti peperoncino. The man clearly liked variety, and always put together a selection of small dishes. Lately, he seemed to be particularly taken with spaghetti peperoncino – a pasta with chilli, garlic and olive oil. Peperoncino was also a favourite of Mitsuri's son Kōsei, and she was just thinking it might be nice to make it for dinner that evening, when she had a sudden idea.

Oh! This was her chance to speak to the man. But was it okay to ask? She faltered for a moment, but really her mind had been made up from the moment she had the thought.

'Um, excuse me!' she called out to the man, who was scanning the drinks in the beverage section, and he slowly turned. The eyes under his floppy fringe met hers. Mitsuri was startled for a moment, and it occurred to her that she and the man had never faced each other properly. He was so covered in hair that she hadn't noticed previously, but he seemed surprisingly youthful. Was he around the same age as Shiba? There was something special about those determined, dark eyes.

'What is it?' the man asked quietly.

'Um, you're a junk collector, right? I was wondering if you accepted broken bicycles.'

The other day Kōsei had come home with a broken bicycle. It had been wrecked somehow, and the frame had been crushed beyond any likely hope of repair. She thought they should get rid of it, but somehow it was still lying around in the yard.

'I do, but where is it?'

I got more than a syllable! Feeling a small sense of accomplishment, Mitsuri replied, 'At my house.'

23

'And your house is where?'

'About ten minutes from here on foot.'

She told him the address, and the man nodded. 'I'll come around soon.

'If you have other things you want to toss, I can take them at the same time. Bicycles are free, but for some items there may be a recycling fee, just be aware of that.'

'Oh. Okay.'

Deep down, Mitsuri was quite surprised at the gentleness of the man's voice and manner. She had imagined he would be brusque and unfriendly, even when he was at work.

'Uh, hold on . . . oh, wait . . . here it is.'

The man fished around in his overall pockets and pulled out a piece of paper. 'Right, here you go,' he said and handed over a business card with the same lettering that was printed on his back: 'Whatever Guy'. Then, in small letters, a mobile phone number.

'If something comes up, you can reach me here.'

'*Junk removal and problems* . . . Um, so what kind of problems do you mean?'

This was the question she had been wanting to ask for so long. She raised her gaze from the business card and looked at him.

'Whatever's bothering you, I take care of it,' he replied. 'When I go to older people's homes, I get asked to do a lot of chores or odd jobs. Moving furniture, shopping, that sort of thing. So I figured I might as well write that.'

Makes sense, Mitsuri thought. 'Oh. There's no name here, on the card . . .'

The man scratched his cheek. 'When I ordered the cards I forgot to put that in.' He looked a little embarrassed. Then added, 'Tsugi'.

'Sorry?'

'You can call me Tsugi.'

Tsugi. An unusual name, Mitsuri thought. *I wonder what characters he uses to write it? Harbour-tree, City-castle, something like that?* Just as she was about to ask, a string of customers entered the store.

'Sorry, I have to get back to work now. But it was nice to meet you.'

Mitsuri wanted to talk more with Tsugi. Reluctantly, she returned to work.

The best part of Mitsuri's day came at 10 p.m., when her husband went to bed. She called it her Golden Time. She arranged her things neatly on the dining table: a laptop, a tablet, a half-read manga and her phone. All she needed was a cup of freshly brewed coffee and she was good to go.

'Lots of material today, that's for sure.' Mitsuri took a sip of hot coffee and giggled to herself. Just learning the name of the young beautician would have been wonderful enough, but that he was already under the clutches of their Phero-Manager, that was a real coup! And on top of that, she had got a little closer to the mystery man.

'Ayumu is definitely going into the Friday instalment.'

The laptop was powered on, with the browser open to the top-ten list on Pixiv.com. Pixiv was a website for artists, devoted to sharing original manga comics online. Mitsuri ran her finger down the list to third place: 'Phero-Manager's Indecent Diary'. She giggled again. *Who would have thought that the manga that I drew could have become so popular? It's like a dream.*

Mitsuri loved manga truly, madly, deeply. She had been drawing her own comics since middle school. She kept it up through high school and college, and even started submitting her work to manga magazines, although she never made the final cut. Then she fell head over heels in love with a man she had met, and they were married. Before she knew it they were blessed with a child, and after that the days seemed to fly by in a frenzy. Eventually her relationship with her husband settled into a pleasant routine, while their only child began to crave independence, and she remembered her old drawings. Once she started to feel that she had some time to herself, naturally, the first thing she thought of was manga.

We live in an amazing time, Mitsuri thought. Anything you make, you just post it on the internet and everyone can see. Back in the day she would publish fanzines with friends, desperate to get their work out, but if they didn't sell, they'd end up in a stack of remainders. They were all driven to tears, hoping for someone – anyone – to read them. Now the number of readers was growing all the time, and she got all sorts of encouraging comments: 'So much fun!', 'Can't wait for the next instalment.' It was really a wonderful time.

'Well, all of that is thanks to the Phero-Manager, anyway,' she said to herself.

Sometimes you need money to fully enjoy a hobby. Mitsuri had originally taken the job at the store because she wanted a tablet, but she thought it was fate that she met Mr Shiba there.

When Mitsuri learned that Shiba was just the manager – a hired hand like the rest of them – she was moved. What a perfect, perfect manga character he was! A convenience-store manager, throwing love bombs everywhere – just perfect. It was too funny! Even while she was clocking in for job training, she was also clocking her boss, gathering notes for her new manga.

The more she got to know the store manager, the more interesting he was. Although the aura surrounding him was the last thing you'd expect at a convenience store, he served customers with the greatest care and courtesy. In the Tenderness chain's annual customer service competition, he had been inducted into the Hall of Fame. Strangely, although his entourage of rabid fans continued to expand, girls in high school and junior high were repelled by him – they called his special chemistry 'facial harassment'.

His private life was a mystery. First he would show up at the store on his day off, and then he'd say he was taking a break and they wouldn't see him for several days in a row. One day Mitsuri spotted him at the Kanmon Strait Museum, walking arm in arm with a beautiful woman in a kimono, and the next, she saw him being carried into the Mojikō Premier Hotel by a man even more muscular than Nomiya. Finally, her curiosity got the better of her and she had to ask: 'What kind of people are you associating with?' He brushed off the question with a laugh, saying 'We have to start by clarifying what "association" means between the two of us.'

Before she knew it, Mitsuri had become obsessed with Shiba, although it had nothing to do with love, or even lust. How could she not make this person into a manga? Shiba would be the main character, and the setting, of course, had to be the convenience store. It would depict the daily life of the Phero-Manager and the people around him. The title was a perfect fit: 'Phero-Manager's Indecent Diary'. She was confident as soon as she began to draw it that there would be interest, but she'd never thought for a second that it would be so popular, even after several years.

Does this store manager exist in real life? If so, please tell me where the store is! #badthoughts

When Mitsuri saw the DM someone had sent to the Twitter account linked to her profile, she laughed. In the beginning, as the manga was slowly starting to grow in popularity, she came clean about the project to Shiba, asking for his consent to continue her work.

'I'll stop if it makes you uncomfortable,' she said, head bowed, but Shiba's eyes lit up.

'That's fantastic!' he said. 'Feel free to use me as much as you like, but please leave out the name of the store, just in case.'

'Absolutely, of course,' said Mitsuri firmly. Comments had already started to arrive from people wanting to locate the actual Phero-Manager. She was well aware that to share the location of the store in real life would cause an uproar. After Mitsuri promised to protect his privacy, Shiba lightly replied, 'Well, okay then.' And that was the end of the matter.

'He does exist,' she replied to the fan, 'but I can't tell you where. If this becomes a nuisance to the store manager I'll have to cancel the series, so please give up your search.'

She typed the reply for the umpteenth time, sipping her coffee. Then, as she was responding to the last of the comments, Kōsei appeared. He opened the refrigerator door, chugged some milk directly from the carton and turned to Mitsuri, glowering. 'Manga again? Act your age, Mum, don't be such a freak!'

'Didn't I tell you not to be rude about your mother's hobbies?' Mitsuri pressed her lips together in annoyance. Her son always seemed bothered about her manga. Although when he was little, he would always talk about how 'Mama was really good at making pictures'. It was adorable, but if she reminded him of that now, Kōsei would make an even more terrible face, so she decided to keep it to herself. 'If you don't like what you're seeing, then go back to your room, please.'

'I'm going there whether you ask me to or not,' he replied. 'Oh, by the way, did you ask a junk collector to pick up the bike?'

'Why?' she asked, surprised.

'Just as I was getting home from school a little truck pulled up.' Kōsei took another gulp from the milk carton. 'The guy said that you'd asked him to pick up the bike and if it was okay to take it now. That's why.'

'W—was he wearing a beard? Like Mr. Shōhei?' *He couldn't have come already!*

But Kōsei nodded. 'His beard looked like Old Red, but aside from that he was totally different. He was really young, you know?' He paused. 'Not that it really matters, but he was interesting. Also, he seemed kind of cool.'

'Cool?'

Another surprise. But you could hardly see his face!

'I think there's a good-looking face under that beard. It's for the best that women can't see it,' he said matter-of-factly.

Grown-up words for a boy who just turned sixteen, Mitsuri thought.

'Anyway, I gave him the bike, so . . .' And with that, Kōsei returned to his room.

'Wow, that was fast.' Mitsuri took the card she had been given earlier out of her bag and looked at it. She hadn't been aware of it until now, but apparently she had been looking forward to contacting him. She found herself slightly disappointed. 'My funny-guy sensor is going off . . .'

Tsugi had something special about him. She could feel it.

★

A few days later, Urata, who was always first in line for the bento lunches, didn't show up. The other members had all picked up their lunches and finished eating, and still there was no sign of him, so Mitsuri called the phone number they had on file. There was no response. She told Shiba, who thought he should go over to Urata's apartment to check on the situation. Urata's place was about a ten-minute walk from the store.

'He probably just overslept, or had a medical appointment, or something like that,' he said.

Similar incidents had happened before, and each time it turned out to be a simple miscommunication. Mitsuri assumed this one would be no different. 'See you soon,' she said lightly, but about fifteen minutes later, she heard an ambulance siren in the distance, and her legs went weak.

'Oh no, I hope . . .'

Instantly her head was full of unpleasant possibilities. She exchanged glances with Nomiya, who had just come in to work. 'I've got a bad feeling about this,' muttered Shōhei, who was buying a bottle of Banana Latte, his drink of choice. Mitsuri put a hand to her chest, heart racing. She had always known in her head that something like this might happen someday, but it was still upsetting.

The ambulance probably had nothing to do with Urata, she told herself, but it seemed like it had been forever, and Shiba hadn't returned. Her anxiety increased.

'I'll just go check on them,' said Shōhei, who had been keeping an eye on the dine-in space. Mitsuri bowed her head, saying 'Sorry for the trouble.' Shōhei pedalled off on his cargo bike, and when he returned a scant ten minutes later a single look at his face told Mitsuri that her fears had become reality.

'It seems he collapsed at home. Mitsuhiko said he would go with him.'

'Oh. Is it . . .?'

'Mitsuhiko will probably let us know more soon. Let's wait to hear from him.'

It was about two hours more before Shiba checked in. 'He's okay,' he said, in a voice both exhausted and relieved. 'The prognosis is still unclear, but he survived.'

Apparently Urata had suffered a stroke and collapsed. If he had been taken to the hospital just a little later, he might not have survived.

'I've just contacted his daughter in Yamaguchi Prefecture,' Shiba said. 'I'll stay here until she arrives.'

'I understand,' Mitsuri replied. 'It must be hard for you too. Hang in there.'

Mitsuri had taken the call in the staff room. When she returned to the front of the store, there were a number of people standing by the checkout counter. She panicked, thinking she had left customers waiting, but it was Shōhei and the members of the Ladies' Association. They had surrounded Nomiya and were grilling him.

'What could have happened to old Urata?'

'I finally got him to talk the other day, but he didn't say anything about being ill.'

'The body wears out when you get older, you know. You have to be careful!'

Mitsuri waded into the chattering ring of people. 'I'm told Mr Urata will be okay,' she said, 'It's a good thing the manager discovered him so quickly.'

The faces around her brightened.

'Oh my, yes indeed!'

'You get a lot of unpleasant news at this age, but at least it wasn't the worst news, if you know what I mean.'

'It's just like that dear man, isn't it? Always looking out for his customers.'

In no time the subject had moved on to singing Shiba's praises, and after everyone had enjoyed the conversation for a while, they went home.

Eventually the evening staff arrived for their shift. After Mitsuri had completed the changeover, she stepped into the staff room, and found Nomiya still there, although his shift had ended before hers. He was sitting in somewhat of a daze, staring at his phone on the table in front of him.

'What's wrong, Nomiya?' He looked up slowly at the sound of Mitsuri's voice, his face twisted in pain.

'Hey, are you feeling sick?' she asked in surprise, but he shook his head. She asked him again what was wrong, and with a weak voice he responded: 'Mr Urata.'

'I get it. It all happened so quickly, it was a shock. But we're lucky it ended well, right?' *And our lunch service worked pretty well, too, didn't it?* Mitsuri almost added, but thought better of it. Nomiya looked up at Mitsuri through tearful eyes. He bit his bottom lip as if trying to restrain the tears, but they kept coming.

'Hey, there. Hey. What is it?'

Mitsuri wasn't sure why Nomiya was crying. She took a seat opposite him and waited for him to calm down. At last, he opened his mouth. 'I . . . I always ignore people's signs.'

'Signs?' Mitsuri parroted, tilting her head in confusion. Still in distress, Nomiya gazed down at his own tears on the table in front of him.

'In high school, there was this guy I'd always practise with. Takagi. At some point I realised that he was in bad shape. He wasn't moving right and seemed worn out, and, well, also he told me himself he had been feeling weird lately. But I didn't think about it much, just figured he was fatigued, or needed sleep. If I had just told him then to go to the hospital, his illness might not have got so bad . . .'

Nomiya gulped, as if trying to swallow his tears.

'I, I told him . . . I told him that when we got to university we'd keep wrestling together, but now he can't do anything like that anymore. I feel so bad about that.'

Mitsuri looked at Nomiya. *So that's what happened. That's why he gave up wrestling.*

'I . . . that's bouncing around in my head and I can't get it out. I wanted to make sure that if something like this ever happened again I wouldn't regret it the same way as last time, but . . .'

His hands clenched on the table. His fists, large and rugged as two boulders, were trembling.

'The other day when I brought Mr Urata his lunch, he said, "My head hurts."'

'His head?'

'You remember there was a day when Mr Urata's mood was worse than usual? That day, I asked if something was bothering him. He yelled at me and said his head hurt and he couldn't help it, could he, and if I kept talking to him like a loudmouth it would only hurt more, so would I please just shut up. So finally I got ticked off, and stopped talking. Then he told me to leave because I was ruining his lunch, so I did . . .

'Here,' Nomiya said, and held out his phone. It seemed he had been looking up information about strokes. One of the warning signs was a headache, it said.

'I did the exact same thing again. I spent so much time in my head about it, thinking no way ever again will I let this happen. I was sure that was enough, but I was a total failure. Just because I got a little mad . . .'

'Hey, well, you know Mr Urata is always in a bad mood. If I'd been in your shoes, I think I would have done my best to ignore him too.'

Mitsuri thought back to that day. Certainly Mr Urata had been in a foul mood from the moment he had entered the store. But she too had paid it no mind, thinking it was just the usual state of affairs. If Nomiya was at fault, then she was equally so. But Nomiya stood up so forcefully his chair knocked backwards on the floor with a loud bang.

'That's not the point!' he shouted. 'It's got nothing to do with what someone else would do! To tear myself apart about this for so long, and then when the crucial moment comes, to make the same mistake again? – I can't forgive myself, and there's nothing I can do about it!'

Mitsuri could do nothing but goggle at his fierce display. When he noticed her look, Nomiya's face contorted again.

'I can't help shouting, do you understand? I'm furious at myself. Really, I'm the worst. I am.' With that, Nomiya fled the room. Mitsuri hurriedly chased after him, but when she exited the store he was nowhere in sight.

She went back into the store and turned to Hirose, who was now working the checkout counter. 'Hey, do you know which way Nomiya went?' He shook his head.

'What's up with him? He blew out of here on his moped like his life depended on it.'

Oh, that's dangerous, she thought. Hirose's concerned tone only heightened Mitsuri's anxiety. Nomiya was tormenting himself. She couldn't leave things like this.

34

What to do? What to do?

She wanted to contact Shiba, but he was probably still at the hospital. So what could she do . . .? She thought frantically, and then the white piece of paper popped into her mind.

'The business card!' she exclaimed reflexively, rummaging in her handbag. Snatching it out, she dialled the number on the card. A few rings, and then she heard a low voice on the other end of the line.

'Hello?' she said. 'This is Mitsuri, the clerk at Tenderness.' Her heart beat just a little faster. 'Um, remember I was asking you about what sort of problems you handled? Well, I've got one here. I was wondering if I could ask you a favour.'

There was a low chuckle on the other end of the line. 'What do you need?'

The dine-in space at Golden Villa Tenderness was fully kitted out. There were five counter seats with a view of the street outside, and two four-top tables. On each of these was a small vase for a seasonal flower – currently sunflowers – and a box of tissues. At one end of the room was a hot-water dispenser for tea, and a toaster, along with a rubbish bin. There was talk among the building residents of installing a television in the room as well. Fidgeting in a seat at one end of the counter, Mitsuri stared out the window, oblivious to all else.

The sun had completely set, and a cream-coloured moon hung in the sky. A gentle night breeze flowed in through the open doors. Mitsuri fiddled with her phone, killing time, her eyes focused blindly on the screen.

'Oh!'

As Mitsuri's gaze swept the scene outside for what seemed like the hundredth time, her face brightened. A familiar mini-truck had pulled slowly into the car park. In the back of the truck were a washing machine, a vacuum cleaner, and Nomiya's motorbike. The heavily bearded driver noticed Mitsuri watching him and raised a hand. Next to him she could see Nomiya, head sagging.

'Oh, you found him! Thank you!' She jumped up and ran towards the little truck. As he exited the truck, Tsugi's big beard split into a toothy grin.

'He was making a face like he was going to die, but he didn't!'

When Mitsuri had called Tsugi, she asked him if could find a missing person, and he had replied simply, 'Of course.' In fact, he had added, it was his speciality.

Mitsuri told him she wanted him to look for Nomiya, and he quickly replied, 'Ah, the muscly part-timer,' as if he understood. He had shown no interest in the staff, so she hadn't thought he would actually grasp the situation at all.

'He was so mad at himself that he panicked and disappeared on his motorbike,' Mitsuri had explained. 'I'm afraid something awful could happen to him. Can I ask you to look for him?'

Tsugi was silent for a moment, as if he were considering. 'Got it,' he replied. 'Where are you calling from now? Ah, Tenderness, as usual. Okay, can you wait there, please? I'll bring him as soon as possible.'

'Oh, is that . . . are you sure?'

'I told you, I'm good at this.'

He had seemed confident, but she never expected him to find Nomiya so quickly. 'I'm glad you're safe.' She smiled at Nomiya as he clambered out of the truck.

'Sorry,' he replied in a faint, embarrassed voice, hanging his head. 'Mitsuri, you should be home at this hour. It's my fault you're not.'

'I already went home. I made dinner, and came back, so it's fine. Don't worry about it.' She smiled at the young man's concern for her, even at a time like this, and continued. 'You must be hungry. I'd really like to take you somewhere to eat, but Phero—, um, the manager will be coming back soon. So let's wait for him in the dine-in space and I'll get you something from the store.'

When she had contacted Shiba to let him know what was going on, he'd told her to have some food, and wait there for him. Regarding Nomiya's disappearance, he wanted to know who she had called for help. He seemed surprised at the answer. Shiba said he had always figured the two of them would meet at some point, but, well, what timing! Anyway, from what he knew the guy would find Nomiya quickly enough, no doubt, so she had made the right choice, but well, hmm . . . She got the feeling somehow that Shiba would rather not have involved Tsugi.

I wonder what's up between those two? Curiouser and curiouser. Beating back the devil that was starting to dance in the corner of her mind, Mitsuri smiled at Tsugi. 'Would you join us, Mr Whatever Guy? It's on the house, courtesy of the manager.'

'As I said, call me Tsugi. And thanks, I suppose I can't say no to that.' His tone was a little informal but added nothing to her knowledge of him. And the way he further said, 'Actually, I'm pretty hungry,' and patted his belly was quite normal, not strange at all.

'Nomiya, why don't you wait in the dine-in area while I get some food? How about the pork cutlet bowl? That seems to be your favourite lately.'

Nomiya shook his head. 'I've lost my appetite.'

'But you hardly touched your lunch. You should eat something.' Usually he could put away as many as three servings in a flash. *Won't his muscles wither away if he misses a couple of meals?* she wondered.

'But I don't want to eat—'

'How about a sandwich? Pasta salad?'

If he eats just a bite, it could jump-start his appetite. Mitsuri suggested everything that she could think of, but Nomiya wouldn't yield.

'Why don't I just go get a few things?' Tsugi, who had been watching the exchange from the sidelines, broke in. 'You talk to the kid. I'll buy the food.'

'Okay, but . . .'

'It's fine, it's fine. We'll settle up the bill later. Okay, Mitsu?'

With that, Tsugi disappeared into the main store with his lopsided, easygoing gait.

'He's a strange one, isn't he?' Nomiya said under his breath. 'I was sitting in Mekari Park, not thinking anything, just staring out at the ocean, when he came right up to me just as if he knew exactly where I'd be. He said "Mitsuri is waiting for you, so it's time to go."'

Mekari Park was famous in the area for its beautiful nighttime views, but how in the world had Tsugi known the young man would be there? It was unbelievable, Mitsuri agreed, nodding, but at the same time, the devil of curiosity was dancing around like crazy on her shoulder as she wondered about Tsugi. *Mitsu? He called me Mitsu. Isn't that a little too intimate?*

She was sitting across from Nomiya at one of the fourtops in the dine-in area when Tsugi returned, carrying a large plastic bag in each hand. 'I've got food!' he said cheerily. 'I bought a ton. Shopping with other people's money is the best!'

He flopped down next to Nomiya and started pulling all sorts of foods from the bags, one item after the next. There was a large peperoncino pasta and an assortment of sausages – two of each. There was a spaghetti carbonara and a *katsudon*, breaded pork cutlets with egg over rice. A container of kimchi, a ham-and-cheese sandwich, piled high with lettuce, and some soft-boiled eggs. There were three servings each of crème caramel pudding and *dorayaki*, sponge-cake sandwiches stuffed with red-bean filling and whipped cream.

'Right! Now we eat!'

Mitsuri couldn't help but smile at his giddy high spirits. He sounded like a child with all his favourite foods laid out before him.

'Don't hold back, Mr Tsugi. You must be hungry!'

'Okay then, let's dig in. You there, which do you want?' He turned to Nomiya, but when Nomiya shook his head, Tsugi reached for the spaghetti carbonara. He also broke open the sausage assortment and topped the pasta with them, and on top of those he placed a soft-boiled egg.

'A meal fit for a king. That's happiness.'

With a smile, Tsugi happily laid into the food. He dunked the sausage in the sauce and ate it, inhaled some of the pasta, stopping halfway through to gently break the soft-boiled egg he had added to the dish. 'Ummm, good,' he murmured, chewing on pasta coated in bright yellow egg yolk.

'You enjoy eating, don't you?' Mitsuri said, watching Tsugi eat with gusto, and he nodded between bites.

'The greatest pleasure in life is to eat good food while talking about how good it is.'

He polished off the carbonara and reached for the peper-oncino. Watching Tsugi enjoy his meal, Mitsuri began to feel hungry, even though she had eaten a light dinner while she was home. She reached for a pudding, since there were three of those.

'Nomiya, please have something too.'

Nomiya must have felt at least a little bit hungry watching the two of them, but he still wouldn't touch anything from the array of foods in front of him. She could see a glimmer of desire flickering in his eyes as he watched Tsugi packing away his feast, but he didn't even bother to pick up his chopsticks. 'I'm okay,' he kept repeating stubbornly, no matter how often Mitsuri pressed him.

'You can starve yourself, kid, but the old man's condition won't change!' Tsugi spoke brusquely, as if he were irritated by the endless back and forth. In response, Nomiya's eyes filled with tears. Mitsuri hurriedly held out a handkerchief, but Nomiya wiped his eyes with the back of his hands. 'I'm really sorry,' he said. 'Sorry I caused so much trouble for everyone.'

'It's really okay,' Mitsuri reassured him. 'You know how much I like nosing into other people's lives. I probably worried too much about you. I'm sure you would have been fine on your own.'

'. . . I just don't understand. I'm so pathetic! Why do I have to be this way?' Nomiya bit his lip in frustration.

'I think it's because you're such a kind young man. You can't beat yourself up like that just because you didn't notice. Next time will be different.'

'The next time wasn't different, for me,' Nomiya said in a pained voice. Mitsuri searched for the words to respond.

'First of all, I'm not kind,' Nomiya continued. 'I'm selfish. In Takagi's case, I didn't think about anything but winning my tournament. When it was Urata's turn, all I thought about was talking back to a cranky old man. I feel bad about that now though.'

'Look, none of us are saints. I can be self-centred myself. And this time in particular, it's really not your fault. What if you had noticed and suggested that Urata go to the hospital? He probably wouldn't have listened to you anyway. So you can't fret about it like that.'

Nomiya just shook his head and kept crying as if he couldn't even hear Mitsuri's words. She sighed to herself. How could she make him understand?

'You should try it like this. It's really delicious!' Tsugi interrupted.

While they were talking Tsugi had polished off his peperoncino, and placed the *katsudon* in front of Nomiya. Then, on top of it, he deposited a generous portion of kimchi. The golden-brown of the cutlet was perfectly balanced by the yellow egg yolk and green scallions, and with the bright red pickles as a garnish, Nomiya couldn't help but say 'Wow.

'What are you doing? I can't eat something like that!'

'You can. It's delicious!'

Tsugi held out a pair of chopsticks to Nomiya. 'Take them.' When Nomiya seemed reluctant to take them, Tsugi paused for just a moment, then pressed them into his hands, saying, 'Now eat. Or it will get cold.'

Tsugi's tone sharpened, and Nomiya accepted the chopsticks as if compelled. Then, gingerly, he lifted a piece of cutlet, covered with kimchi and egg, onions and sauce, but his face darkened.

'Hold on,' Tsugi quickly intervened. 'I'm forgetting something important. Wait a minute . . . here you go.'

Rummaging through the bags he pulled out a small packet of mayonnaise. He opened it and squeezed it back and forth over the kimchi-covered cutlets. Nomiya said 'Wow . . .' again, but then in an abject voice, continued, 'I meant to say, I don't deserve to eat anything like this.'

Frowning at the bowl of food, Nomiya's expression changed slightly. Curiously, Mitsuri watched him as he gazed intently at the *katsudon*. 'That's it,' she murmured. Was it the delicate latticework of mayonnaise lacing the top that whetted his appetite? She had to admit it looked delicious.

Nomiya silently conveyed the fully dressed morsel of pork to his mouth. He chewed, and then took another, larger bite. He was gathering momentum steadily.

'Good, isn't it?' asked Tsugi, and Nomiya nodded vigorously.

Once he started eating it was like a switch had been flipped. Nomiya bolted down the *katsudon* with even more vigour than usual. In an instant, more than half of it had vanished. But in the middle of all that, suddenly, his chopsticks stilled, and again, the tears began to flow.

'I . . . I'm stuffing myself when I should be concerned. It just seems . . .' Once again, Nomiya faltered.

'Move your chopsticks,' Tsugi responded curtly. 'It's natural to feel that good things are good,' he said with some exasperation between bites of the sandwich, into which he had inserted the leftover sausages.

'Say your parents die. You're still going to get hungry. If you can't taste what's good, something really is wrong with you. What I mean is, to eat without enjoying yourself is to disrespect the food.'

Making short work of his sandwich, Tsugi then placed a peperoncino pasta in front of Nomiya, saying, 'Here, this is your share,' and adding forcefully, 'Now, don't think. Eat!' Under heavy pressure, Nomiya lifted his chopsticks again. 'The more we suffer, the more we should eat. If you don't get enough nutrition, it distorts your thinking.'

Nomiya finished the *katsudon* and reached for the pasta. Tsugi plunked down a sausage on top. Nomiya, who had been eating in silence for a while, mumbled something. Mitsuri pricked up her ears, trying to hear what he was saying.

'. . . it's good.'

Tsugi nodded. 'Isn't it? Now pay some attention to your food.'

Nomiya continued to eat without speaking. Mitsuri felt that something like life was slowly returning to his face. Then she took a surreptitious glance at Tsugi. *What an extraordinary person.*

'When I told you to eat, I had no idea how much! How many servings was that?' Mitsuri giggled, then she looked over at the side door to the store. There stood Shiba. He looked a little tired, which was not surprising, since he had been detained since noon.

'Sorry I'm late. Mr Urata's daughter likes to talk. So we talked, for quite a while, and time kept passing.' Shiba seated himself next to Mitsuri, and Nomiya broke off from his meal again, but Shiba urged him on. 'Eat, eat!' He waited for Nomiya to finish, a gentle smile playing across his face, then spoke.

'Listen to this. Mr Urata says he looked forward to it.'

'Huh?' Nomiya looked up.

'Mr Urata said he looked forward to visiting the store every day. He told his daughter on the phone! "The staff are always cheerful, and they smile at me even when I'm in a bad mood," he said. He got to know people in similar situations to his, and it made him want to get out of the house more often.

'Also, he has a grandson who's a high-school junior.' Shiba chuckled to remember it. 'The kid came to the hospital too. He was on his school rugby team, a total muscle man. He said his grandfather was always talking about how much he resembled Nomiya.'

'. . . me?'

'He told his grandson that there was a kid working at the store who had a much better physique than him, but for some reason he had given up on the team and was just frittering his time away. Apparently he was really worried about it.'

'Come to think of it,' Nomiya said quietly, 'when I first started here, he asked me if I did any clubs. I told him I used to be on a wrestling team, but now I've quit, and he scolded me. He said it was a waste, not making use of my gifts. Then after that, whenever he saw me, he'd say my muscles were a waste, and that I had better things to do than working for pay.

'I thought he was saying all that just to be mean,' Nomiya said, downcast.

'I guess he really had high hopes for you! He had a gruff way of showing it, so you didn't get it. It wasn't easy to understand. It was hard for me, too.' Shiba spoke gently.

'It's hard to know what's inside a person. If you judge people only by their words and faces, you miss the really important things. But then, what should we do instead? I think it's best to let people's actions speak for themselves. Mr Urata actually enjoyed coming to our convenience store! That's the real story, isn't it? Every day, he was the first one in. So when it seemed like he just kept mocking Nomiya, that must have been Urata's way of cheering him on.'

Nomiya's expression twisted oddly.

'Now, here's my idea. Mr Urata is alive and well, and when he recovers a little more he'll be able to have a conversation. Why don't you visit him for a little talk?' Shiba smiled. 'What do you think?'

He put his hand on Nomiya's, which were clasped together on the table. 'You can have regrets in life, but that doesn't mean you can't do something about them. It's okay.'

Nomiya closed his eyes as if he were thinking just a little, then pieced together a few words in response: 'I do want to go. I want to go see Mr Urata. I want to speak to him properly, and I want to apologise.'

Shiba smiled.

'Why don't we go together next time? I'm sure Mr Urata would like that.'

For the first time that day, something like a smile flitted across Nomiya's face. Mitsuri heaved a sigh of relief to see him brighten up, even just a little.

'So it's settled? In that case, have a *dorayaki*!' Tsugi held out one of the sponge cakes to Nomiya. Nomiya smiled in thanks and then shook off Shiba's hand, which was still clasping his.

'This kind of thing is a clear case of sexual harassment.'

'Ack!' Shiba let out a helpless croak. Watching the scene, Tsugi burst into laughter, and Nomiya turned to him, continuing, 'Mr Whatever Guy, looks like you ate my share of the pudding. I love pudding – I want some more, please!'

Now it was Tsugi's turn to howl.

★

The Golden Villa Tenderness branch was always understaffed. This was because so few people could withstand Shiba's charms. After Nomiya resigned – a friend had begged him to rejoin the wrestling team – the burden of covering the various shifts at the store had fallen largely on Mitsuri and Shiba.

'Ugh, I'm exhausted. Mr Shiba, please hire someone quickly!'

'I wish I could. Lots of people show up for the interviews, but it's not that easy to find someone who can actually do the job.'

The staff room was empty except for the two of them, who had been working without a day off for who knows how long. Resting her face on the table, Mitsuri heaved a deep sigh. Shiba sighed too, as if in reply. When Nomiya left, they had hired a middle-aged gentleman who had taken early retirement, but somehow the man's wife had fallen for Shiba, and after one thing led to another, it ended in a divorce. To avoid a crisis, they had to let the man go. The staff had been running themselves ragged trying to do their jobs while also stopping to mediate fights between the wife, who had turned into Shiba's stalker, and her furious husband.

'Manager, can't you wear a horse mask or something like that while you work?' Mitsuri asked in despair. 'We need to hide that face of yours.'

'Mrs Nakao, if I do, you'll have to change the name of your manga to *The Horse Manager*, okay?'

'Yuck. On second thought . . .'

The two of them sighed. Then there was a knock on the door, and Hirose's head popped into view. 'Manager, the

Whatever Guy came and asked for you. He's waiting in the dine-in space. Is that okay? Should I tell him you're not here?'

'No, tell him I'll be there in a moment,' Shiba replied. He pulled himself together and stood up.

'Oh! Excuse me,' Mitsuri asked, 'but is it okay if I come too?'

'That's fine, but . . . Mrs Nakao, why do you look so pleased?'

'Well, I haven't seen him since that night.'

After Nomiya had settled down, Mitsuri had thought it would be a great opportunity to ask Tsugi a few questions, but a work call came in and he had to rush out. After that it was like the line had gone dead somehow, and he stopped coming to the shop. She wondered why.

'Well, you know me. I was worried about him.'

'Hmm . . . I see "new material" written all over your face. That's it, isn't it?'

'No! That's not it, at all.' Mitsuri gulped. She'd been found out, she thought, but tried to cover it up anyway. 'Um, look – I never had the chance to pay him back for the food that night.'

'Oh, I've already paid him, so you're fine.'

'Huh?' she said, involuntarily. Were they meeting outside the shop somewhere then? Mitsuri's imagination was already percolating when Shiba said, 'I guess it's probably time I came clean.' He paused. 'Mrs Nakao, you are the shop's senior employee. It's been four years, hasn't it? That's a decent stretch, wouldn't you say?'

'What?'

'There's something I've been hiding from you.' With a sigh, Shiba left the staff room. Head spinning in confusion, she followed him to the dine-in space, and there was

Tsugi, wolfing down a bento lunch. It was the same pork cutlet bowl slathered with kimchi as the other day, and for some reason Shōhei was sitting opposite him.

Tsugi was wearing the usual coveralls, but this time they were caked with mud, as if he had been wandering around in a mountain forest. Green leaves protruded from his unkempt hair, and the strong arms jutting from his rolled-up sleeves were covered in scratches.

'Hey. Sorry to pull you away.'

'It's not a problem, but what have you been up to? You're a mess.'

'Am I? Oh, on the way here, I was helping a few woodsmen. In return they gave me some wild boar meat. Need any?'

'No, I don't,' said Shiba, but Shōhei grinned. 'I'm partial to boar, myself,' he said.

'Then you take half. Or maybe we can have it all at your place? It's good for grilling.'

'Ah, that'll do!'

'Oh? Shōhei knows Tsugi?' Mitsuri piped up in surprise from behind Shiba, where she was standing. She didn't know they knew each other that well. Seeing Mitsuri, Tsugi said 'Ah, hello,' and bowed his head in greeting, then added to Shiba, 'Sorry, I thought it was just you.' Shōhei too, hurriedly said 'Whoops, sorry,' and lapsed into silence.

'No, it's okay. It's okay. I decided I couldn't keep it from her forever, so I brought her in.'

Shiba glanced back at Mitsuri.

'So here goes, Mitsuri. This man,' he said, gesturing towards Tsugi, 'he's my older brother.'

'Huh?'

For a moment, the word 'brother' failed to compute.

'My second-oldest brother, Nihiko.'

She looked back and forth between Shiba and Tsugi, in turn. Out of the corner of her eye she could see Shōhei grinning widely. No, wait a second, the two of them looked nothing alike. Nothing alike at all. Could the walking pheromone factory and this gruff, dishevelled man be brothers?

'Uh, but he said Tsugi . . .?'

'That's his nickname. There are five of us. Ichihiko, Nihiko, Mitsuhiko, Yohiko. Using the Japanese for one, two, three, four. But adding *hiko* this, *hiko* that all the time got too complicated. So we just call each other Ichi, Tsugi, Mitsu, and Yon. I guess our parents got lazy,' Shiba said, looking a little embarrassed. Mitsuri's mind was swimming. It was too much for her to take in.

'Wait a minute. Um, you said five brothers? Are any of them like you? Uh, if it's five, then who's the fifth? And what's he called?'

'The fifth is a sister. Her name is Jewel.'

'I'm sorry, that's a lot, isn't it? I'm still trying to put it all together.' Mitsuri staggered over to the table and took a seat opposite Tsugi. So that was why he had called her 'Mitsu' earlier, wasn't it? It was a family habit. Behind his hair, his eyes flickered with amusement. Mitsuri noticed something in those eyes. The true nature of the discomfort she had felt earlier. His eyes were the one way that Tsugi really resembled Shiba.

'They surprised you, didn't they, Mitsuri? Me too, when I first heard.' Shōhei laughed, and rumpled Tsugi's leaf-strewn hair. 'It seems like a story someone made up, doesn't it now? That Mojikō's most suspicious man is brother to its most mysterious.'

'Although he always says that he realised it right away,' Shiba noted.

'Anyway, why did the three of you keep it a secret from me?' Mitsuri puffed up her cheeks and pouted a little, despondent over her lack of observational skills.

'Because it's a real pain,' Tsugi replied. 'I can't tell you how much trouble I've got into just because I'm this guy's brother. Once a woman chased me around with a razor – just because she thought I might look a little more like my brother if she shaved my beard!'

'Yipes.' Mitsuri shivered in spite of herself. But it wasn't impossible. She had seen Shiba's fans go too far like that every day.

'Don't blame it all on me,' Shiba said. 'I've been through a thing or two just because I'm your younger brother. I had to fight off a few delinquents and pay off a few bills that I certainly don't remember racking up.'

In the end the brothers came to the same conclusion.

'It's best for everyone if we act like total strangers,' said Shiba. 'So if possible, please don't spread it around.'

'I agree. It just creates unnecessary commotion,' said Tsugi.

'Gotcha. I won't let it get out.' Even if the story leaked only to the residents of the Golden Villa apartments, there would surely be trouble. At least three of the ladies there would fight tooth and nail to be the one to care for their dear Mitsuhiko's older brother.

'On another subject, Mitsu. I came to give you this.'

Tsugi took a large Tupperware container out of a paper bag. He lifted the lid. Inside, it was filled with *ohagi* – rice-flour dumplings wrapped in red-bean paste – packed in neat rows. The rich, red-bean paste gleamed in the light, glossy and sweet.

'Wow,' Mitsuri said reflexively. 'Those look delicious.'

'They're our sister's speciality,' Tsugi said, a note of pride creeping into his voice. 'I was home this morning and, well, our sister is big on Mitsuhiko. She gave me these, said "Take them to Mitsu." If I didn't bring them to you quick, I'd be in trouble, so I came by.'

'You know I love little sister's *ohagi*,' said Shiba. 'But she doesn't need to make so many!'

He explained that his sister, Jewel, was only seventeen. As he was presented with his much younger sister's handiwork, a look Mitsuri hadn't seen before stole across Shiba's face. If the members of his fan club could see him now, they'd be off their rockers, she thought.

'Have you had some, big brother?' Shiba asked Tsugi. 'Since you went to the trouble of bringing them, let's eat together.'

'She made me eat the funny-shaped ones until I was half dead,' Tsugi complained. 'But I guess I could have a few more.'

'You too, Shōhei, and Mrs Nakao,' said Shiba. 'How about it? I won't be able to finish them on my own.'

So the four of them purchased paper plates and chopsticks from the store, and ate the *ohagi*. The elegantly sweet red-bean paste and the light, springy rice dumplings were delicious. *No wonder they call it her speciality*, thought Mitsuri, helping herself to more.

'So how's the little macho man doing? Is he doing his best on the wrestling team?' Though he had claimed to have eaten *ohagi* until he was half dead, and gorged himself on *katsudon*, Tsugi was stuffing his belly with the rice dumplings as though it was his first meal of the day.

'The kid knew how to handle customers,' Shiba replied. 'We lost a talented employee.'

'That's true,' Shōhei added. 'Although he's in such good shape, I might just let him inherit my post as Mojikō's top informant!' The older man, too, was downing the dumplings with a vigour that belied his age.

'To tell you the truth, it seemed like he didn't want to give up the job here, but now that he's getting serious about wrestling, it would be hard to do both. Not much we can say about that.' Shiba, who was carefully lifting a dumpling to his mouth, suddenly paused and smiled.

'Oh, that's right. He said something that made me really happy, you know.'

Mitsuri looked at Shiba.

'He said, "Everyone who comes to our store lives every day of their lives to the fullest. When I gave up wrestling I thought my existence had become meaningless, but after spending all day helping people get through their days, I started to feel like it was good to be alive."'

Mitsuri's eyes crinkled merrily. Nomiya had said that working at the store was his first job. Before that, it had been all about wrestling for him. This oversized boy, unfamiliar with everything at first, trying so desperately to serve customers. She remembered how his face shone the first time a customer complimented him on his good service.

'A long time ago, there was a girl who said something like that,' Shiba said with deep feeling.

'That one?' Shōhei said, a note of nostalgia creeping into his voice.

Tsugi took an emphatic bite of an exceptionally large dumpling and gazed out at the car park.

'When I heard what she had to say, I decided I'd give this job everything I had. Helping people is a good thing, isn't it? Even if it's just for the tiniest moment in their lives.'

Shiba's voice echoed gently in Mitsuri's ears. She had never imagined the man felt this way about his work. And with some embarrassment, she had to admit that she had become too used to the work herself, thinking only about completing her roster of daily tasks without incident. She, too, needed to change her way of thinking.

'Those words made me who I am today,' Shiba said quietly, as if speaking to himself. 'I'm glad the store exists.' There was no hint of the usual sex appeal or anything dubious on his face. Mitsuri felt like she was seeing his true nature, as fleeting as a drop of dew hidden in a beautiful rose. Perhaps all those people who felt so much for him were simply seeking a glimpse of what she was seeing now.

And, she thought, *he really loves his job.*

'Well, I like this job too,' she said aloud, 'but working like this with no relief? I'm sorry – it's too much!' Mitsuri took a joking tone, because she knew that she'd never be that close to him. She wasn't that sort of person. The person to do that would have to be special to him. She might not have had great observational skills, but she had accumulated enough life experience to see that.

'Hey, now!' The blossom had closed, and Shiba was back to his usual self again. He placed a hand on his chest and laughed. 'Don't say that! I'm doing the best I can with the interviews.'

'Mitsu, maybe you ought to wear a mask or something, hey?' Tsugi joined in. 'Like a horse or a big Buddha.'

'Leave off, brother!' Shiba protested. 'Mrs Nakao said the same thing.'

'No – if anything, it should be one of those full-body cartoon costumes.' It was Shōhei's turn to chime in. 'I have a friend at an event company. Want me to ask?'

'Shōhei, you too? Give me a break!'

Listening to the friendly banter, Mitsuri laughed. She had the feeling that the shifts to come would be more fun. The mysterious brothers had more surprises, mysteries, and drama in store, no doubt, and she wanted to know it all. After all, it was good material, wasn't it!

Yes, Mitsuri Nakao was living a full life. *Ah, but I wonder . . .* she thought to herself, *I wonder if it's okay for it to be this full!* Popping another dumpling in her mouth, Mitsuri laughed merrily.

Chapter Two

The Convenience Store
Coffee of Hope

Yoshirō Kiriyama was eighty per cent egg sandwiches and coffee. To be precise, special fluffy egg sandwiches and premium coffee. Both were popular offerings at the Tenderness convenience-store chain.

Yoshirō worked at a *juku* – an afterschool test-prep academy. It was in Nozomigaoka, to the southwest, so he took the train, but before heading out, he always stopped for a late lunch at Tenderness. He bought the same thing every time, and at the same branch. The Golden Villa Tenderness in Mojikō, about halfway down Ōsakamachi Avenue. It was a little out of the way from Yoshirō's rooms at the Sea Breeze Villa apartments, but he was a regular customer there.

It was just past 1:30 p.m., and the lunchtime rush had begun to subside. The automatic doors slid smoothly open and Yoshirō heard the familiar melody play as he stepped inside. His whole body relaxed as the cool air flowed over his sweaty skin. The theme song of a recent TV drama played quietly in the background, and Yoshirō went straight to the refrigerated foods section. There were rice balls, pasta, and a wide assortment of other foods in the case, but without hesitation, he picked up an egg sandwich and examined the colour of the eggs and bread. Yes, good again today, as always. He selected a two-pack of sandwiches and headed to the register.

The clerk was waiting there, a regular-size coffee cup already in her hand. He'd seen her before – a woman in her thirties with a name tag that read 'Nakao'.

Nakao took the sandwiches and entered the items on the register with a practised hand.

Watching her calm face, Yoshirō wondered idly what she thought of him. By chance he had turned on the TV the previous day, and they were talking about how store clerks would give nicknames to customers who made a strong impression on them. Like 'Red Tee' for the one who always wears the same t-shirt, or '#39' for the one who never says anything except the number of the cigarette pack he wants from the rack behind the counter. *They might have a name for me,* he thought. *Whenever I'm here I get the egg sandwich and coffee. Something like 'Breakfast Combo'? Or maybe something simpler, like 'Specs'.*

Yoshirō paid the bill and Nakao put the sandwich in a bag and handed it to him, along with the empty coffee cup. Usually at this point she would say, 'Thank you very much,' but today, instead, she cleared her throat and said, 'Excuse me . . .'

'Y-yes? What is it?' There was no way she could have known what he was thinking, but he was a little embarrassed anyway for some reason, and his voice cracked slightly as he spoke. Nakao flashed him a gentle smile and handed him a sheet of paper.

'We're getting new coffee machines next week. This is the announcement flyer.' Yoshirō looked at the paper. His eyes widened.

'Ah! You know them, don't you?' Nakao said happily. 'Sachika Coffee is supervising the whole operation. Isn't that amazing?'

'But that's . . . wow.'

Sachika Coffee was a hidden gem in Hakata, a bustling district in Fukuoka, on Kyūshū's northwest coast. Every serious coffee lover knew it. The proprietor was a coffee master, having received extensive training at the well-known Caffe Greco in Italy, and he was particular about his brew. He purchased the beans at their place of origin, roasted them locally on site, and produced a special blend that was strong on the palate, with a spicy finish. The trend lately was towards fresh, acidic coffees with fruity notes, but Sachika Coffee continued to offer the more traditional dark roast, and discerning customers would travel from far and wide just to enjoy their brew.

Yoshirō, too, held strong opinions about coffee. In a crowded field, Sachika Coffee's premium blend made for a superior cup. He thought there was nothing in the world quite as wonderful as time spent eating a warm egg sandwich with a cup of Sachika Coffee premium blend in the old shop, a wonderfully preserved relic of the early twentieth century in the Shōwa Modern style.

He continued. 'That's a real shock. You got approval from the master himself?'

In the centre of the flyer he recognised the stern, venerable face of the old coffee master. The man was said to take great pride in the Sachika Coffee name. He had received a number of offers from companies who wanted to mass-market his products, but he had never before agreed to such a thing.

'I just can't believe it. How in the world did it happen?

'It seems Niseko persuaded him, somehow. Um, that's our *counsellor*,' Nakao said in a meaningful tone, stifling a giggle. Nakao usually handled customers calmly, in a manner befitting her age, but now and again her girlish side would emerge. Catching a glimpse of the innocent-seeming smile, Yoshirō let out a noise of surprise.

'They make really great coffee, don't they?' Nakao said. 'I'm looking forward to this myself.'

'They're famous. But why . . .?' Abruptly, Yoshirō thrust the flyer back at her.

'Oh!' Nakao said, eyes widening in surprise, and Yoshirō began to speak at rapid-fire speed.

'Look, it's just that the master there makes delicate changes every day to the roast and the brewing time. Folks who don't appreciate the depth of flavour say it's too bitter, or whatever, but it's not like he's just steeping a dark roast for a long time. It's a subtle process. If they tried to get a machine to serve something like that, his long-time fans would be up in arms! People would say Sachika Coffee had sold out. Why would he choose to do something like that, that affects the reputation of such a prestigious store? I'm a fan myself, you know, and I think it's a real shame.'

Nakao's round eyes blinked rapidly. Seeing her confusion, Yoshirō came to his senses and ceased his monologue. Rubbing his head with a little embarrassment, he offered an awkward apology: 'I . . . sorry about that. It's just, maybe I like it too much? So I got kind of worked up . . .'

'No, no, don't worry about it. It's that kind of a place, isn't it?'

Nakao's kind face shifted to a placating smile as she added brightly, 'But I'm sure our version will taste great, so please give it a try when it becomes available.' In the face of her unfalteringly professional attitude Yoshirō became embarrassed. He had let his emotions get the better of him. 'Sorry,' he croaked weakly one more time, then left the register and proceeded to the coffee station.

He set the cup in its place and waited for the machine to do its work. A little song played to let him know when the coffee was ready. He was about to reach for a plastic lid from the shelf nearby when someone pressed one into his hand. He turned in surprise, and there, holding the lid, was a man with a smooth look, standing a little too close to Yoshirō and peering into his eyes.

'Oh! Er, what . . .?'

'Good afternoon, Mr Kiriyama. Going to work, I see.' A honeyed voice, then a gleam of white teeth. A small mole at the corner of his right eye was hidden from view by laugh lines. Yoshirō responded 'Yes, well . . .' his voice a little too high.

Yoshirō had never met a movie star or male idol in person, but he thought they must all be creatures like Shiba, descendants of the same tribe, wielding some kind of special powers.

'Mr Kiriyama? Is something wrong?'

Again, his face moved a little nearer, and Yoshirō's heart started to race. *No need to get so close!* He tried to reply coolly, not wanting to let Shiba know the effect he was having, but in the end, he just stammered. 'N-no . . . nothing'

'That's good. Here, take the coffee lid.' Not wanting to talk anymore, Yoshirō nodded, took the lid, and carefully fitted it atop the steaming cup. He came face to face with Shiba nearly every day, but he never really got used to it. With an easy motion, Shiba took a duster to the counter next to him.

'W-well, time to go.'

'Yes, thank you. Come back soon!' Shiba saw him off with an easy smile, and Yoshirō moved to the dine-in space, which had a door separating it from the store. There were spaces like this in some of the other stores, but this one was always comfortable and carefully maintained. He entered the room. A woman who looked like a cleaner was mopping the floor, in a flowered apron. She smiled at Yoshirō. She bore a slight resemblance to his mother who lived in Ōita, on the southeast coast where he grew up.

The woman must have been done with her cleaning, because she quickly put away the mop, and exited through a door leading back into the building. The room was now empty, and Yoshirō perched on a seat at the end of the counter. The countertop was perfectly clean, not even a drop of water on it. He deposited his messenger bag on a stool and brought the food bag over to the toaster. He took out one of the sandwiches and toasted it. *50 seconds at 1,000 watts*. After toasting the sandwich to a light golden brown, Yoshirō returned to his seat with it cradled in his hand.

He sank his teeth into the sandwich. His mouth filled with the fragrant bread – crisp on the outside, fluffy on the inside – and the warm egg salad. It was delicious again today, as always. The bread had a delicate sweetness and the nutty scent of wheat. The mild egg, with just the right amount of salt and a hint of mustard tickling his nose, was a perfect match. Yoshirō made quick work of the two halves of the first sandwich and was about to reach for the coffee when he paused for a moment. 'I suppose it's true, isn't it?' he said quietly to himself. 'This sandwich would pair really well with Sachika Coffee.'

The egg sandwich at Tenderness was somewhat similar to the hot egg sandwich at Sachika Coffee. If you toasted it, they became even more alike. The premium coffee at Tenderness complemented their egg sandwich, naturally, but nearly every day Yoshirō thought about how much deeper and richer the flavours would be if it were Sachika Coffee's special blend. He wondered if the company had also caught the eye of this 'Niseko' because of this egg sandwich.

'Not a chance.' Yoshirō gave a dismissive laugh. But in some part of his heart he couldn't help but believe it. Niseko's taste in coffee had to be very similar to his own. Lifting the cup to his mouth, Yoshirō thought back to the day he had first tasted the coffee at Tenderness, and how the flavour had surprised him.

There had been coffee machines in convenience stores for quite some time now, but Tenderness introduced them about three years later than most. When the long-awaited debut arrived and Yoshirō finally tasted the coffee, it made him just a little bit happy. The rich flavour and aroma of the carefully roasted beans suited him well, and at long last the convenience store had reached the point where it could offer this kind of quality at an affordable price. The thought of it was surprisingly moving.

After that, he started buying coffee at various Tenderness stores almost every day, but one time he happened to stop by one particular branch of the chain, and the coffee there, although broadly similar to the Tenderness coffee he had been drinking up until then, had some definite differences. A rich, clear flavour, as if he were drinking something a step up in quality. He was surprised enough to ask the clerk: 'Did Tenderness get different beans?'

In reply, the clerk beamed – now that he thought about it, it was Nakao back then, too – and asked, 'Is this your first time visiting this branch, sir? You must have noticed the flavour. But the beans are the same. They're the premium coffee beans in exclusive use at all the branches.'

'But then, what about the taste?' Yoshirō had pursued the issue. Nakao's eyes crinkled happily. Then she whispered, as if she were letting him in on a great secret. 'Actually, at our store we pick over the beans. We're the only ones that do it.'

'Huh.' He made a noise of surprise. Picking was the process of sorting the beans by hand, removing the ones that were broken, insect-damaged, or irregular in size. This eliminated odd flavours and odours, significantly improving the taste of the coffee. However, considering the daily volume of coffee sales at the convenience store, it seemed like a ridiculous amount of effort.

'Really, you do that?' he asked.

'It's delicious, isn't it?' Nakao responded. 'We do it every night. We also use a sieve and sort them by size. It makes a surprising difference in the taste, doesn't it?' She added, 'But I don't do it myself. It's our store manager.'

Could there really be a store manager who cared enough to take on such an exhausting task? Yoshirō was moved in a way that reminded him of the day when he had tasted Sachika Coffee's original blend for the first time. *Imagine, there were actually people out there who loved coffee the way he did!* But when Nakao actually pointed out the manager, Yoshirō couldn't believe his eyes. There was this man, giving off a sort of pink aura, surrounded by elderly women. The women were all at least seventy years old, or maybe even older than that, and were besieging the man with expressions no different from what Yoshirō would see on the faces of the girls he taught at the *juku*.

'Oh, Yoshiko, did you switch to a new lipstick? It looks lovely!'

The man spoke with a captivating smile, strangely reminiscent of a blooming rose.

'Yesss!' A woman – Yoshiko, presumably – let out a half-whisper that was closer to a silent shriek. Then all the ladies around her began to clamour in loud, giddy voices completely incompatible with their years. Yoshirō simply couldn't believe the scene before him. Was this some sort of ladies' night out on the town? Yoshirō rubbed his eyes and looked twice, but it was definitely a Tenderness shop, and the man was wearing the same Tenderness uniform as Nakao.

'Um, are they shooting a movie or something?'

'Nope, just a normal day for this store.'

Nakao spoke calmly. Yoshirō was confused. This scene, the mobbing of a teen idol on tour, normal? And what's more, the man in the centre of it all was the manager of a convenience store?

'It's kind of hard to explain, so maybe let's rewind the conversation back to coffee.'

Okay, let's just pretend I didn't see that.

'Ah, yes. Well, why bother yourself over this nonsense?' he asked.

Nakao let loose as if she couldn't wait any longer.

'Ah, sorry. We followed an advisor's recommendation. Seems Chairman Horinouchi of the Tenderness Stores calls him his counsellor. Counsellor Niseko.'

Tatsuhige Horinouchi was well known in Kyūshū. His small local market had grown into an extensive chain of convenience stores throughout the island. He was an energetic older man who was noted for appearing in the company's TV ads. *Caring for people, caring for you: Tenderness.* Yoshirō could picture his familiar figure, his powerful voice pronouncing the company's slogan.

'Counsellor Niseko said we should do it. That since we went through all the trouble to get good beans, we should take the time to pick them over. So we're trying it out here.'

Yoshirō took another sip. Was it a ludicrous amount of time and effort? No, when he tasted the difference, any doubts melted away. Yoshirō breathed a sigh of agreement, but Nakao frowned slightly.

'The problem is, if all the stores do the work we're doing, they won't be able to make ends meet. And then we would no longer be able to price it at 150 yen. So it seems like the best path going forward is to focus on having the beans picked at the plant, right after they roast them, instead of at the stores.'

A few months later, the coffee began to taste better at all the Tenderness stores, just as Nakao had predicted. But Shiba never stopped picking and sorting the beans himself, so the coffee at his branch was still special – head and shoulders above the rest.

Yoshirō was so impressed by the taste of the coffee that he added a visit to the shop to his daily commute. Sometimes he'd talk with Nakao and Shiba. Along the way, Nakao eventually explained that the mysterious Niseko was not an employee of the chain, but rather just an enthusiastic customer.

'Chairman Horinouchi set up a PO Box because he wanted to hear from customers directly. Messages go straight to him, without anyone interfering. This Niseko writes to him all the time, and has a lot to say.'

She explained that Niseko had acquired the title of 'Counsellor' largely due to the suggestion that the store carry baby food. Nakao, whose son was now in high school, folded her arms at this point in the story and said in a serious voice, 'Baby food isn't easy.'

'It's really hard to make something that you can feed a baby,' she continued. 'My husband was always quite the chef, but when it came to baby food, he said himself that he was at his wit's end. There were all sorts of problems. We needed to use sterilised jars, but we kept running out . . . Well anyway, we heard that Niseko wrote to the chairman, and said she wanted him to sell baby food at the store.'

You should provide food for babies, too, said the letter. It went straight to the chairman, and he responded.

He created a Baby Corner in each of the Tenderness stores, stocked with powdered milk, nappies, and baby food in sterilised jars. What's more, he began to stock special bento lunches, mildly seasoned with soft textures. These were for younger children, and the elderly as well. So the original impetus for the Tenderness chain's goal – to become a convenience store that cared for people – came from one customer's letter. In the wake of this, the chairman began to really look forward to Niseko's letters.

'Wow. Niseko, huh?' Yoshirō murmured, fiddling with his cup.

So this Niseko person was the reason Yoshirō was making his daily detour to the Golden Villa branch. He had no idea what sort of person Niseko was. Shiba had once let slip in passing that Yoshirō and Niseko were about the same age, but other than that, he hadn't a clue.

Niseko was no older than Yoshirō, but had the power to move an entire convenience-store chain. And now, the stubborn master of a coffee shop as well. So Niseko was surely not only a person of common sense, but also one of energy and influence. Who was it? He really hoped they could meet somehow. Yoshirō felt sure Niseko would be able to size him up accurately, help him take stock of his life, and advise him on what was lacking. There was so much he needed, to grow and improve, and Niseko could offer advice to him just as well as to Tenderness.

Or was that all just wishful thinking?

With a wry smile, he stood and took his remaining sandwich pack over to the toaster. Toasting it just as before, he returned to his seat. Downing his warm coffee between bites of sandwich, he gazed out the window.

The sharp early afternoon sunlight heated the asphalt on the street outside. Hot air rose shimmering from the ground, while the cars above spewed exhaust fumes as they passed. There were few pedestrians. A woman passed quickly by, carrying a small parasol that seemed of little comfort in the bright sun. *The weather will cool down after the O-bon festival in August*, Yoshirō told himself, but even now, with September just round the corner, the hot summer days continued. There were daily reports of people collapsing from heatstroke. People were talking about it all over – *The weather's extreme this year! Well above average. A real heatwave!*

But to Yoshirō, the scene seemed no different from the year before. Not the view out the window, the coffee in his hand, the colour of his sandwich. And he himself was the same. After his meal, he'd get on the train, go to work, prepare his evening lecture, and talk to middle-school students about how to write the perfect short essay, just as he had done many dozens of times before. In the evening he'd grab a perfunctory diner meal for dinner, or head home with whatever was on sale at the supermarket. Today one year ago, he was exactly the same. Would he be here a year from now, too, staring out the window at the same scene? He didn't like it, but he didn't know what to do about it, either.

Yoshirō watched as a young man in a tank top dashed into the store. He was wearing a baseball cap and his face underneath was flushed bright red. Then a mini-truck rolled into the car park. He had seen it a few times before – he thought it was probably from some sort of junk collection company. A washing machine and some steel oil drums were loaded in the back. A bearded man climbed out of the driver's seat. He wore a light green coverall with the sleeves rolled high and the words 'Whatever Guy' written in white letters on his back. Whenever he saw it, Yoshirō thought about what a strange name it was for a company. The man glanced up at the blazing sky, then disappeared into Tenderness with an easy stride.

The side door from the store opened and the young man he had been watching earlier entered the dine-in space. He sat at the opposite end of the counter from Yoshirō and reached into his plastic bag. He took out a fizzy drink and the latest issue of a weekly manga magazine for boys. He ran his hand happily across the cover, which featured the main character brandishing a sword. Yoshirō recognised the series – it had been made into an animated film the previous year. He quietly examined the young man. *The kid must be a real fan, too*, he thought. After devoting a sufficient amount of time to the magazine cover, the boy turned the page. Ignoring the sweat running down his temples, he started to read, and in no time he was lost in the world of the manga, contentment spread across his face.

By force of habit, Yoshirō reached for the sketchbook that he kept stowed away at the bottom of his messenger bag. Then he caught a faint scent of curry. He looked around. The bearded man from before had entered the dine-in space. The man looked around the room, and with a grunt and a nod, sat down right next to Yoshirō. *There were plenty of seats at the empty tables behind them*, thought Yoshirō, *so why'd you have to sit next to me?* He shot an accusatory glare at the man, but the man paid it no mind, and reached into one of the bags he was holding.

With a gesture that radiated pleasure, he pulled out a black curry with wagyu beef and a small pack of red *fukujin-zuke* pickled vegetables. From a second bag, he pulled a one-litre bottle of sparkling water. He took about half of the pickles, heaping them alongside the steaming curry sauce. He gave a long, satisfied look at the way the bright red of the pickles stood out against the velvety black curry, and then slowly, taking time to savour the food, the man began to eat. Either he was very hungry, or else he just really liked curry. Periodically, he would close his eyes and give a heartfelt nod. He ate the pickles straight, and then tried them mixed together with the sauce. The man ate continuously, admiring each subtle variation, one by one. The whole experience looked so delicious that Yoshirō couldn't help but stare.

Yoshirō ate egg sandwiches just about every day. It made him happy, but as he watched the man, it occurred to him that a little curry once in a while might be nice, too. The dark black roux, which had never held the slightest

68

interest for him, and the bright red pickles – they were too bright, really – were stirring his appetite in an unexpectedly powerful way.

The man ate the curry with gusto from start to finish, then cleared his throat happily and drank some of the water. Then he put his hand back in his bag and drew out one of Yoshirō's favourite egg sandwiches. The man peeled back the plastic and took out the sandwich, and then, deliberately, as if he were analysing it, he also peeled apart the two slices of bread. *What?* thought Yoshirō, but before he could react, the man had scattered the leftover pickles from the curry on top of the creamy egg filling of the open sandwich. Looking at the vivid contrast between the intensely red pickles on that background of pastel yellow, Yoshirō said 'Whoa!' out loud. What was this guy doing?

As if noticing his existence for the first time, the man turned towards Yoshirō. The man looked first at Yoshirō's bemused face and then down at the contents of his own hands, and the corners of his mouth lifted into a grin. The face beneath the well-tanned skin and long beard was unexpectedly youthful. With an innocent smile, he asked, 'Any food allergies?'

'Huh? Uh, no, but . . .'

'Okay, then give that here.'

The man pointed to the half-eaten sandwich, still in Yoshirō's hand. Almost against his will, he held it out and the man said quickly, 'Open it, open it!' Under pressure with no time to think, Yoshirō pulled apart his sandwich into two pieces and the man just as quickly scattered some of the pickles inside.

'Ugh,' Yoshirō groaned.

'Eat' the man said simply. 'Try it. It's good.'

The man reassembled his own sandwich with expert precision and took a big bite. Yoshirō could hear the crunch of the pickles as he chewed. Watching the smile lines gathering in the corners of the man's eyes as he enjoyed his food, Yoshirō put his own disassembled sandwich back together. After some hesitation, he bit into it nervously.

'Well?' asked the man. 'It's good, isn't it!'

Slowly Yoshirō nodded at the man, who now had a little egg in his beard. Gradually a smile dawned on his face. The combination was surprisingly good. It was sweet and sour, with an appealing texture. He had never for a moment considered having it this way, but somehow he also felt like he had tasted it sometime before. Something . . . what was it? Then he remembered. It was the special tartare sauce that his mother would always make for him at home. It was like that, with minced pickled radish or something in it.

'Pickled wasabi isn't bad either, but these are good for colour, don't you think?' The man finished his sandwich and drank down the rest of his water in a great gulp. Draining the litre bottle easily, he gave a deep sigh of satisfaction. He cleared up his rubbish, said 'Well, gotta go,' and took his leave. But then he suddenly turned back to Yoshirō.

'I get it.'

Yoshirō stared at the man and shook his head in confusion, not understanding what he meant. The man raised his voice. 'You toast the egg sandwich. I get it!' And this time he left for good, 'Whatever Guy' gleaming in the sunlight as the man disappeared into his truck. The vehicle pulled slowly out of the car park and was lost in the flow of traffic along the roadway.

Yoshirō watched him go, dumbfounded by this strangely vigorous mystery man. Then he took another bite of the half-forgotten sandwich he was still holding in his hand and gave a little laugh.

'He's right. It's pretty interesting,' he said. 'Maybe it goes well with curry, too.'

The aroma of curry lingering in the room complemented the egg sandwich well. Next time, he thought, he'd try the man's combo himself. After his strangely satisfying meal was complete, Yoshirō looked at his watch and saw that it was almost time for his train. He hopped out of his seat and left in a hurry.

*

How many people in the world find their dream job? We ask middle-school students to talk about their dreams for the future, but how many of them actually make those dreams come true?

Work was over, and the second to last train of the day was nearly empty. Yoshirō slumped in his seat, staring vacantly at his own reflection in the glass of the window across from him. Exhaustion showed on his drained face, and his skin was oily with sweat. *Have I become an old man already at thirty-three?* he wondered. By this point in his life, he should have made great progress along the road towards fulfilment of his dreams. But the ideal self that he had pictured so many times in his young head was nowhere to be found.

In the window reflection, he suddenly saw an image of himself as a boy. He had been an unexceptional child. In every activity you cared to name, whether it was athletic or academic, his performance had always been unremark-able. He had an unassuming personality, with nothing to distinguish him throughout his school years. So he lacked confidence, and his catch-phrase became 'Me? I dunno . . .' But there was one thing that he was truly proud of, one dream that he believed would definitely come true. He wanted to become a manga illustrator, drawing comic books.

He had nurtured his dream since he was just a kid in fourth grade. *Someday the world will be spellbound by my manga.* He had won a few prizes for his artwork, and for as long as he could remember, wanted nothing but to sit in front of a sheet of drawing paper. It was his clear purpose in life; there was nothing else. More important than being selected for the track team, or coming first in his class, it was the thing that allowed him to be himself.

But his dreams hadn't come true, not at all. Instead, he'd graduated from an ordinary high school, attended a run-of-the-mill college, and ended up working as a test-prep instructor at the *juku*. Even that job was just something he fell into: someone had recommended him and he was hired, no more than that. Still, he didn't intend to stay there forever. He continued to pursue his dream while he worked, and if he succeeded, he would quit without hesitation. Or that's what he told himself.

Maybe I shouldn't have been so half-hearted about it.

'Professor Kiriyama, why did you take this job?'

The words from about a half-hour ago echoed in his mind.

His lecture was over and he was seeing off his students, who were heading home as always. Yoshirō called out his farewells from behind as they climbed into shuttle buses and family cars, when several of the girls in his class approached and surrounded him. They exchanged glances among themselves, some of them smirking, and eventually one of them seemed to gather her courage and addressed him.

'This class is no fun at all, and you're not even trying. It feels like you're just here for the paycheck.'

Yoshirō understood what she was saying and yet, at the same time, the words didn't sink in. The smile froze on his face. Looking at him, the girl continued. 'I wouldn't want to live like that, no matter what.'

The girls around her burst into laughter. Seeing their sincerely happy but somehow unpleasant smiles, he felt a chill running from the top of his head down to the tip of his toes. Yoshirō scratched his head and somehow managed an audible chuckle.

'Is that so?' he asked. 'Sorry about that. I'll try to be a little more careful in the future.' Looking a little uncomfortable, the girls dispersed to go home. He smiled at their backs as they left, but his legs were trembling.

Yoshirō had always intended to do his best at the test-prep job. But he had only ever meant it to be a temporary position and it was hard for him to take working with the children seriously. In the end, the students saw right through him.

Yoshirō took his phone from his pocket. Today they had announced the second round of cuts in a large manga competition. He called up the list of finalists, but his pen name wasn't on it. How many times now had he failed to make the shortlist?

Maybe everything that had happened recently was a sign that enough was enough. It was time to let go of his dreams – actually, past time, so maybe it was a warning. Yoshirō put away his phone with a sigh. *A middle-aged man who turned his back on reality to chase dreams that will never come true. A hopeless husk with nothing to show for his name.* He hated to admit it, but that was who he was now. It was just too pitiful.

He was seized by a sudden impulse to pull the sketchbook from his bag and tear it to shreds, but another voice inside him called out to stop. He froze, hand halfway into the bag, unable to move an inch either way.

At Mojikō Station, a crowd of students in uniform and women in business clothes with tired faces, presumably on their way home from work, streamed out of the train. Yoshirō exited a little behind them and walked sluggishly down the platform. At the ticket gate, he glanced backwards. The front of the train was directly behind him, its flattened red-and-black face staring right back at him.

Mojikō Station was the first stop on the Kagoshima Main Line, which ran from Kitakyūshū in the north all the way down to the city of Kagoshima on the southern tip of the island. Since it was the starting point, the tracks ended right in the station. Yoshirō didn't know all that much about trains, but there weren't a lot of places where one could get a good look at the front of the trains up close like that. Actually, the scene was quite popular with tourists, who would often take photos from just outside the gate.

When he first moved to the area for work, Yoshirō, too, was surprised by the sight, and found it fascinating. When he stood at the beginning of the tracks, he felt a surge of happiness at the thought that his personal potential could run on forever from there.

But now it only seemed like the end of the line. Just as Mojikō Station was both the starting point and the terminus for this train, Yoshirō's possibilities were not stretching off endlessly, but instead gasping their dying breath. He would just keep on doing the same thing, one day after the next.

It was departure time. The bell rang, and the red-and-black face receded into the distance. Yoshirō shook his head once, then left the station.

Summer's lukewarm evening breeze touched his cheeks. He could smell the salt from the ocean. On the streets, teeming with tourists during the daytime, scarcely a soul could now be seen. He bought a can of beer at a convenience store by the station and made his way towards the seaside across from his home.

The Mojikō station house was built in 1914 during Japan's Taishō era and featured an unusual Neo-Renaissance design. It was a national historic landmark with a distinct retro feel, and the area around the station house was dotted with a number of old buildings from the late nineteenth century to the pre-war period. The buildings, including the station house, were lit up as they usually were at night, but due to the late hour, all was still. It was as if they were holding their breath. Yoshirō opened his beer and nursed it, sip by sip, as he headed down to the waterfront. He passed by a few couples gazing out at the night ocean.

He grimaced at the beer – he wasn't much of a drinker – and looked up at the sky. The stars were twinkling, and he could hear the sound of the waves rolling gently in. He stopped and cast his gaze out over the sea. Across the channel he could see the city lights of Shimonoseki. Shortly after he had arrived in Mojikō, he'd taken a ride there, on the ferry that ran across the channel. The boat had also stopped at Ganryū Island, which lay between Kyūshū and the mainland. The island had been the site of a famous duel between two great samurai, Miyamoto Musashi and Sasaki Kojirō.

The dusty tale had been tucked away in the back of his mind, half forgotten, but when he had disembarked and was actually standing on the soil there, he felt strangely elated. He had been riveted by statues of the two warriors, swords raised in mutual combat. *One day*, he thought. *One day I'll be a real illustrator, and turn sublime moments into timeless images like this. Thrilling scenes to give young readers goosebumps, take their breath away, to rise up unbidden in their memories for years to come, even as adults, and they'd talk about how great they were.*

He heard a disgusted laugh and then realised it was his own voice. Trying to silence it, he upended the can of beer into his throat, but instead choked on the bubbles. He doubled over coughing, hands braced on his knees, when he heard a voice.

'Kiriyama, isn't it?'

He wiped his mouth and turned. There was Shiba, surrounded by several older women. Instead of the usual Tenderness uniform, he had on a casual shirt and jeans. The ladies were dressed in finer clothes. Did the guy moonlight as a host at some sort of ladies' club? Were they his patrons? Yoshirō couldn't shake the thought.

'Kiriyama, what are you doing here?'

'N-no, I think that's my line.'

'Are you a friend of our dear Mitsuhiko?' The ladies were bubbly. Yoshirō always wondered where in the world these ladies came from. Shiba always seemed to have an entourage of at least one or two of them in tow. Was it some sort of package deal?

'He's a customer at the store,' Shiba answered on Yoshirō's behalf.

'Oh!' As if she had just remembered, a woman in a kimono exclaimed, 'He's the egg sandwich boy, isn't he?'

How did she know that? Yoshirō was at a loss for words. Watching his mouth open and shut silently, the other ladies murmured their assent: 'It's true!' 'That's him.' Everyone

76

seemed to know who he was, but Yoshirō hadn't a clue as to how. As he desperately searched his memory, Shiba smiled.

'These are the good people who manage the dine-in space next to the store.'

Ahhh, that was it. When he looked at them carefully, he noticed the face of the woman who had reminded him of his mother.

'Oh, do you all work there? Thank you. I eat there all the time.'

'Oh dear, no. Nothing like that!' The woman who looked like his mother waved her hand in front of her face to dispel the idea.

'We all live in the Golden Villa apartments. That dining room was a social space for residents, but we opened it to the public.'

Yoshirō raised his eyebrows. He knew that the upper floors of the building were reserved for seniors. Right, so then it made sense that the upstairs residents were in the store all the time.

The woman who looked like his mother continued. 'I started doing it for the sake of our dear Mitsuhiko, but you have no idea how much spice it's added to my life.'

The ladies all laughed, and in his sweetest voice Shiba said, 'I don't know how I'd survive without you,' before he turned to Yoshirō. 'They keep it spotless in there, so the customers love it, for one thing—'

'Just hearing that from you is thanks enough. And then on top of that, you take us to dinner!'

The ladies explained that Shiba had just taken them out for a fancy dinner at a local place specialising in *fugu* – blow-fish. So, Yoshirō thought idly, it wasn't that Shiba was a kept man, but still, it was somewhat of a weird relationship.

'Ah, yes, yes. But young man, you need to eat something else once in a while, don't you? It's not healthy to eat nothing but egg sandwiches and coffee!'

One of them admonished him, as if just remembering, and the rest of them nodded deeply in agreement.

'At least add a salad.'

'Or vegetable juice, that would be fine, too.' They all chimed in, sounding exactly like his mother, and Yoshirō was a little embarrassed. When he ate alone, he usually just wanted to finish fast and use the time for something else – for manga, basically, but what was the point of saying that now?

'Well, I'd better get going,' he said, and started to take his leave. *I guess I should stop going to that store from now on,* he thought. *It'll be a shame to miss all that delicious coffee, but it's out of the way.*

As he turned to go, Shiba said, 'Seems like food is always a low priority for artists.' Yoshirō froze and turned back. Looking half apologetic, half embarrassed, Shiba continued. 'I'm a fan of your drawings, Mr Kiriyama. The truth is, sometimes I sneak a peek at them from behind when you're working on them.'

As confessions go, it was a mild one, but Yoshirō felt as if his body, flushed with alcohol, had cooled instantly. He exhaled, his breath catching like a draught of cold air in the back of his throat.

Shiba continued, a note of passion creeping into his voice. 'You have your own style, don't you? They're warm, and gentle, and I think they're sweet. It's nice that you have something that you can get lost in that way, isn't it?'

What was this emotion? Something halfway between anger and shame forced its way up into Yoshirō's throat.

He felt as if he could hear the laughter of his students echoing in his ears, loud voices barking at him, engulfing him. And beyond those voices, Shiba too was laughing.

'Shut up!' Yoshirō screamed, waving his arms wildly in front of him, as if he were trying to scare away some creature. 'Shut up! Shut up! You don't know me at all, so you can't say that!'

He raised his voice so loud he surprised himself. The ladies' eyes flew wide open, and a couple walking by cast a startled glance his way. His whole body trembling, Yoshirō opened his mouth again.

'I'm trying really hard to live my life, okay? I've got my own problems! Maybe it's hard for people like you to get it, but I'm killing myself here just trying!'

As his emotion mounted, his eyes began to water. Yoshirō bit his lip, but this had been a weakness of his since he was a kid. He whirled and fled. The dam broke and the tears he was trying to hold back flowed freely. *How pathetic,* he thought to himself. He was certainly old enough to know better, so what was he doing?

He ran until his breath came in ragged gasps and his poorly toned legs screamed in protest. When he finally stopped, he found himself near his own apartment. Shoulders heaving, he wiped away the accumulated mix of sweat and tears. In contrast to his physical state, Yoshirō found that a strange composure had settled over him, and he dragged his exhausted form back to his apartment.

In the kitchen, he drank water, lots of it. Halfway through his third glass, he took a deep breath. Cup in hand, he headed to his room. He settled himself at the black desk that had been with him since his student days and cast his eyes downwards. In front of him was a draft of the story he had been drawing until late last night, the hero a young swordsman, his blade swinging valiantly through the air.

'They always make fun of me.'

He ran his fingers lightly over the swordsman's face. He had always loved to draw, but never knew that it could be an actual profession until third grade, when a new friend – his name was Mogi – transferred to his school and taught him about artists. Mogi came from Tokyo, and announced he was going to be a manga illustrator when he grew up. He already owned pro-grade art supplies: a G-pen, a round pen, screentone sheets and Kent paper. He knew how to use everything properly and could even draw all the heroes from the weekly issues of *Jump* magazine.

Yoshirō had never seen drawings or tools like that before – they were the real thing. Thanks to Mogi, Yoshirō too now had a dream. He might have come to it on his own, but Yoshirō imagined that it was Mogi's arrival that enabled him to really go for it. Mogi's presence in their shared dream loomed large in Yoshirō's mind.

In high school, the two of them each started submitting work to publishers, but Mogi was always the one who came closer to winning the big prizes. His finely detailed drawings had become more impressive since elementary school, and his character designs were brilliant. Before long he'd been paired with an editor and was told he'd make his debut while he was still a student. Yoshirō was full of pride for his friend.

But at some point, Mogi seemed to start thinking of Yoshirō as a burden. He stopped asking him to help with inking drawings, and then he even stopped sharing his drafts. By the time Yoshirō realised he was no longer being consulted, Mogi had already found engagement elsewhere, as an assistant to a manga artist in Hakata. At times he would even skip school to work with the man, bowing his head in quiet apology to Yoshirō, who was perplexed by the change in his friend.

'We won't learn anything if we take our advice from people whose abilities or situation are too different,' Mogi said to him. 'Besides, haven't you had enough of this? You've always pushed yourself to the limit, haven't you, listening to my stories.'

It had been many years since Mogi had moved from Tokyo to the rural town of Ōita. But he spoke in clear language, free of dialect, and chose his words with care. There was no disguising the pity in his voice.

Yoshirō couldn't draw the way Mogi did. No matter how he practised, he didn't seem to improve, and his work was always panned. He had managed to make it to two competition finals, but after that, progress was slow. He didn't have Mogi's talent. There was simply no way he would ever be able to create gorgeous, stylish pictures like those splendid works of art, unless he could find a way to be reborn as someone very different from who he was then. That being the case, he had no choice but to draw his own pictures, in his own way. Instead of making himself miserable over what he couldn't draw, he decided to focus on what he could draw. That's how he kept himself going, and Mogi understood how he felt. Or so Yoshirō thought.

'There's probably something else you . . . that is, a different kind of talent that you have. Right? So I think it would be wrong of me to lead you astray, down my own path. And me too – I want to be with the kind of people who can understand me on a deeper level.'

'But you said my work was interesting, didn't you?' Yoshiro said in a trembling voice. Mogi always had something kind to say about Yoshiro's work. How happy it had always made him! He knew there was no way he'd find success as an artist as quickly as Mogi had done. But it would be nice if Mogi would at least do him the kindness of letting him help out as an assistant. No matter how desperately Yoshiro tried to find the right words, Mogi just shook his head.

'Your skills are weak, but your personality is too strong. Besides, I can't let someone who's basically an amateur touch my work. It will hurt the quality.'

Yoshiro was stunned at the flat refusal, but Mogi continued. 'You're not going to succeed in this business relying on the kindness of others! I'm serious about becoming a manga artist. This isn't a game!'

'I'm not playing around either,' Yoshiro retorted. 'I mean it . . .'

Yoshiro had always wanted to be a manga artist. He wanted to say so, but the words stuck in his throat and wouldn't come out. Mogi burst out laughing. The laughter seemed to ooze from his mouth of its own volition.

'Oh please, stop,' said Mogi. 'You've made a terrible mistake. Do you understand that your actual skills are at the level of an elementary student's notebook scrawl? It's a miracle that you ever made it to the finals at all!'

Mogi laughed in Yoshiro's face for a little while longer, then shut his mouth as if he had got bored of the whole thing. 'Well, let's each live our lives in the fields that suit us.' Then he left, and Yoshirō and Mogi never spoke another word to each other.

Soon after that, a manga artist from Hakata – where Mogi used to go – became a popular author. His series became a regular cover feature in the magazines and was even made into an anime that was super popular with the kids. Mogi might have worked for him as an assistant until his early mid-twenties. For a while, Yoshirō used to recognise his touch on backgrounds and minor characters, but after a certain point those disappeared completely. He never saw Mogi's pen name anywhere. What field suited him now?

Yoshirō lifted a pen from the desk, but his hand wouldn't move. He had been working feverishly until yesterday, with the intention of entering the next open contest, but his passion seemed to have vanished overnight.

He had been mocked, he had failed to get the results he wanted, and still, he had been utterly unable to give up manga. He had worked hard, in his own way, but maybe it was time to quit. He had to rethink his life. He had the feeling that if he didn't, a day would come that was even worse than the present one.

The young swordsman was looking at Yoshirō. It seemed to him that he was saying, 'Sorry, pal.' *Maybe I shouldn't draw anymore*, he thought. It was so complicated, so many things overlapping, including all those past wounds, and so painful. Maybe this was the end.

The young swordsman said nothing. With a sad look on his face, head bowed slightly, Yoshirō stepped away from the desk. That night he crawled into bed without taking a bath.

★

Yoshirō had decided it was time to go home. He'd quit his job, let the apartment go, and move home to his parents' place in Ōita.

The day arrived quickly, and he sent his bags ahead of him. Standing in the middle of his empty apartment, he felt like he might cry. What had he been doing here for all these years?

I don't think I'll be back here again. Yoshirō began to walk, holding his small bag and putting the apartment behind him. The plan was to catch a connecting train to Ōita where his parents lived, but he was finding it hard, somehow, to just up and leave, and he couldn't quite bring himself to go straight to Mojikō station.

He wandered aimlessly until he found himself in front of the red-brick building of the former customs house, gazing blankly at the sea. The water was beautiful, sparkling as it caught the summer sunlight, and Yoshirō squinted a little. Although the seascape was the perfect scene to lighten the heart, his spirits sank lower and lower. Going back home meant he'd be leading a boring life that wasn't very different from life here, that was for sure. *Now that I've abandoned both my work and my dreams, what will I do . . .?*

'Aha! Found him!' Suddenly a rough voice called out behind him, and when Yoshirō turned, he saw an old man astride a red cargo bike. Yoshirō had seen the man before, in the area around Mojikō station. He dressed strangely, and Yoshirō was sure he had heard students calling him 'Old Red'. As he was thinking this, the man called out to him. 'Professor! Hey, Professor! Mitsuhiko said you haven't been around lately! He's worrying about you.'

Who was Mitsuhiko? And more to the point, how did this Old Red fellow know him? Yoshirō stared back at him in surprise. 'Don't go!' the old man shouted. 'Don't leave! Don Juan is down in the dumps because he said something rude to you, Professor!'

At that point, it finally dawned on Yoshirō that Mitsuhiko must be Shiba. Now that he thought about it, he had a feeling that was what those ladies down on the waterfront had been calling him, too.

Since that day, he hadn't been to the Golden Villa store, or any Tenderness store, for that matter. That must be what Old Red was talking about. *Butt out, old man*, he was about to reply, but thought better of it. After all, he was leaving, anyway. Better just to be polite. He tossed the man a quick head bob and Old Red smiled in satisfaction. His already severe face became downright menacing when he smiled, and Yoshirō was a little startled.

'Good. Now go make it right.'

Yoshirō nodded a few more times, then suddenly broke away and fled towards Mojikō station. He dashed through the ticket gate without the slightest hesitation, and quickly boarded. He didn't look back, even once the train had started moving.

After he left Mojikō, a month passed in the blink of an eye. Yoshirō was leading a boring life at his parents' house, as he had predicted. At first his elderly parents were overjoyed at their son's homecoming, but that quickly shifted to a litany of complaints: 'Isn't it about time you found some work?' 'You know, this all happened because you're single.' And so forth. He visited Hello Work, the government employment centre, but he couldn't find the right job, and there wasn't much he could do about that.

Things weren't great at home, so he'd go out, but there was nothing much to do within walking distance. How was he supposed to kill time in a place with nothing but mountains, rice paddies and a few family farms? Mojikō wasn't a big city, but it had at least been fairly convenient in that respect. Daily life there was free of even the most minor inconveniences, and all the pleasures of Hakata were less than an hour away by train. Tenderness coffee was a five-minute walk from his front door. It had become such a regular part of his life that he had taken it for granted, but he realised how lucky he had been to have that small luxury so close at hand. Particularly now, when the nearest convenience store was twenty-five minutes away, and that was by car.

He sprawled on his bed, gazing at the ceiling. He couldn't stop wondering how this had become his future. Where and how did it all go wrong? *What if I had never met Mogi? If I had never had the crazy dream of being a manga illustrator?* But no matter how he thought about it, the truth was, he had always loved manga.

'I'm such a fool!'

As he was muttering to himself, his mother Satomi called out, 'Yoshirō! Are you there? I need your help! We're throwing out the old reception set in the barn.'

He looked out the window. An orange hue was beginning to steal across the sky. Why were they clearing out the barn at this hour? But if he asked that, Satomi's good mood would turn bad quickly. With a sigh, Yoshirō went outside.

'Mum, what do you . . .?'

Scratching his head, he entered the barn. Just then, a loud voice called out 'Yep, that's the guy!' He looked over.

It was none other than the bearded man who was eating curry next to him, that time at the Tenderness.

'Gotcha! I thought you'd be somewhere around here.' The man bounded over and gave Yoshirō a few hearty slaps on the back. 'I've been searching for you.'

'Ow! Um, okay, what the heck . . .?' That the man remembered him at all was strange enough, but Yoshirō couldn't for the life of him figure out what the man would want with him. 'What do you mean?' asked Satomi, who was standing in front of a dilapidated faux-leather sofa.

'I've been searching! For him,' the man cheerfully replied. 'Me, I've always been really good at treasure hunts, hide and seek – finding things is my speciality. So I was pretty sure I could find him.' The man gave a deep belly laugh. Then he turned to Satomi and started issuing instructions: 'Okay, Auntie – before we do all that, let's get this into the truck. Hold it right there.' *This is all happening too fast*, thought Yoshirō, gingerly rubbing his back.

'M . . . Mum? You know this guy?'

'Oh yes, he's the handyman. We call him *the whatever lad*. He comes around from time to time. There are a lot of seniors in the area, so it's useful to have a young man to come and do some of the heavy lifting, don't you think? You're a little too weak and not that much help, so . . .'

After this cutting remark, Satomi asked, 'And you? How do you know Mr Shiba? Are you friends?' Before Yoshirō could answer, the man gave a calm nod.

'We shared some egg sandwiches.'

Yoshirō wanted to ask if that alone qualified them as friends, but the name that Satomi had called the man drew his attention.

'Shiba?'

87

He knew that name. Wasn't that . . .? But before he could ask, the man responded, 'Oh, he's my brother. My younger brother, the store manager.'

'You don't look like him.' He blurted out the thought before he could stop himself. They were nothing alike, not at all. He couldn't believe that they were brothers, this dishevelled, shaggy man and the other one, who seemed to have sex appeal baked into his every fibre. The man must have been used to such a reaction; he simply nodded, and said, 'We have the same two parents. Brothers for sure. Yep, call me Tsugi.'

Before Yoshirō could respond, the man – Tsugi, apparently – carried off the sofa with his mother's help. From outside the barn came Satomi's voice, 'Yoshirō, you help too!' Yoshirō hurriedly picked up a small ottoman.

After they had somehow managed to fit all the furniture into Tsugi's truck, Satomi pointed to a stack of cardboard boxes piled up at one end of the barn, and said to Yoshirō, 'Now, what about these? He also takes paper for recycling. Should we have him take these?'

Yoshirō was at a loss for words. The boxes contained all of his accumulated drafts and artwork. He had intended to burn them in a corner of a field that Satomi was tending, but he hadn't been able to bring himself to do it. So instead he had carried them out to the barn, where at least they'd be out of sight.

'Seems they're too much for you to handle yourself.' Satomi added.

'Uh, yeah. I guess so, but . . .'

Looking at the large cardboard boxes, Satomi said, 'Even at your age, you still love 'em, don't you? It would have been nice if you could have made a living off 'em. But it didn't work out. Life is like that. Only a handful get to put rice in the pot by doing what they love.'

Yoshirō hung his head at his mother's sober tone. The woman knew her son well. She understood that he had sacrificed both food and sleep to his passion for manga.

Her tone softened. 'It's time to let it go.' Yoshirō tried to nod.

'You don't have to let it go.'

Yoshirō turned and found himself face to face with the bushy beard. Tsugi was busy guzzling an energy drink, but between gulps he managed to ask, 'What if you just kept on doing it? It's just drawing, right? If you've been able to do it this long while holding down a job at the same time, I think you'll manage.'

'But I . . . Well, it's a question of talent . . .'

'Talent is being able to keep going,' Tsugi said, simply. 'Successful people all say that. They just had to find a way to keep going, no matter what. If you can do that for long enough without reward, can't we call that talent?'

Yoshirō bit his lip. Then he managed to squeeze out a few words. 'But it's true. I have no talent,' he said. 'I'm bad at it. Really. I'll never be able to be a manga artist.'

'Is that so? My brother said your pictures were good. He liked them, at least. Although he can come off as a little bit of a smooth operator, somehow, so he can be hard to believe.'

'Oh! It was the same with you, wasn't it?' Satomi said, 'At first we were all quite concerned about this peculiar young man coming around.'

Tsugi laughed. 'Yes, that's right. Seems like peculiarity might run in the family, you know?'

SONOKO MACHIDA

'If it's a family matter, your brother must be a good person,' said Satomi. 'We all look forward to the days you come round, now.'

All Tsugi said was 'Is that right?' but he looked a little pleased, nonetheless. Then he turned to Yoshirō.

'Anyway, my brother meant what he said. But seems like he didn't get it across to you. He wanted to apologise, but it looked like you were gone for good. He was really worried, you know. He thought maybe it was his fault you disappeared. So that's why he put me on the case. I'm glad I found you!' Tsugi let loose a toothy grin. Then he latched on to Yoshirō's arm. 'Let's go for a drive. To Mojikō.'

Tsugi spoke in an offhand manner, but Mojikō was close to a three-hour drive from there, even on the expressway.

'W-wait a minute.' Yoshirō tried to demur. 'Let's not jump into anything we'll regret. Plus, it's already getting dark.'

'It's no problem. I have to come back this way, so you can spend the night there and I'll bring you back tomorrow. That should do it.' Tsugi looked back at the mini-truck behind him. The truck bed was already full, but according to Satomi, there were other households waiting for him to visit.

Tsugi continued. 'You can stay at my brother's place. Just between us, he actually lives in the Golden Villa building, on the fourth floor. He gets a discount on the rent, but it's a nice big place. So, Auntie – can I borrow your son?'

'Yes indeed,' Satomi readily assented. 'I've had enough of him loafing around with that hang-dog look on his face. Oh! And if you're going down to Mojikō, get me some of those local sweetcakes, the ones shaped like blowfish. I like those quite a bit.'

Yoshirō was disconcerted by this unexpected turn of events, but Tsugi had a firm grip on his arm and wouldn't let go. An hour later, Yoshirō was riding shotgun in the mini-truck, speeding north on the expressway to Mojikō.

'How did you find me?' he asked, gazing at the scenery as it flowed past.

Tsugi gave a satisfied laugh. 'I told you, didn't I? Finding things is my speciality.'

'Yeah, but it's just unbelievable. I didn't tell anyone where I was going.' The test-prep academy had his home address, but the Shiba brothers wouldn't even have known where Yoshirō worked. As he puzzled over how in the world they could have found him, Tsugi gave him a quick sideways glance, then said, 'Old Red. He told us that you had given up your room and were leaving Mojikō. You can learn pretty much anything if you ask that man.'

'Wow.' Yoshirō remembered the man's tough, bearded face. He had always thought the guy was kind of comical, wandering around all day in his funny get-up, but now he was sounding more like some sort of intelligence agent, or a member of some shadowy organisation that watched over the streets of Mojikō.

'But even Old Red didn't know where your hometown was. And then, my brother said you were probably from Ōita. Seemed like he recognised your accent.'

That night, when he had got so upset and shouted at Shiba, his local dialect must have come out. He hadn't noticed.

'My work takes me all over Kyūshū. So recently I looked for you whenever I was in Ōita. Aside from that tip, I've mostly been following my nose. But I found you, so that's no small thing.

'It's all about my animal instincts,' he added, his mouth spreading into a wide grin. Observing his gruff, forthright manner, Yoshirō doubted for a moment whether this man could really be the other Shiba's brother. But then, who but Shiba's brother could have such a peculiar ability?

'Right, then,' he continued, 'it's time I had a look at these drawings, too. I'm sure they're in that bag of yours.'

Yoshirō had a bag with a change of clothes in his lap, and sure enough, he had also packed a sketchbook with his drawings, as Tsugi had guessed. He opened the bag and pulled the book out. He ran his hand softly over its old, faded cover.

When the time finally came for him to leave Mojikō, Yoshirō had barely been able to stroll by the old customs house, and nothing more. Since he now had the chance to visit all the places lodged in his memory, he had taken with him the volume that held the deepest sway in his heart.

'This is the first sketchbook I bought after I moved to Mojikō.'

He had purchased it at an old stationery store in the shopping district. The proprietor seemed an ill-tempered man, but after Yoshirō had made his purchase, the man had said, 'There are a lot of picturesque landscapes in these parts, so make good use of it.'

'I grew up deep in the mountains,' Yoshirō said to Tsugi, 'so just being by the sea made me happy.'

Maybe the new surroundings would prompt a change in him, too, he thought. He could still remember the thrill he felt at the time. As he turned the pages, the scenery of Mojikō unfurled before him. Children playing on the giant octopus slide at Saltbreeze Playground, and the night view at Mekari Park. A sleeping cat with the Sankiro social club in the background, and a penguin at the Kaikyokan aquarium. When they paused at a traffic light, Tsugi paged through the book and made a sound of pleasant surprise.

'I told you, I'm no good.' Yoshirō insisted.

'No, they're not bad, are they? They have charm.' He didn't know if it was Tsugi's unaffected manner of speech, or something about his temperament, but Yoshirō found that he accepted the compliment without resistance.

'Thanks. But I'll never be a professional. My pictures don't have whatever it takes to make the cut at a commercial magazine.'

Mogi's words came back to him and a wave of sadness washed over him. Mogi had been hard on him, certainly, but he wasn't wrong.

'I don't get it,' said Tsugi, tilting his head in confusion. 'Making it your job, or making a meal out of it, or, uh . . . making the cut at a commercial magazine – are those things that important?'

'Well, aren't they?' Yoshirō raised his voice as if he couldn't believe what he was hearing. 'Isn't that the way it works? I always dreamed about drawing a manga that all the kids were crazy for, and so—'

'And so . . .' Tsugi broke in, 'are you saying your dream is equal to all that other stuff?'

Yoshirō became still. Tsugi scratched his dishevelled head furiously. 'Aren't things like food and work the extras that get thrown in after your dream?' His voice was so gentle it was almost like he was talking to himself, and Yoshirō could say nothing in response.

'Ta . . . talent is . . .' he gasped, as if trying to breathe.

'So listen. I'm telling you I think your pictures are good,' Tsugi continued. 'My brother, too. To say you want to be accepted by everyone, that's not easy. But now, you have at least two people saying you're good. Don't you need to start somewhere?'

93

Yoshirō thought that was a little idealistic. But he could say nothing in reply.

At a loss for words, he flipped through his sketchbook, page by page. He gazed, captivated, at the pictures he himself had once drawn.

Yoshirō was halfway through the book when there was a loud exclamation from Tsugi, who hurriedly pulled onto the shoulder of the road and stopped the car. Yoshirō looked at him in surprise. Eyes shining, Tsugi commanded, 'Turn back a page!' Yoshirō wasn't sure what he wanted, but he opened the book again and flipped to the previous page.

'Uh . . . here?'

It was the scene of the duel between Miyamoto Musashi and Sasaki Kojirō. Once he saw those two bronze statues he knew he simply had to draw them, come hell or high water. He didn't have the skill to sketch them in fine detail, so he just did it his own way. Tsugi gazed happily at that picture.

'It's good. Really good. Is that your style? I see it. I think these two are great.'

'Really? Musashi and Kojirō?'

Tsugi pulled back onto the road. 'My old man liked them a lot. When he was in a good mood, he'd always do it for us – the duel at Ganryū Island.'

'He'd do it?'

'Well, according to him, it was like his version of *kamishibai*, the puppet shows he'd see in the streets when he was a kid. He would beat the table with some rolled up paper and tell us the story. "Kojirō waited on the shore for his nemesis. At last, Musashi appeared! He stood tall in the bow of his small boat. Kojirō shouted: *You there, Musashi! Do you fear me? Are you trembling?* Mad with impatience, Kojirō unsheathed his long blade – *the hanging pole*, he called it – and flung its scabbard to the sand. Musashi mocked him: *If you're ready to throw away your scabbard, then you've already lost!*"'

Tsugi let his voice swell into a chant as if he were in a real drama in a theatre. 'I'm not bad at it myself,' he laughed, 'because I've already heard it dozens of times. And every time, I adored it.'

Tsugi pointed to the open sketchbook in Yoshirō's lap, and said earnestly, 'It's good, that one. It's nice and warm, and I think it's really good. You want something that children will love? How about *kamishibai*?'

'Ha! You think I should do puppet shows?' Who needed a Shōwa-era relic like that now? Yoshirō laughed, but at the same time his heart gave a little jump. Maybe there were other jobs out there involving pictures that children would love?

'Well, you could do something besides *kamishibai*, I guess.' Tsugi's voice startled him out of his reverie.

'There might be something.' Yoshirō replied. Could there be? He didn't know. The sea breeze came flowing through the open window of the car and he looked outside.

'Ah, Mojikō already.'

The mini-truck slipped into the store car park. As Tsugi cut the engine, his brother Shiba popped eagerly out of the store. Catching sight of Yoshirō in the passenger seat, he smiled like a flower bursting into bloom. Yoshirō recoiled for an instant, at this smile that seemed more appropriate for a long-lost lover than anything else.

'Older brother! Thank you!'

'Pretty amazing, aren't I?'

'I never thought you'd get him here!' Shiba bowed his head deeply to Yoshirō, who was climbing awkwardly out of the passenger seat. 'Please forgive me for my words the other day. I spoke out of turn.'

95

'Oh, um, forget about it. I got fairly worked up, too, didn't I? Sorry about that.' As Yoshirō bowed his head in return Shiba noticed the sketchbook in his hand and heaved a sigh of relief.

'Ah, good! I was worried that you'd quit drawing on my account.'

'No, it's fine.'

Tsugi had wasted no time ducking into the store, leaving Yoshirō alone with his brother. Presently, he stuck his head out of the dine-in space and shouted to Yoshirō, 'Hey! Let's eat, I'm starving!'

'What about me, older brother?'

'Nope. Buy your own.'

'Oh, that's harsh!'

Listening to the two of them banter, Yoshirō laughed. They may have been completely different types, but they sure sounded like brothers.

'Yoshirō, be quick! Coffee's getting cold'

'Oh! The Sachika coffee! You got it?'

At the side entrance to the store a banner hung down, reading 'New! Now Selling Sachika Coffee. Sole Authorised Vendor'. Yoshirō still hadn't had a chance to try it, he had been so far away from the store.

'I'll be right there!'

Hurrying over, he entered the familiar dine-in space to find hot coffee and egg sandwiches – two for each of them – lined up on one of the four-top tables. Not to mention the bright red *fukujinzuke* pickles.

'Ha! That's a combination I know.'

He wanted to toast the egg sandwiches immediately, but first he just had to try the coffee. He seated himself across from Tsugi and reached for the cup. It was a high-quality cup with a touch of luxury and the Sachika logo embossed in it. He traced it with his finger, then popped off the plastic lid. Yoshirō breathed in as the fragrance gently spread and made a little noise of surprise. 'Hm?'

'Taste it.'

He turned. Shiba was standing nearby, watching him. Yoshirō turned his gaze from the manager's meaningful smile back to the coffee cup and lifted it carefully to his mouth. At the first sip, a shiver of excitement ran through him. There was a heady aroma, reminiscent of wine, and a burst of fruity acidity. A sudden, delicate flash of bitterness, then the lingering sweetness of the coffee fruit.

'But . . . this is single-origin coffee, isn't it?'

The clean, clear taste was unmistakable. Could this really come from Sachika Coffee's master of the dark roast? It was completely different from any Sachika coffee that Yoshirō had ever tasted.

He took a sip, tilted his head again, then one more sip, his eyes widening. The coffee he knew from Sachika and the coffee he was tasting now didn't match up neatly at all.

'He's got a really bad rap in some parts for selling out the Sachika Coffee name.' Shiba, who had been watching Yoshirō carefully, blurted this out, then frowned. 'Some of their more intense fans even picketed the store to protest.'

So it went that far. *It was possible*, thought Yoshirō. He had wondered about the public reaction himself when he had first heard about the plan. On top of that, fans of Sachiko Coffee's famously robust flavour might feel disappointed, or even betrayed, by the sharp acidity of the new brew.

'Don't overthink it, just taste it. It's amazing! The flavour really suits the sandwiches.'

Before he could blink Tsugi had thrust a toasted sandwich in his direction, his face full of confidence. Yoshirō
accepted the sandwich and bit into it cautiously. He chewed
slowly and took a sip of the coffee. For a while, he said
nothing. Then he cracked a slight smile.

'Ah, there's something . . . what is it?'

Although the flavour was different, there was something essential about the coffee that hadn't changed. The
fragrance of the bread and the sweetness of the egg filling
came through perfectly, and the presence of the coffee
wasn't diminished in the slightest.

'How . . .? It's delicious.'

It was a new flavour. How was this possible?

'Originally, it was the higher-ups at the Tenderness chain
who had requested a custom single-origin coffee,' Shiba
said. 'Apparently, the master at Sachika Coffee thanked
them for the request. He said that he was grateful to take
on a new challenge at his age, while still doing what he
loved. And that if they were going to do it, they should
search out a flavour that would be loved by one and all.'

Yoshirō peered at the cup in his hand. The master was
already a stooped old man. He had grown weaker, too.
The last time Yoshirō visited the shop he had mentioned
with a shrug of the shoulders that his hospital visits had
been increasing of late. They had persuaded that man to
take on a venture like this?

'The average number of customers here at the Tenderness
is at least eight hundred per day. Of those, about a hundred
and fifty buy coffee. When you consider how many branches
altogether there are in the chain, this makes for a vast number
of people. Personally, I wondered if it was possible that a
single flavour could satisfy all of them. Still, it's become

very popular. It has its critics, but sales have been excellent.'

Yoshirō took a bite of the sandwich and drank his coffee. A feeling that could only be described as passion was building inside him. Even that old man was happy to take on a new challenge. And he got results.

'It's amazing,' said Shiba. 'I hear he's planning to carry a selection of the best single-origin coffees at his own shop. He's now on a trip to source the beans. That's pretty cool, isn't it?'

The cup in Yoshirō's hand was empty. As he looked at it, he found himself starting to despair again. Could he ever have got that far in life? Would he ever express in his own work just a small fraction of the artistry that he had just now tasted? Unable to do even that, he had left everything in his life a half-baked mess, but despite that, hadn't he been hurt enough?

He removed the sketchbook from his bag. Yoshirō gazed at the old volume for a while, then called out to the store manager. Shiba had changed out of his work uniform, and was happily munching on some pickled *takuan* radishes that Satomi had given to Tsugi before they left. In one hand was a can of beer. *That was fast.*

'Excuse me, Mr Shiba? And Tsugi, too. My pictures – you really think they're good?'

'Of course.' Shiba nodded. 'I only managed to steal a quick glance now and then from behind you, so my opinion doesn't count for much, but I would never make such a hurtful joke. I always thought they were good!'

'Oh, Mitsu,' interrupted Tsugi. 'Did you see that one? There's one that's real good. Yoshirō, show him.'

Yoshirō opened his sketchbook as requested. The samurai sketch of Musashi and Kojirō made Shiba instantly happy, just like his brother.

'Wow. The *kamishibai* that dad used to talk about must have been just like this, you know?'

'I thought so, too.'

Their faces lit up as they looked at the picture that Yoshirō had made. A smile rose of its own accord on his face. The whole reason he wanted to draw in the first place, he recalled, was to see faces like these. He wanted to draw pictures that would make people really feel something. Maybe it didn't have to be kids' comics, after all.

'Maybe I should keep on drawing . . .?'

The quiet remark didn't elude either of the brothers. Although they didn't resemble each other at all, a single look passed between them as they said in unison, 'Sounds good.'

'Now then, shall we go somewhere for a drink?' asked Shiba. 'Kiriyama, I owe you an apology, so it's my treat.'

'Personally, I could really go for some *fugu*,' interjected Tsugi.

'I'm talking to Kiriyama. Big brother, you can pay for yourself.'

Together with the two peculiar brothers, he walked out into the town of Moji at nightfall. A cool sea breeze flowed gently by. As they immersed themselves in the familiar but beautifully illuminated cityscape, Yoshirō laughed out loud for the first time in a long while.

Looking back, he could see the bright lights of Tenderness casting off into the darkness. Their coffee gave him courage, that was certain. If he needed courage in the future, wherever he was, he could always visit Tenderness. Feeling just a little bit happy, he gave a slight bow to the banner fluttering in the wind.

Chapter Three
A Melancholy Strawberry Parfait

The high-pitched shriek from the garden was unmistakable.

'No, no, no! I've just about had it! Your father, he doesn't get it at all. They won't grow like this!' Michiyo's voice was growing more heated by the moment, so with a sigh, Azusa closed her book and stuck her head out through the patio door.

'What's the matter, Mother?'

'Oh, Azusa. Listen to me. Yesterday, your father wanted to help in the garden, right? So I asked him to plant the beds, but he's being so careless!'

Michiyo wore a pink gardening smock, and the round face under her wide-brimmed straw hat became even rounder as she pouted. 'Look!' she said, pointing with the tip of her trowel towards her carefully tended garden plot. The plot was neatly divided into sections for flowers, vegetables and herbs. Michiyo was pointing at the herbs. It looked like there were a great variety planted there, but Azusa couldn't tell one from another. Look as she might, she had no idea what was wrong.

'Careless, you said? Did he forget to cover them with dirt or something?' Azusa didn't see any exposed roots, but she couldn't think of any other reason. Michiyo raised her volume as if she had utterly lost her patience and said, 'It's about compatibility of course! Isn't it obvious? I taught you about compatibility in herbs, didn't I, Azusa? Just look at the positioning of the lemon balm and rosemary here. It's just like your father. He says *leave it to me, I'll take care of it*, but what was he thinking?'

Michiyo was talking as if she couldn't believe her eyes, but Azusa still didn't see the problem. She was about to ask again, but she thought better of it and stopped. It would just fan the flames of her mother's fury. When Michiyo's horticultural pursuits were treated lightly, her anger could flare up instantly, without warning. Sparks flew in all directions, and Azusa had been the victim of second-hand burns this way more than once in the past. But she had to say something. 'Dad's a total mess,' she blurted out, 'it really sucks, doesn't it?' Then she fled to her room.

Azusa flopped down on her bed and took up her phone. As she lay there on the bed, she tried searching for 'herb compatibility' on the phone.

'Hmm . . . it's about *preferred growing conditions*, maybe?'

Apparently herbs had preferences. They liked different conditions – dry or damp, sunny or shady – and if you planted things with different preferences together, they might wither or fail to grow properly. *Right, of course, so that was it.* Azusa kept scrolling aimlessly, then paused.

'Wow, mint is intense!'

She had landed on a feature titled 'Dangerous Herbs'.

'Mint is a herb that grows with excessive vigour. It can cause great trouble when planted together with other species. If not controlled properly it may overrun neighbouring herbs, leaving only mint in the pot. Moreover, when planted in the ground, its rhizomes spread densely, rapidly expanding its breeding area.'

Hmm, she murmured to herself, and jumped to a different site. There was a dramatic story about how someone had planted mint in their garden. It had overrun the gardens next door and caused trouble in the neighbourhood. It was known, somehow, that while mint had amazing benefits – including possible uses as an insect repellent, antibiotic and anti-inflammatory – it was also a difficult plant to manage.

When Azusa pictured mint in her mind's eye, she imagined it perched daintily atop a slice of cake, or else on a bowl of ice cream. It was a leaf with an assertive, breezy flavour that completely cleared her palate. Also, her toothpaste tasted like dried mint. It made sense to her that with a presence like that, it would also have a strong life force. Azusa exited the browser and returned to the lock screen on her phone. The image there was a photo of Azusa striking a pose in front of a tulip field, together with another girl, the two of them leaning cosily in towards each other. She gazed at the pretty face next to hers.

'It's a little like Mizuki.'

Mizuki Murai did everything properly. Nothing she said was ever wrong, and sometimes she even corrected the teacher. Her grades were always at the top of the class and she was the star of the volleyball team. Every semester she was assigned some important role at school. She was a central figure in the class. Whether it was the annual talent show, the music recital or some other event, everything always went well, so long as they did what she said. So everyone deferred to her. Mizuki wielded immense influence over the top class in middle school, which was also Azusa's. *Mizuki is like mint*, Azusa thought.

Next, Azusa thought of another classmate. Nayuta Taguchi. *If Mizuki is mint, then what is Nayuta? Will she be overrun by mint? Or will she and mint be able to co-exist as friends? No,* Azusa thought, *probably neither one.* Those thick eyebrows and dark eyes were too wilful to be affected by mint in any way.

'Yeah, it'll be okay.'

Because that girl, she's strong. Talking to herself, she felt a knot form in the pit of her stomach. It was a sudden pain she had been experiencing frequently for a while now. Clutching her stomach, she curled up like one of the rhinoceros beetle grubs they found sometimes in the garden. In her mind's eye, she saw Mizuki's face, Nayuta's face and then a third face, a man's kind face. She shook her head, saying *No, no, no.* The pain persisted for a surprisingly long time, and as Azusa lay there in its grip, she seemed almost about to cry. *I'm no good,* she thought.

Before entering the classroom, Azusa took a deep breath. Then she forced her mouth into a smile and, in a small voice, said, 'Okay.' She held the smile in place. It was a little ritual Azusa performed daily.

She opened the door. Some of her classmates had arrived early and looked over at her. For a second her legs froze, but then she looked around and saw smiles on everyone's faces. She breathed a sigh of relief.

'Morning!'

'Good morning, Azusa!'

Several of the girls had formed a circle at the front of the classroom by the window. In the centre of it was Mizuki. With her lovely eyes set in a perfect oval face, she looked somehow more grown-up than the other students. Her glossy black hair was tied back, and her long, elegant lines were reminiscent of the actresses that performed the male roles at the Takarazuka theatre in Tokyo. She seemed a class apart from the girls around her. Azusa remembered the article she had read on her phone yesterday. No doubt about it, Mizuki was like mint.

'Morning, Mizuki! Hey, how was yesterday's Virtual World concert?' In response to Azusa's question, Mizuki's face lit up.

'It was so good! The set list was awesome!'

Virtual World was an alternative band that had recently become popular. Its members played hard rock music while wearing grungy rabbit costumes, and they wielded an outsize influence over middle- and high-school students. Mizuki, a huge fan of the band, was no exception.

'Ooh, Mizuki, that's so great!' A flutter ran through the other girls in the group. 'You got tickets?'

'It really was great,' Mizuki responded, a little boastfully. 'Kanako miraculously managed to get hold of two tickets, so she took me. I already wish I could turn back time to yesterday. Right, Kanako?'

Mizuki put her hand on Kanako's shoulder as she spoke, while Kanako nodded happily beside her.

'It was literally the best thing ever. Actually, at the end I got so excited that I started hugging Mizuki!'

'It's true. And Kanako was crying like crazy, too, weren't you!'

'I was! Because it was totally intense!'

As Kanako was nattering away with Mizuki, she flashed a quick glance at Azusa. Azusa pretended not to notice the meaningful look, and responded innocently, 'That's great, really.' But behind her fixed smile, she thought that Kanako was going to be trouble. Azusa had never heard anything about Kanako being a fan of Virtual World, so she must have got the tickets just for Mizuki, she was sure.

'Ooh, next time I want to go with Azusa! She's a huge fan of Virtual World, too, right?'

Kanako's expression clouded as Mizuki spoke. Without letting her smile drop, Azusa nodded: 'Sure. Definitely, let's go. That would be so much fun.'

Kanako looked at Azusa again, her gaze now turning ugly. Disregarding this as well, Azusa made her way to her own seat at the back of the classroom, farthest from the window. Kanako was obsessed with Mizuki and was always at her side. And she hated Azusa, who was Mizuki's childhood friend.

Kanako wants to take my place, thought Azusa. Mizuki's special friendship meant security in the classroom – throughout the entire grade, really. And Kanako was always worrying about what everyone else thought. *I'm sure she can't help but be jealous of my position. She'll use tickets or anything she can get her hands on to try to replace me. But I don't think it'll be that easy.*

Azusa and Mizuki had been friends forever. Their mothers were close friends from high school. When she looked at the old photos, Mizuki was always there, standing right beside Azusa in every one. Mizuki was born nine months earlier, so there were photos of the two of them from the very day Azusa was born. They were literally together from birth.

Azusa was small and slow to mature, often lagging behind the other children. They wouldn't let her play tag with them and refused to play house with her as well. She was always in tears about this or that. Mizuki, on the other hand, was a natural leader. That was probably why it fell to Mizuki to look out for her, always taking charge for as long as Azusa could remember. Her mother, Michiyo, too, constantly told her, 'Stay close to Mizuki. Listen to what she says!' So she never thought it was strange to have Mizuki telling her what to do. For Azusa, Mizuki's authority had been absolute.

Or so Azusa thought, transferring her pen case and textbook from her book bag to her desk drawer. Their mothers were still close and didn't hesitate to let people know they were lifelong friends. They looked forward to handing down that friendship to their daughters. When the two women got all starry-eyed and talked about passing the torch to the next generation, Mizuki always gave an exasperated laugh and said, 'Our friendship and your friendship are two different things. Don't mix them up. I care for Azusa regardless of how you feel. Because we're perfectly compatible, that's why.'

Azusa always nodded at that point, but the truth was she thought their mothers were right. The two of them would never come close to their parents' friendship. If they hadn't been childhood friends, they probably wouldn't even be as close as they were now. Mizuki liked to say they were compatible, but the truth was, their favourite things, their personalities, the way they spent their free time – these were all completely different. To be honest, Azusa didn't even like Virtual World all that much, either. The pack of expressionless rabbits were creepy, and the music – well, mostly, it was just loud. But Mizuki's authority was absolute, so she couldn't say that. She had to find a way to like them, or else.

So, will I stay in Mizuki's shadow forever, Azusa thought, *and keep on living the way she tells me to? Is that okay?*

The mood in the classroom shifted, and Azusa lifted her head. Nayuta had just entered the classroom. In her gym top with thick black hair cropped short, she looked at first glance like a boy. She took a seat in the centre of the classroom without speaking to anyone.

'She's not in her school uniform. Again!' Overhearing Kanako's comment, Azusa shifted her gaze back to the group of girls by Mizuki, now all wearing looks of stern disapproval. 'Why isn't the teacher warning her? She's breaking the rules!'

It wasn't the first time Azusa had heard such loud, tactless remarks. Nayuta would come to school in her gym clothes, not a uniform. Someone in Mizuki's entourage would see her, and start going on about uniform this, uniform that, like a broken record until Mizuki chided them. Today again, Mizuki said, 'Come on, guys,' settling them down. 'I told you, it's not a violation! She's wearing official school gym clothes, so basically it's fine.'

According to school regulations, students were allowed to wear designated gym clothes to school, except on days with special events, when they had to wear their uniforms. Azusa hadn't known that until recently. She knew it now, of course, because of Nayuta.

There had been something funny going on with Nayuta since March, or around then. She cut her waist-length hair short and started wearing gym clothes instead of a blazer. She came to school late, left early, and was frequently absent. She had never been the most social student, but lately she had taken it to the extreme, rejecting even the most innocent overtures. When asked what was wrong or why, she insisted that it was nothing. At first, Mizuki and her crowd were worried about her, but Nayuta's stubborn refusal to tell them what was going on annoyed them, so that now, two months later, they were mostly just critical. It was because she disrupted the class, they said, and made everyone worry with absolutely no explanation.

Their teacher said nothing about it, and he must have had his reasons. Azusa gazed at Nayuta's back, in the chair diagonally in front of her. Nayuta had probably heard Kanako talking about her, but she looked completely indifferent, not reacting in the slightest. Azusa wished she could ask her where that strength came from. She didn't care about the hair or the uniform. She just wanted to know how Nayuta was strong enough to keep looking straight ahead under those circumstances.

'I mean, is she ignoring us?' Kanako said in a scandalised voice. 'Not even a good morning! She's the worst.'

Listening to Kanako put Azusa's teeth on edge. Wasn't it strange that Kanako was so sure she deserved a greeting? If greetings were important to her, she should be the first to speak.

'It's true, isn't it? Who does she think she is?'

'Over here! Look at us, pretty please!'

The girls around Mizuki picked up the chant, while another group, instead of trying to put a stop to it, looked on, smirking. A boy in the class muttered under his breath, 'Girls are trouble.'

'Don't worry about it, everyone,' Mizuki said with a sigh. 'If she doesn't want to do it, you can't force her.'

'Mizuki, you're too nice!' Kanako replied, with a petulant look. 'She's acting like she's above us!'

'But now people might think we're ganging up on her. It's not true, but we don't want anyone to get the wrong idea, do we?'

Mizuki put on a forced smile, while Kanako and the others glared at the boy who let the comment slip. Watching this, Azusa was annoyed all the same. Unconsciously, she clenched her hands into fists. *Mizuki also thinks that she should be the one to be greeted first. She thinks that's only right.*

'Azusa, you're spacing out. Are you okay?'

At the sudden voice, Azusa came to her senses. She looked up and Mizuki had somehow slipped out of her circle of friends and was standing next to her.

'Are you okay? You were staring at Taguchi.'

'Oh? Um, I . . . I was just looking. I don't know why.' She hadn't been aware that Mizuki was watching her, so she was a little flustered.

'Don't act like you're interested in her,' Mizuki said. 'She wants to be in our circle, and she's got her eye on you. She wants to use you as a way to get in with us. If that happens, I know you'll be sorry, so . . .'

Surprised, but trying not to let it show, Azusa quietly asked, 'You don't want to include her?'

To that, Mizuki replied, 'Isn't it obvious?' as if shocked. 'That's the kind of naïveté that she's trying to take advantage of, Azusa. Look, we've held out a hand to her so many times, but she's always the one to reject us, isn't she? And that hurts. It's important that you understand that.'

Mizuki was speaking loud enough that Nayuta could surely hear. 'Well, I know you're the kind of girl who will say the right thing when the time comes, aren't you, Azusa?' She smiled. Listening to her, Azusa knew her face was hardening. Her stomach twisted, and she placed her hand there. It hurt. It hurt.

'I know you'll be okay, Azusa, but I can't help worrying. You understand.'

'Oh . . . okay.'

'Anyway, don't waste your time worrying about her! You're just so nice that you're easy to take advantage of. Right?'

Would she listen to Mizuki and live the way she was told? Did she truly think that was the right thing to do? Her stomach was in knots again. But she nodded, slowly. She nodded and thought to herself, *is this really right*? Oh, her stomach hurt so much.

★

Azusa's guilty pleasure on Tuesdays was an evening trip to the convenience store. It was her day off from *juku*, and it was also the night her mother Michiyo worked late at her part-time job. She changed her clothes hurriedly and, grabbing her purse, hopped on her bicycle. Her destination was the Golden Villa Tenderness branch.

En route, she passed a convenience store a three-minute walk from her home, and another one that was a ten-minute bike ride. This one was a twenty-minute ride, but there was a reason for that. She couldn't let anyone know where she was going.

Azusa took after her mother, so as one might expect she shared Michiyo's round face and a slight tendency towards chubbiness. Because she also had fair skin, the local boys teased her when she was little, calling her *daifuku*, sweet rice dumpling. Mizuki would stand up for her, and offer words of consolation: 'Azusa, you're not fat, really, not at all!' But several months ago that all changed, thanks to Michiyo.

'Azusa is looking a little heavy compared to you, Mizuki, dear,' Azusa's mother had remarked to Mizuki. 'Can you help make sure she doesn't snack between meals?'

'Leave it to me,' said Mizuki. It was no secret Azusa liked sweets. Maybe she had been eating too many of them? Thus began Mizuki's strict supervision of her diet. Azusa's mother watched her like a hawk at home, and Mizuki attended the same *juku* after school, so Azusa was under constant surveillance everywhere. Tuesday evening was her sole chance to escape and sample her beloved convenience-store treats to her heart's delight, free from both sets of eyes.

Furthermore, the Golden Villa Tenderness offered a dine-in space next to the store. It was a perfectly clean, comfortable place. And if she ate everything there, she didn't need to worry about bringing home evidence of between-meal snacks. For Azusa, it was ideal.

As the familiar sign came into view, Azusa's pedalling legs pumped harder. *Yes, it was there! The Spring Strawberry Cake Parfait.*

She left her bike in the rack and entered the store. A melody played as she went through the door, and a man at the checkout counter called out mildly, 'Welcome!' Azusa headed without hesitation to the sweet section.

'Aha! Got it!'

Finding the sought-after treasure, Azusa called out in happy triumph. She had been waiting forever in anticipation of the spring special, a strawberry shortcake parfait, and there they were, arranged neatly on the shelf right in front of her. And next to them were fresh-baked strawberry *dorayaki*, sweet and spongy pancakes sandwiched together with cream and strawberries, that had also been on her list. Without hesitation she claimed one of each and moved to the beverage section. She picked up a bottle of her favourite flavoured milk and headed to the register.

The store manager was standing at the register with an odd smile on his face. The man gave her an itchy feeling down her spine when they stood close. Azusa was used to it at this point, but at first the manager's strange aura had felt so oppressive she avoided the register when he was there. Mizuki would probably tell her she shouldn't frequent a place run by such a suspicious man, Azusa thought idly, as she completed her checkout. Actually, Mizuki would more likely scold her for being in a store like this at all. She'd probably report it to Michiyo, and Azusa's allowance would be docked. She'd been very careful so far not to let that happen.

She took her bag and headed through the connecting door to the dine-in space. An elementary-school boy was sitting at the corner of one of the four-person tables, immersed in a handheld video game. There was a half-eaten portion of *yakisoba* noodles on the table. Azusa took a seat at the counter, away from the boy, and removing her long-anticipated sweets from the bag, she set them in front of her. She wavered between them just a little, then picked up the *dorayaki*. Between the spongy pancakes was a single, perfect strawberry, large and red, nestled in pink cream and glossy, sweet red-bean paste. She could feel the weight of it in her hand, and the contrasting colours peeking out from the opening of the pocket made her glow with joy. She took a large, enthusiastic bite.

The fluffy sponge, the fresh cream, and the mild, tender red beans merged into a single, deep sweetness. Behind that, the fresh tartness of the ripe local strawberry tickled her senses. Azusa closed her eyes in delight.

Oh so delicious. Happiness.

Azusa's guilty pleasure came just once a week. She wouldn't trade it for anything. She finished off the *dorayaki* dreamily and drank her flavoured milk. Juice and sweet drinks had also been forbidden, so it was extra good. She let out a single, sweet sigh, then reached for the main course: her cake parfait. She opened the plastic lid of the transparent cup, and then spent a while just looking at it. The cake was diced and soaked in strawberry juice. It was submerged in layers of fresh cream and strawberry sauce, with three large, perfect local strawberries enshrined atop the parfait, dusted with powdered sugar like a fine sprinkling of snow. Over that, there was a garnish of chopped pistachio nuts. It was adorable to the eye, but also seemed to be begging her to eat it.

Azusa looked at it, then pulled out her phone and took a photo of the parfait. It would be good to look at when she was really craving something sweet. She continued to sip her milk, all the while taking photos of the parfait from a variety of angles. Finally, she started to eat. The strawberries were at once gently sweet and brightly tart. She was spellbound. Then, as if from a great distance, she was returned to the world by the sound of someone entering the dine-in space from the store. She glanced over.

'Oh!' she said. The person who had just entered was none other than her classmate Nayuta, still clad in gym clothes. Nayuta noticed Azusa, and in turn, replied: 'Oh!'

'H-hi . . .'

'Yeah.'

Any other classmate would probably have sat down next to Azusa. But Nayuta looked around the room, then settled herself into a seat at the opposite end of the counter. As if she had totally forgotten that Azusa was there, she opened a can of unsweetened coffee and took several large swallows. She seemed so grown up, Azusa couldn't help looking at her. Nayuta exhaled, and put down the can, then noticed Azusa was watching her. 'What?' she said.

'No, I, uh . . . That's amazing,' Azusa replied. 'I can't drink coffee.' Azusa wasn't sure of the right thing to say, so instead she said the first thing that popped into her head. 'I can't drink it without milk and sugar. I like coffee jellies, though, and mocha ice cream.'

Nayuta gave her a curious look, then laughed. 'Seems like you like the sweet stuff.' Her gaze drifted to the parfait and flavoured milk, and Azusa gave a start.

'Oh! Um, don't tell anyone about that!' Her voice came out louder than she had intended, and the boy broke contact from his game to look over at her. Nayuta stared at her blankly. 'I'd rather you didn't talk about it. Um, that I was here, eating sweets.'

Sweets were forbidden, Azusa falteringly explained, and Nayuta asked, 'Why?' Her tone was so short and sharp that Azusa was at a loss for words, but Nayuta continued. 'Did the doctor say you can't?'

'Oh, no. Nothing like that! That's . . . well, it's because I'm fat. Mother says I shouldn't have snacks.'

She cringed in embarrassment to hear herself say it. She lowered her gaze, but Nayuta said flatly, 'That's just crazy.' Azusa looked up again. Her classmate smiled at her.

'If that's how it is, I won't tell anyone, and you can eat whatever you want. But Higaki, you're not fat.'

Nayuta was looking at Azusa's body as she spoke. 'I guess it might seem that way, because your figure has curves.' She spoke with simple candour, and it made Azusa feel a little better. She herself was well aware that her weight was normal for her age. Compared with Mizuki and her model's body, Azusa might seem heavy, but nobody would call her overweight.

'Th–thank you.'

'There's nothing to thank me for. Oh, and don't worry, I won't tell Murai either.'

As Nayuta spoke, Azusa's stomach started to hurt again.

'Um, Mizuki, she . . . that's, I mean . . .'

Should I apologise? I never tried to stop Mizuki and her crowd from saying what they did, not even once. The words got stuck in her throat. But as Azusa struggled to say what she was thinking, Nayuta's expression took on a bored look. She picked up her can and drank the remaining leftover coffee.

'It doesn't matter. None of it makes any difference.'

Azusa was surprised at how Nayuta spoke, as if she were trying to push her away. Her coffee finished, Nayuta stood. She tossed the can in the rubbish bin. Then she turned round.

'I don't care what they say. There are more important things to do than worry about what other people think. I don't want to be sorry later that I missed something really important because I was focused on things that didn't matter.'

Nayuta said this in a firm voice, and then she left. She came into view again a little later, riding away on a bicycle. As Azusa watched her go, she mulled over what Nayuta had said. *Am I too focused on what other people think? I don't think so, but I guess it's possible.* When Nayuta said that to her, Mizuki instantly came to mind. Azusa didn't always worry too much about what Mizuki thought or felt, did she? Well, actually, she did. There was a time, once, when she had done exactly that, and look what happened then.

Professor Kiriyama, why did you take this job? It was something that had happened during the summer holidays last year, a question Azusa had asked her instructor at the *juku*. Why in the world had she said a thing like that?

The instructor, whom Mizuki had hated, was a mild-mannered man.

'He has no ambition, and doesn't care about his job,' Mizuki said, fuming. 'Our parents pay for us to be there, and it's not cheap. We make the effort to be there for class, and we depend on the instructors to teach us. I think it's weird for him to act like it's such a chore. I won't stand for that kind of attitude in class.' When she heard from someone that he liked to draw, she was dismissive: 'A teacher should love teaching. Anything else is weird.'

Just like at school, Mizuki was the centre of attention at the *juku* as well, and none of her friends there would dare disagree with her. So on that day, when Mizuki said everyone should tell the teacher face to face that he should rethink his classroom attitude, nobody tried to stop it, and a group of students surrounded Kiriyama. Azusa was among them, as usual.

The group was having fun, laughing as they imagined the look on their teacher's face when they confronted him, but once they were actually standing before Kiriyama, and he asked them what the matter was in his kind voice, they faltered. Although they generally agreed with Mizuki, none of them were seriously concerned about the classwork. They were just going along with her for the fun of it.

In truth, Azusa liked Kiriyama's classes. Although he wasn't as upbeat as some of the other instructors and didn't tell jokes or anything like that, his careful and deliberate teaching style suited Azusa well. But she couldn't say anything like that to Mizuki. She had never even considered going against Mizuki, ever.

So once Kiriyama was there in front of them, everyone exchanged nervous looks. Azusa was just thinking that it would probably be best for everyone concerned if they didn't go through with it and left things as they were, when there was a whisper in her ear. It was Kanako.

'Sometimes you should speak up, Azusa. It's lame to spend all your time hiding in Mizuki's shadow.'

Startled, Azusa turned to see Kanako's malicious grin. *I don't hide in Mizuki's shadow!* She was about to say as much, but then it occurred to her that some of their other friends might feel the same way, so she shut her mouth. *After all, I'm Mizuki's oldest friend, and she does look after me, so nobody would openly attack me, but still . . .* But still, Azusa thought, it wouldn't be strange if that bothered them. And maybe Mizuki, too. How could Azusa say for sure that any of them didn't think so?

Even Mizuki might be annoyed with me. The thought of that really scared her, and before she knew it she had opened her big mouth.

'This class is no fun at all, and you're not even trying. It feels like you're just here for the paycheck.'

For a moment, the girls were all in a flutter. Azusa usually just stood by quietly, an accessory to Mizuki, but now she was lighting the fire. Then, as if a switch was turned on, they all began attacking Kiriyama, criticising him about this or that. Azusa heaved a deep sigh of relief as Mizuki patted her on the back.

'Way to go, Azusa! You said everything I wanted to say, just like my oldest friend should!' Mizuki congratulated her happily and Azusa smiled back at her awkwardly, thinking, *Well, obviously. Don't I always?*

Kiriyama looked shocked for a moment, but then laughed.

'I'll try to be more careful in the future.'

His response was gentle as always, and he saw them off in the usual way, saying, 'Get home safely.' Everyone seemed a little bit bored after that, but Azusa was deeply relieved. *Good. It wasn't a big thing.* She started to feel as if what she had said wasn't so serious after all.

But then Kiriyama quit his job and left the *juku*. The other teachers said it had something to do with a family matter, but Azusa thought that was unlikely. She was almost positive Kiriyama left because of their critical comments. *And the person who made that happen was me, and nobody else. I changed Kiriyama's life.* When she said so to Mizuki, full of remorse, the latter replied, 'I'm glad you did. We did the right thing then, and you said the right thing. I don't feel the least bit guilty about any of it.'

But she couldn't stop asking herself questions. *Why did Kanako's words goad me on like that? Why didn't I try to stop Mizuki from saying we should talk to Kiriyama?* Azusa thought Mr Kiriyama was a relatively good teacher, and if she had said so, things might have gone differently.

There was a sudden noise, and Azusa snapped out of her reverie. She looked round. The boy with the video game had finished his meal and was getting ready to go.

He quickly disposed of his rubbish and then took off. Listlessly, Azusa stared at the table in front of her. There was the cake parfait, now warm and soggy. She had been so excited to eat it, but suddenly she had lost her appetite. She dumped the remains in a plastic bag and stuffed it in the bin.

The following Tuesday, Azusa saw Nayuta at Tenderness again. This time, Nayuta was there first, and she was drinking unsweetened sparkling water. She said hello before Azusa could speak.

'Oh, um, hi,' Azusa responded.

Nayuta hadn't come to school since the previous Friday. The teacher had said it was due to a cold, but Nayuta didn't look the slightest bit unwell, sitting there sipping her soda water. She was dressed lightly, in a t-shirt and knee-length shorts.

The dine-in space was empty aside from the two of them. Nayuta was in a seat at one end of the counter by the window. Azusa sat at the opposite end. While she was taking the treats from her bag, she thought for a moment, then said, 'You haven't been in school.'

'I've been busy,' Nayuta replied, and shrugged. 'I don't have time for school.' She hiccuped a little from the soda water and Azusa gave her a sidelong glance. She looked a little bit tired. Azusa wanted to ask why, but thought better of it. Instead she asked, 'Do you want some of my strawberry éclairs?'

'Huh?' Nayuta responded dully.

'I got the Tenderness *petit éclairs*,' Azusa continued. 'There are four. We could split them, if you want. See?' Azusa showed her the éclairs, covered with pink chocolate and neatly arranged in a spacious box. She laughed. Nayuta was silent for a moment, then mumbled, 'One is plenty. Sweets aren't really my thing.'

'Oh, I wondered about that. Because you're always sugar-free. But these éclairs aren't all that sweet, so try one.'

She opened the box and beckoned Nayuta over to the adjacent seat. Suddenly happy without knowing why, Azusa held out the box of éclairs with a smile. 'Thank you,' said Nayuta softly, taking one. She took a bite, and said, 'It's really sweet . . . but it's good.' She gave Azusa a kind look.

'I heard it's good to eat sweet things when you're tired. Nayuta, you seem a little tired.'

Nayuta's eyes opened just a little wider. 'You think so?' she asked. Azusa bit into her own éclair. 'Your eyes are bleary,' she replied. 'My mum gets like that around the eyes when she's tired.'

'Hmm. I hadn't noticed,' Nayuta said quietly. There was something soft and tired in her voice and face. In school lately, she had always had a severe look about her. This was probably because there had been such a tense, unsociable atmosphere in class, Azusa had thought, but she wondered now if there wasn't some bigger reason. Still, Nayuta probably wouldn't tell her about it even if she asked. So Azusa offered her another éclair instead.

'They're delicious, aren't they? Have one more.'

'Another? One was enough for me. There won't be enough for you, Higaki.'

'That's okay. I also got a milk pudding.'

'You really do like sweets, don't you? Well, if you're sure you don't mind . . .' Nayuta reached for a second éclair. 'I never thought they'd taste this good,' she said with a hint of shyness. Azusa laughed.

After eating the second éclair and finishing her sparkling water, Nayuta said, 'Well, break time is over,' and stood up. 'It's nice to do this sort of thing sometimes, isn't it? Thanks for sharing with me, Higaki.'

'Please, don't worry about it.'

Nayuta tossed the soda bottle into the rubbish bin. Watching her from behind, Azusa hesitated briefly, then asked, 'Is coming here a break for you?' Nayuta turned to face her, and Azusa quickly added, 'If you don't want to talk about it, that's okay, too.' Nayuta looked at her for a moment, then nodded.

'Yes, a break. Mum says that if I don't take a break and get some fresh air, I'm going to come undone.'

'Um . . . you really have to work that hard?'

Nayuta's face hardened. But then after a bit, she nodded. 'But it's something I want to do, so it's good.'

Nayuta spoke so fervently that it was almost as if she was taking an oath. Azusa couldn't ask anything else after that. She felt like it would be too rude to pry.

'Then I hope you do your best.'

That was all she could say, Azusa thought.

'If you need to take breaks like this, it must be a tough job. Just don't push yourself too hard, okay? Well, anyway, I'll be here at the same time next Tuesday. Come have another cake with me.'

Azusa didn't think she could do much to help, but she made the offer anyway. Nayuta stared at Azusa as if she had just seen something unbelievable, then a shy smile escaped her. Azusa was stunned.

'Thank you. Well, see you Tuesday, I guess.'

With a slight wave of her hand, Nayuta left. Thinking of that smile, Azusa broke into a little smile of her own.

The following week, and then the week after that too, Azusa met Nayuta at Tenderness on Tuesdays, and together they ate cake. The springtime strawberry series disappeared from the display case, only to be replaced by early summer specialties – sour-orange parfait and fresh loquat fruit jellies. Nayuta appeared less and less often at school, her features always veiled with tiredness. But when she saw Azusa she would smile, however faintly, and together they would eat their treats.

'Higaki, you really like sweets, don't you?'

'Yes. I do.'

Today they were sampling the new 'Feather-Light Cream Puffs'. In addition to the two of them, the dine-in space was also hosting a bearded man in heavy work clothes. He was ploughing through a bento dinner with gusto. Azusa had her back to the man, and she herself had a mouthful of cream puff.

'Do you go to other sweet shops?' Nayuta asked her, 'Or cafés?' Mojikō was a popular tourist destination and featured a variety of bakeries and candy stores. Azusa shook her head no. She frowned briefly, and then laughed.

'My mother says I can't go there alone until I'm in high school,' Azusa explained. She'd been told it was okay to go places together with Mizuki, but now that snacks had been banned, that was an impossibility. There were mountains of things she wanted to try – fruit parfaits, pancakes of all sorts, and so on – but for now, at least, she had had to give them all up.

'Convenience store sweets are delicious, though, so I don't really mind. Also, I especially love the sweets here at Tenderness.'

The Tenderness sweets were delicious – both the regular ones that they carried all year long, and the seasonal specials.

Azusa thought that the seasonal fruit series, in particular, was a collection of masterpieces. And to be able to eat things of that quality at a convenience store! It was so, well . . . convenient. It was more than enough, so how could she complain?

'Besides . . .' Azusa looked down and silenced herself. After some hesitation, she said, as if confessing, 'Actually, when I grow up, I'd like to work at Tenderness.'

'You want to work at a convenience store?' Nayuta asked, in a tone of some disbelief.

'Well, not exactly. I want to do – what do they call it? – "product development" for Tenderness. I want to work in the dessert department there, or something like that. I want to make the best cakes.'

Ever since kindergarten, Azusa had dreamed of becoming a pastry chef. The first thing she remembered writing was an essay about building a shop that looked like a gingerbread house. Her dream was well known both to her parents and to Mizuki as well. But now Azusa was beginning to think she might not even need her own shop.

'That's good.' At those simple words, Azusa looked over at Nayuta, who was nodding in admiration, a little cream stuck to the corner of her mouth. 'It's very good, I think. That means all the Tenderness stores throughout Kyūshū will be yours, won't they, Higaki?'

Azusa said, 'That's right!' Her face brightened. She never thought anyone would understand her plan so readily. Without thinking about it, she leaned forward.

'It would be good to put a lot of work into building a single store that was my own, but, you know, convenience stores would also be good. I really look forward to tasting the treats here every week the way we do. I want to make sweets that those sorts of people – people like me – can't wait to try.'

This was the first time Azusa had shared her dream – the outlines of which were just starting to become clear to her – with anyone. She couldn't help but be happy to receive such a positive response. Seeing her so pleased, Nayuta smiled.

'It's good that you have a dream, Higaki.'

There was something lonely about that smile. 'How about you, Nayuta? Don't you have a dream?' Azusa asked.

Nayuta frowned and said, 'For now, I can't think of one. I'm pushing myself to the limit right now, just trying to deal with what's right in front of me, so I can't think at all about what comes next.'

Hands rubbing her cheeks and speaking tentatively, Nayuta didn't seem at all her regular self. Azusa thought now might be the time to ask her what had been going on. She waited a moment, and then when it seemed right she asked.

'Nayuta? It seems like you're working awfully hard on something now. What's going on?

Nayuta's expression clouded.

'Oh hey, I'm sorry,' Azusa added quickly. Apparently it had been a bad time to ask, after all. 'If you don't want to talk about it, that's fine.' But Nayuta shook her head.

'It's okay, Higaki,' Nayuta said in a weak voice. 'You're easy to talk to, so I can tell you. Actually, to be honest, I've been thinking I really want to tell someone about it.'

She sighed, then continued.

'Actually, I'm pretty wiped out. Even though it was my decision in the first place, I'm not really any good at it. The truth is—'

'WHAT ARE YOU DOING?'

Azusa and Nayuta trembled in shock at the sound of the icy voice. Standing in the doorway was Mizuki. She strode over to Azusa and roughly struck the half-eaten cream puff from her hand. Then she slapped her on the cheek. The noise echoed through the small room.

'Sneaking around behind my back?' Mizuki hissed. 'That's as low as it gets!'

Azusa was simply dumbfounded. Now Mizuki turned to Nayuta, and lowered her voice. 'And you, Taguchi.' She addressed her by her last name. 'You skip school day after day, and then you have the nerve to come here with Azusa, and just sit around eating cake? Well, you can do what you want, I don't care, but do me a favour and don't go dragging other people into it. It's a real pain.'

Azusa stared at Mizuki's angry profile, hand pressed to her cheek where she had been slapped. How, why was Mizuki here? She had a strange feeling she knew, and let her gaze stray past Mizuki through the window to the answer. She bit her lip. There, standing in the corner of the car park, was Kanako.

'Kanako told you . . .?' Azusa said, half to herself. Mizuki shot her a look.

'Yes, Kanako told me. That you were sneaking off to meet Taguchi. And that you were having all sorts of fun gossiping about us.'

'We were just eating cakes together. Is that against the rules?' Nayuta didn't mince her words, but Mizuki just laughed at her scornfully.

'Obviously. You're not even coming to school! And when you do show up, you disrupt the atmosphere and then act like you don't even care. A person like that has no excuse to be hanging out in a place like this. It's strange you think you can dodge all your responsibilities and then claim all the privileges anyway.'

Mizuki didn't stop there, but instead continued speaking at a breakneck pace.

'And on top of that, you're a bad influence on Azusa. She's not the sort of coward who would slip away from me and her parents to go off and eat cake somewhere, so the fact that she's doing it is evidence enough of that. As far as the gossip is concerned, I'm sure it was a one-way street from your mouth to Azusa's ears. So I'm sorry, but please leave her alone.'

Her tirade complete, Mizuki turned to Azusa. 'Okay, we're leaving now.' She grabbed her wrist and gave it a tug. 'For your sake, I'll look the other way just this once. I don't want to have to tell Auntie Michiyo about the snacks. Come on now, let's go.'

Her wrist was in a vice grip, her cheek burning. Even from this far away Azusa could see the nasty grin plastered across Kanako's face. It was an ugly look. Mizuki herself was still angry, and behind her, Nayuta just looked sad. Mizuki's barking voice was still echoing in her ears. It was too much. Azusa shook off Mizuki's hand.

'I'm with Nayuta because I want to be, Mizuki,' Azusa said quietly. 'I can't do what you're telling me to do.'

'What? Did you not hear what I said?'

'Mizuki, you need to apologise to Nayuta. Apologise for saying she's a bad influence. I invited her to join me because I like her.'

Azusa knew her voice was shaking. She had never talked back to Mizuki before. And she had certainly never imagined asking her to apologise. Mizuki, for her part, was equally confounded, and gave her a long, hard look, as if trying to determine the true identity of the person talking to her. Without breaking eye contact, Azusa said once more:

'Apologise, Mizuki.'

'Take your fight outside.'

The deep voice came from the man who had been eating his lunch so happily earlier. He picked up the cream puff, which had fallen to the floor, and said, 'Take all that outside. There are other customers here.' He gestured towards the side door with his chin, tossing the cream puff in the bin. The man called 'Old Red' had appeared in the doorway. The three girls stared at him.

'Now, now, friends,' he said with a mischievous look on his face, 'No fighting, no biting. All you need is love!'

'Outside, I said!' The man who had thrown out the cream puff flapped his arms as if he were shooing away flies. Mizuki was the first to move.

'I'm done looking after you! Since you won't let me, anyway.' She stormed out the door and raced past Kanako, who hurried after her, while Azusa watched through the window, stunned.

'Uh . . . um . . . I'm sorry,' Nayuta apologised to the man, and he turned to her.

'It's a public place, keep that in mind,' he said calmly, and left it at that before turning to the other man. 'Hey, Old Red, it's about time you got here! Or actually, you should have stopped them a while ago.'

The man spoke as if he knew him well. Entering the room, Old Red replied lightly, 'If I'd done that, those girls would be crying now.' He turned to Azusa. 'You okay, missy?' he asked, as if he had been watching the whole interaction from somewhere. 'You took a real smack on the cheek, didn't you? You weren't about to let her get away with that a second time, were you!'

His raucous laughter roused Azusa from her daze. Nayuta, too, peered at her face and asked, 'Are you okay?'

'Oh, Nayuta . . . I'm sorry,' Azusa stammered. 'About Mizuki, I mean.'

'There's nothing to apologise about, Higaki. But are you okay? Talking to Murai like that.' Nayuta spoke worriedly, thinking about the way Mizuki had run off. 'You shouldn't have tried to protect me.'

Azusa's whole body began to shake. She felt like her heart was beating at twice the usual rate. *Now I've really done it*, she thought. By tomorrow she would have lost her comfortable spot at school. And at the *juku*. And become a target for Mizuki's attacks.

'Thank you.' Nayuta took Azusa's trembling hand. She wrapped it in her own, slightly hardened hands. 'Thank you for sticking up for me before. It made me happy.'

Nayuta, who never wavered anywhere, anytime, even in the face of the most malicious attacks, was looking at her with tears in her eyes. Azusa started to believe that she had made the right choice. She had finally taken a path that didn't lead to regret.

'I'm really sorry, Azusa, but I can't go back to school yet. So you might be on your own.'

'No, it's all right. I'll be okay.'

I acted of my own free will, Azusa thought. She tried to smile at Nayuta, but somehow it didn't come out properly. It just looked like her mouth was twisted upwards at the corners.

'If you can get through your hard time, Nayuta, then I think I can get through mine.'

'Well, I . . . Oh, that's me.' Nayuta wiped her tears and pulled her phone from her pocket. She looked at the screen and her face changed hue. She quickly pressed the button to take the call.

'Hello, Mum? Uh-huh. Yes, I understand. I'm coming now.'

After hanging up, Nayuta lowered her head. 'Sorry,' she said. 'I have to go home now. I'm sorry to run out, especially now.'

'Don't worry about it. But what's wrong?'

Nayuta returned her phone to her pocket and pulled out a bicycle key. She bit her lip tightly, then managed to squeeze out a few words: 'He's in critical condition,' she said. 'It's my dad. He's got terminal cancer. He said he wanted to be at home with us near the end, so Mum and I are his caregivers, just the two of us.'

The words were so foreign to Azusa she had a hard time understanding them. *Critical, cancer, terminal, caregivers.* She'd read them in books and heard them on television dramas, sure enough, but was Nayuta describing her own father?

'Anyway, I have to go. Sorry.'

Nayuta jumped on her bike and left. Suddenly her recent behaviour made a lot more sense to Azusa. Nayuta must have been carrying such a heavy load; it was more than enough to bring anyone to copious tears, wasn't it? Azusa's heart ached to imagine it.

'She said she looked forward to Tuesdays.'

A man's voice. The bearded man was standing there, together with Old Red. His voice, half obscured by his beard, seemed kindly somehow, and, strangely enough, Old Red's eyes were a little red, too.

'We're her break buddies,' the bearded man continued. 'When I asked her if she liked having coffee with a couple of old dudes like us, she said what she really looked forward to were the big dessert Tuesdays with her friend.'

'Did you know about . . . her situation?' Azusa asked.

'Well,' the man said, 'there's a certain look that people get when they're caring for a sick person. A weariness. It was starting to show through in her face, so I figured maybe his condition wasn't going the way she wanted.'

'I knew,' said Old Red, 'but it wasn't the sort of thing to go jabbering about all over town.'

The two men sighed heavily. Azusa looked in the direction in which Nayuta had disappeared. 'I . . . I didn't realise at all.'

'At your age, that's the way it is. That's just how it goes.'

Now it was Azusa's turn to get teary.

'I am the worst.'

I didn't know, she didn't tell me. What in the world was that? Nothing but excuses! I sat back and watched while they all attacked her, just because her behaviour was a little out of the ordinary. And I did nothing to stop it! I sided with Nayuta's bullies.

Her stinging cheek and her usual stomach pain were nothing compared to this. Now Azusa was ashamed. And angry at herself. It was the pain in her heart that was going to destroy her.

At school the next day, it was like Asuza was invisible. She had been totally cut off. In addition, insults were flung at her from all sides, just as had happened with Nayuta. Students who had been perfectly friendly just a day earlier had transformed as if by the flip of a switch, and now mocked her to her face. 'You've really been getting on my nerves lately!' said Kanako loudly, while Mizuki just stood by and watched.

Azuma was shocked by how much things had changed, but at the same time, she was prepared for it. She had watched Nayuta endure this treatment for a long while. *How could I possibly whine about what I'm going through?* Azusa thought. Alone in the classroom, she held her head high and endured. When she thought of Nayuta, her thumping heart would gradually calm down. And then, a curious thing happened. Azusa noticed that the stomach pain which had been bothering her for so long had disappeared. *I don't think it will be back*, she thought. *I'm okay.*

Summer holidays started, but there was no news of Nayuta. School was out, which was a plus, but she still had to deal with Mizuki and her followers at the *juku*, so her situation was basically unchanged. Mizuki had also spoken to her mother. 'Azusa said she's ending our friendship,' she had told her, so Michiyo was in a sour mood.

'Mizuki cried, you know! She said she always looked after you, and you betrayed her. And then you slip off behind her back to stuff yourself with snacks! How could you be so cruel?' her mother asked. Azusa had no idea how to explain the situation, so she said nothing, and her own home became an uncomfortable place for her. Even so, Azusa did the best she could, day by day.

She tried visiting Tenderness, not just on Tuesdays but also other days of the week, but she never managed to find Nayuta. She did run into the bearded man – his name was Tsugi, she learned – and Old Red, often enough that they began to greet each other in a friendly way. But it seemed neither of them had any recent news about Nayuta. How was she doing? Was she okay?

Azusa learned nothing about Nayuta's situation until August, when she and her fellow students returned to their classroom for a mid-summer school day.

'Due to family circumstances, Miss Taguchi has transferred to another school.'

The classroom had been buoyant, as if it were a floating island in the middle of the summer holidays, and merry voices rang out on all sides. But the words of their homeroom teacher, Professor Fukawa, introduced a note of gravity, and the class quieted down.

'Together with her mother, she had been working hard to care for her ailing father. He passed away not long ago, and the two of them have moved to Nagasaki, where her grandparents live.'

Fukawa had a daughter in elementary school. Perhaps he had a special feeling for the situation, because the rims of his eyes turned red as he continued.

'Miss Taguchi said she didn't want to regret missing those moments with her father, so she took time off from school and focused all her efforts on helping him to cope with his illness. I told her I'd let the class know about her situation, so that you would all understand what she has been going through. She didn't want to be pitied. It made her feel weak, she said.'

Nayuta had cut her hair because it got in the way when she was nursing her father. She insisted on wearing gym clothes for maximum freedom of movement when she was needed at the bedside. Fukawa quietly relayed all the things that he had kept to himself until that moment, occasionally wiping his face as he spoke. The students sat silently, heads lowered. Only Kanako, seated directly in front of Azusa, kept shifting in her seat, as if trying to make eye contact with Mizuki, who was seated some distance away.

Azusa felt as if she were far removed from her body sitting in the classroom, while at the same time, she had to work to hold back the urge to cry. Her thoughts turned to Nayuta, whom she would probably never see again. *I'm so sorry*, she thought. *Sorry that instead of helping you, we only added to your pain. I wish I could see you and apologise in person, but I can't even do that. It's so sad.*

'Did you know?'

Azusa was heading home after dismissal when Mizuki and the others called after her. The group surrounded Azusa, their faces stern and suffocating. *That reminds me*, she thought somewhere in the back of her mind, *I also want to apologise to Professor Kiriyama.*

'What do you want?' Azusa asked.

'I'm asking if you knew all this about Taguchi. If you did, shouldn't you have told us?' It wasn't Mizuki, but Kanako who voiced the complaint. 'It makes us seem like we're bad people, and there's no way we're going to allow that. What happened to Taguchi is sad and all, but we didn't know the first thing about it, since nobody told us, and how could anyone expect us to guess?'

Azusa ignored Kanako, turning instead to Mizuki, who was standing next to her. Mizuki simply glared at her, saying nothing. Azusa accepted her look willingly.

'Mizuki, thank you for being such a good friend for so long. I had so many happy times thanks to you. But what you did this time was wrong. Whether you forgive me or not, there are things I had to do for Nayuta's sake. With understanding and kindness—'

Before Azusa could finish her thought, Mizuki slapped

her face again. At the sound of the impact, the corner of Kanako's mouth twitched upwards. Azusa kept her gaze fixed on Mizuki.

'You should try to break the habit of acting on your anger that way, when something bothers you. If you don't, the day may come when someone responds in kind – with even more anger, or violence.'

Mizuki lifted her hand a second time, but then just barely managed to restrain herself. Her face contorted, and then, as Azusa watched, she slowly allowed the hand to fall.

'Okay, Mizuki,' she said, 'see you.'

Azusa slipped between Mizuki and Kanako and was about to leave when Kanako caught her by the shoulder.

'Not so fast! We're not done talking yet.'

'If you think making me out to be a bad person will wipe the slate clean for your own guilty conscience, then do as you like.'

Azusa shook off Kanako's hand, then finally departed. As she walked off, she said quietly to herself, 'It's okay. It's okay.' Her heart was racing and her legs were shaking in a way she hoped nobody noticed. It felt as though if she let her guard down for even a second, she'd collapse on the spot. In truth, she was scared enough to cry. But she thought of Nayuta, and she endured. She had said what she needed to say.

'You can't succeed if you don't try,' Azusa said to herself, and then smiled. Probably Nayuta had done the same to get through her worst moments, one by one. *If she can do it, then I'm not giving up either.*

She stepped out of the school building and looked up at the sky. Tall, cotton-candy clouds floated across a bright blue sky. Birds danced across it, looking just as if they were grazing on the candy clouds.

'I'd like to taste the blueberry parfait at Tenderness,' Azusa said, a sunny note creeping into her voice. Her mood was clearing, just like the sky above her.

★

The autumn specials were arriving in the sweets section at Tenderness. Azusa had continued her customary dessert expeditions there, solo, on Tuesday evenings.

Since she had parted ways with Mizuki and her group, Azusa had made a few changes, and various things had happened as a result. For starters, she had changed her mind about high school. Initially, the two mothers were eager for their own daughters to attend the girls' school where they had become such good friends, and Azusa had acted in accordance with their wishes. But now, Azusa told her parents she wanted to try out for a more prestigious prepara- tory academy. Michiyo was highly opposed. 'You need to mend fences with Mizuki as quickly as possible,' she groused, but Azusa's father supported her ambitious plan. He insisted that parents shouldn't limit their children's opportunities in life, so now Azusa was studying frantically to gain admission.

Rather than maintaining a parallel track to Mizuki and the others, it seemed they were drifting further and further apart. Apparently the girls had expected a hasty apology from Azusa, but she simply continued to attend school as usual, unruffled by anything they might say to her. As the days mounted up, Mizuki became more and more irritated, and when she learned that Azusa was applying to a different high school, she confronted her.

'You're trying to run away from me,' Mizuki said accus- ingly, but Azusa shook her head.

'I'm just trying to walk my own path, instead of one that someone else chose for me.' Then, for the first time, Mizuki cried openly. Afterwards, she began to act as if Azusa wasn't even there.

She led an isolated life at school, but recently some of the children had begun to speak to her.

'I got embarrassed that I was always watching you from far away, and never saying anything,' one person said, and it made her happy.

Azusa rolled up to the bike rack at Tenderness, dismounted, and headed for the dessert section as usual. When she saw the line-up of sweet-potato desserts her face lit up. After a brief struggle, she settled on a baked sweet-potato tart and a sweet-potato cream puff, along with her usual flavoured milk, of course. She was checking out at the register when the store manager, who usually avoided any unnecessary interactions, called out to her.

'Excuse me!' he said. 'Thank you for shopping with us so often.'

'Oh, um . . . Sure.'

'This may seem a little out of the blue, but might I ask you to wait a little bit before eating your pastry?'

His syrupy voice sent a shiver down Azusa's spine. The boys in her class were always hooting and hollering in the most childish ways, and usually seemed more or less like monkeys to her. Was it possible they would grow up to give off this kind of strange appeal? No, she thought. Definitely not.

'Wait a little? But why?' Azusa wasn't sure where this was headed. The store manager frowned slightly and made a gesture as if he were searching for the right words. Even such an insignificant motion as that was compelling, performed by him. Azusa watched, thinking absent-mind-edly, *So this is what it means to furrow one's brow.* She had looked it up online but never really understood it.

'Well, that is . . . do you know the man with the beard? Not Old Red, but the other one, the man with the light green coveralls?'

'Oh, you must mean Tsugi. What about him?'

'He left a message that he wanted to have dessert with you. He should be arriving at any minute.'

It was a little out of the ordinary, but Azusa nodded. It was good to eat with someone else once in a while. She paid for her treats and went to the dine-in space. Taking a seat at the counter, she cast her gaze out the window. The leaves in the trees along the roadside were changing their colours to match the season. Old Red passed by on his ever-present red cargo bike, probably on his way to distribute his tourist brochures. Noticing Azusa, he waved, and she waved back at him.

About ten minutes passed, then a mini-truck pulled into the car park. She could see the logo on the back of Tsugi's coveralls: 'Whatever Guy'. He caught sight of Azusa and waved at her.

Azusa started to wave back, but then gasped in shock. She couldn't believe her eyes. In a flash, she hopped off the stool and was out the door.

'No! It can't be!' she shouted as she ran. Tumbling out of the passenger seat of Tsugi's mini-truck was none other than Nayuta.

'Higaki! It's been a long time!'

Nayuta was smiling from ear to ear. Azusa pounced on her and wrapped her in a tight embrace.

'But how? Nayuta, what are you doing here? I thought you moved to Nagasaki!'

'I hitched a ride with the whatever guy.' Nayuta seemed a little sturdier than when they had parted. She had a healthy glow in her cheeks as she gave Tsugi a grateful look.

'I found him when he was working in Nagasaki and asked him,' she explained. 'I felt really awful about what happened the last time I saw you, Higaki. I needed to talk to you. So I asked him to bring me here.'

'It wasn't easy, you know,' Tsugi said with a wry shrug. 'A funny-looking guy like me, running around with a middle-school girl? I needed proof of identification, and then of course, I had to keep in regular contact on the job. Which reminds me . . .'

Tsugi took out a phone and snapped a quick photo of Azusa and Nayuta hugging.

'Arrived safely without incident . . .' he muttered to himself as he texted. Apparently he was sending the photo to Nayuta's mother.

'Sorry, Mr Tsugi. But I really needed to see her.'

'No big deal. It's my job,' Tsugi responded matter-of-factly. Just looking at the two of them standing there, Azusa felt like crying, but she didn't know why. This happy face, this voice without a trace of grief – she felt like she was seeing the real Nayuta for the first time.

'Hey, Higaki?' Nayuta smiled at Azusa. 'I've wanted to thank you all this time. I really looked forward to our Tuesday meetings. When we saw each other and had our treats, it always made me feel like I might somehow find a way to get through it all. And the truth is, I did.'

As Nayuta spoke, her eyes filled with tears.

'You didn't make me talk about everything, Higaki. You were just there with me. You shared so many sweet things with me. That one gesture was so much help. So that I could see my father off without any regrets. Thank you . . .' Nayuta trailed off as her tears finally began to overflow. Azusa hugged her once more.

'Thank you, too, Nayuta. Being with you made me stronger. I've also been working hard to do my best, without giving up. Ever since then, my very best.'

Still wrapped in her embrace, Nayuta nodded, and before she knew it, Azusa was crying as well, and for a time the two of them just held each other.

Then they arranged themselves at the window counter seats, and ate their sweets, just as they used to do. Thanks to Azusa, Nayuta seemed to have developed a real sweet tooth. 'Delicious!' she laughed, through a mouthful of sweet-potato tart. Azusa laughed as well, happy to see her carefree smile.

'I haven't got used to school in Nagasaki yet. When I'm unhappy, or if I get lonely, I always try to go to a Tenderness store. I buy something sweet, and eat it, and it feels like I'm together with you, Higaki. Isn't that strange?' Nayuta rubbed her face with embarrassment.

Azusa didn't think it was strange at all.

'Me too!' she replied. 'While I was eating I kept thinking about what you would say at a time like this.'

'So we're the same, right?' the two girls said, simultaneously, then laughed. It was good to know that even while they were apart, they had each been thinking of the other.

'Remember when you told me before that you wanted to develop products for Tenderness? I said I thought that was fine, but now, I really, really want you to do it,' Nayuta said. 'Then if anything bad happens, I can always go to a Tenderness store somewhere, eat the cakes that you made, and I'll always feel better. As long as there's Tenderness, there will be somewhere we can meet.'

Azusa took Nayuta's heartfelt words and tucked them away, deep in her heart, as if they were jewels in a treasure chest. She was sure she'd pull them out time and again in the days to come. She felt it.

'I'll do it, for sure. I'm going to make sweets, the kind that will give strength to someone who's struggling.'

'In that case, I want you to focus a little more on Japanese sweets.' A deep voice broke in from the side, and when the two of them spun round, there was Tsugi, laughing.

'I like Japanese sweets,' he continued. 'I wish they'd do more of those, like *ohagi* and *dango*.'

'Of course!' Azusa exclaimed. 'Japanese sweets.'

'Oh!' said Nayuta. 'My mother likes Japanese sweets too.'

'She does? Well, I'll do my best!'

After that, Azusa and Nayuta enjoyed their cakes together, unable to stop smiling at each other. As long as the Tenderness chain was there, as long as they continued to visit it, they'd always be connected, no matter how far apart they were. This they believed with all their hearts.

'Higaki?' Nayuta said. 'Next time, you should come to Nagasaki. You can stay at our house.'

'I'd love to go!' Azusa replied. 'I'll ask Mr Tsugi to take me.'

'Now, wait just a second. I can't play substitute parent every time you call!'

Azusa laughed out loud for the first time in a long while.

Chapter Four

A Soft Egg Porridge for a
Hard Old Man

When he woke up in the morning, his wife wasn't there.

In the living room, a rolled omelette and a piece of grilled salt mackerel were waiting for him under clingfilm on the dining table. Miso soup was in a pot in the kitchen. After reheating them, Takiji Ōtsuka ate his breakfast alone. A faint scent of detergent drifted in through the wide-open patio doors, from the laundry drying outside. He took a quick look: another fine day. Come to think of it, he remembered the TV weather girl saying that the clear autumn weather would continue for a while. The woman, who was younger than his daughter, had said what perfect weather it was for going out, but he had no particular plans, so it didn't matter much to him one way or the other.

Takiji finished his meal quickly and left the dishes to soak in a tub in the kitchen sink. He turned on the TV, listening while he read the paper. He didn't look at the screen until the morning soaps began – he's got hooked on one of them, somehow. The main character was a father, a joker with an overly sympathetic personality, beloved by everyone. Except Takiji. Something about the set-up annoyed him. There were moments when the father seemed happy to be inconvenienced by his daughter's self-indulgent lifestyle, instead of correcting her. Didn't he take any pride in being a father? Or a man? Shouldn't he be ashamed of his failure as a parent to educate his own child properly? Even now, he was tossing off silly wisecracks while his daughter yapped angrily at him. It was the sort of behaviour that caused all the trouble in the first place.

'Damn it. Why do I let this show get me so worked up? Eh, Junko?'

He called out without thinking, then closed his mouth. His wife Junko wasn't there. She'd gone to her part-time job at the supermarket. The job was in the deli section, so morning shifts started early. She would come home in the afternoon, but then rush out again almost immediately, talking about the activities in her women's group. Evening was the only time they could be together, face to face.

The spacious living room was silent but for the voices from the television. Takiji let out a little sigh. Why was he passing his days in such emptiness?

Takiji had worked continuously all his life at one company, an auto parts factory, from college graduation to retirement. The mandatory retirement age was sixty, but he had joined the company's reemployment programme, and worked five extra years. It wasn't right for a man to let his wife and child struggle through life. He had always been guided in his work by that belief. He relinquished his personal days to the company as a matter of course, and devoted long hours to entertaining clients. All household matters were entrusted to his wife, Junko, including the upbringing of their only daughter, Nanao, but that was the natural division of labour between husband and wife, and nothing could be done about that. Men went out and earned a living, women took care of the house. That's just how it was. Junior colleagues at work would laugh at him and ask what era he was from, but thanks to his hard work, Junko had spent many decades as a homemaker, while Nanao had been able to attend the college of her choice. He was also able to put together a modest nest egg, and move them to a retirement home in an apartment building dedicated to seniors. Even better, the place was in Kitakyūshū, 'the number one retirement destination for senior country life'.

Kitakyūshū was nestled between the mountains and the sea, surrounded by the beauty of nature. Despite that, it had a well-maintained infrastructure, and the cost of living there was low. It was a terminal for the Shinkansen 'bullet' train, and close enough to the large city of Hakata that it didn't feel like the remote countryside, or inconvenient in any way. It was an ideal town for Takiji, who had wanted to live quietly in a calm and convenient location after retirement.

Mojikō, the area around the harbour, was particularly nice. The streets of the town were lined with buildings from the good old days, and beyond the picturesque townscape lay the clear ocean waters. And the seafood was delicious. It was a completely different atmosphere from Nagoya, where he had been born and raised, but he was sure they could do reasonably well in the place. He had every expectation of a frugal and tranquil life there, together with Junko. When he'd made the decision to move, he'd had no doubt that his 'second life' would be the stuff of his dreams.

So how, then, had it come to this? Takiji's eyes traced the text in the newspaper as he thought.

Well, for starters, Junko had changed dramatically, it seemed, right after they moved here. The Junko of the present was an entirely different person from the Junko who had quietly and faithfully cared for their home back then, never pushy or presumptuous in the slightest way. It was impossible to imagine the old Junko taking a part-time job without consulting him, let alone her intense dedication to the activities of the building's Ladies' Association. She didn't even go to PTA meetings back then. Of course, that was partially because Takiji didn't approve. It was unthinkable, to him, for a woman caring for a home and family to just leave them behind and go out for drinks. But since they had moved here, Junko actively attended both the part-time staff get-togethers at work and the cocktails with the building ladies. Up until recently, Takiji had been her top priority, but now she had made him into her house-sitter.

'What have you got to complain about?' Nanao, his daughter, had said dismissively. 'She does all the housework before she goes out. She even cooks your meals.'

Nanao had married three years ago. She lived in Ōsaka, but perhaps because she had no children, she came to visit once a month. She spoke sharply to Takiji, who was harbouring some resentment towards Junko. 'You've really been keeping Mother under lock and key. Let her be herself. Give her a little freedom.'

He didn't intend to imprison his wife, and he didn't remember ever forcing her to be a different person. He just acted appropriately for a working man in society, and he wanted Junko to do what was natural for a woman watching over her family and home. Was there anything wrong with that? But when he said that, Nanao responded with a warning: 'Have you heard of grey divorce? A man who neglects his family's needs gets thrown away, Father.' Takiji laughed it off as nonsense, but Junko didn't laugh. She just apologetically said, 'Let me do as I like.'

They're both making fun of me, he thought. It's not like I've been oppressing Junko all this time. I took us all on family trips every year, and she had the clothes she wanted, visits to the beauty parlour, no limits. She had plenty of freedom. Why do they have to make me out to be the bad guy?

Takiji had more to say, but realising that Nanao was just going to take his wife's side, he swallowed his words. Instead, he said, 'It's fine. Do as you like.' *I guess if I can have a second life, then you can too. I can understand that much, at least.*

But if he were being honest, he didn't understand. Every morning there was a fresh whirlpool of dissatisfaction in his chest. How was he to find an outlet for those feelings?

'Maybe I'll go get a drink of coffee or something . . .' When he was alone in the room with nobody there, he quickly started to feel depressed. Takiji left the house, taking nothing with him but his wallet.

Given that he had chosen it for its lovely street scenes, Mojikō was the ideal place for a walk. There were any number of stylish cafés, too, dotting the area. But just to wander in, a single man on his own? That would be far too uncomfortable.

Instead, there was a little coffee shop he'd found just behind their apartment building that had become his regular spot. The old proprietor ran it by himself, and there were always strains of jazz music playing lightly in the background. The interior was somewhat old-fashioned, and with nothing flashy there to catch the eye – what the kids these days called 'Instagrammable'? – there were few customers. Takiji liked it that way.

The only thing was, he felt like a bit of an outsider there. It seemed the proprietor was into fishing, and the walls were festooned with fish prints and photos of fishing boats. And then, too, he and the regulars were always waxing poetic about where they fished, and what they had caught. Takiji had no experience fishing, so he was left out of the conversation entirely. Today, too, a small cluster of customers were going on about *mame aji*, baby horse mackerel that were small enough to cook and eat whole, and what quantities each of the several patrons had caught. He settled into a window seat, ordered a coffee, and for the second time that day ran his eyes over the newspaper he had already read at home.

He needed a hobby, but how to find one?

Takiji looked at a feature in the paper about a dance group for seniors and considered the question. Until now, he had never thought much about anything except work. The days came and went easily enough, and he had no complaints. But now, he wanted something to kill time. Even better if it were something he could banter about with others, like the group gathered here.

The coffee came, and he drank it slowly. His eye fell upon a young mother pushing a stroller outside the shop. *When Nanao has a child, perhaps I'll . . .* He quickly extinguished the idle thought. It seemed Nanao had decided not to have children. He didn't know what her reasons were. She had just told him that she had discussed it with her husband and they had made the decision.

'I have my own life. I'm not giving birth to a child just to make you happy, Father.'

Some of his junior colleagues at the company had chosen a childless life as well. At some point, someone had explained to him that there were couples who deliberately avoided having children. They were called 'DINKs' – double income, no kids. Of course people led all different sorts of lives. He accepted that. But why was it that he felt so lonely when he heard it from his own daughter's mouth? He searched for the right words to explain it to her, but all he could think to say was that having children was a good thing, and just that was enough to make Nanao angry.

'You're always saying that you raised me, Father, but you didn't actually do anything. You think you can just shell out the money and that's enough? Were you there for my first day of school? My track meets? Any of the big events in my life? If a person like that says that children are a good thing, it carries no weight at all.'

He had always thought she was a cute girl, and he had tried his best, in his own way. But still. A bitter taste filled his mouth and he grimaced, then looked out through the window, and his eyes happened to meet those of a boy on a bicycle. The boy's thin limbs poked out of his t-shirt and shorts, and there was a plastic bag dangling from the handlebars of his bicycle. He gave a look of surprise, then increased his speed and rode away. He must have thought Takiji's grimace was directed at him. Takiji stood up, flustered, but the young man had already disappeared.

'Whoops. My mistake.'

He rubbed his head and sat down again. Then he gazed out through the window. He couldn't shake the feeling that he had seen the young man somewhere before.

I don't know anyone in this area. And certainly not any children. But somehow I recognise him. Where could I have seen him?

Suddenly there was a roar of laughter, and when he looked over, the proprietor's fisherman friends were all clutching their stomachs in hysterics. Noticing Takiji's gaze, the proprietor, still smiling, said, 'Sorry, excuse us.' Another of the men said 'Pardon, pardon,' and bowed his head. Draining the remaining coffee in a single draugt, Takiji stood.

'I'll leave the payment here. Thank you.'

I won't come here anymore, Takiji thought. Feeling something akin to irritation, he left the establishment.

★

He and Junko were fighting.

She had announced that she was taking a three-day trip to Kagoshima with the Ladies' Association. Kagoshima was a famously scenic town situated on a bay at the south end of Kyūshū, with dramatic views of an active volcano, and popular thermal springs.

'Mrs Nosé suggested we all accompany Mr Shiba on the trip. He's arranging for a minibus to take us down there – as a thank-you for cleaning the dining area, he said – so it won't cost a lot.'

The Golden Villa Ladies' Association, made up of volunteers from the building, was essentially just a fan club for Shiba. They all adored the fellow, who was no more than a hired manager for the convenience store in their building. Mrs Nosé was the president of the association and the esteemed wife of the building's owner, who was Shiba's employer. The primary activity of the group was to help behind the scenes with store operations, which mostly amounted to cleaning the dining area and car park on a rotating basis. Of course, since it was a service to the community, they weren't paid for the work. Junko pitched in happily, but earned not a single yen for her labour. He had voiced a few complaints about that, but she had asked, 'Would you rather I were stuck in the apartment all day alone?' So he said nothing more about it.

'It's important to nurture relationships with friends and colleagues, but probably not to the point where you have to abandon your home for three days. What's more, to spend a trip fawning over this young man, isn't that in poor taste?'

'*Fawning* is an unpleasant way to put it. But yes. You've seen on TV how they follow teen idols on tour? I won't deny it's something like that.'

Picturing the face of the manager of the convenience store downstairs, Takiji tutted in disapproval. The man had a strange, delicate presence about him.

'A man like that would prey on a woman without giving it a second thought! I've had to deal with hundreds, maybe thousands of people over the years for work, so I should know. The man's no good, he—'

'Oh, stop it! I've heard this story too many times before. Besides, you said the same thing about Kengo, and isn't he a good person?'

Kengo was Nanao's husband. He had found some sort of unserious work as a cameraman that kept him flying all over the country. When they met him at the wedding, his hair was longer than Nanao's. They were still married, and Nanao seemed happy, but Takiji wasn't entirely convinced. Wasn't it possible they were giving up on children because the man lacked a stable job? They made a point of declaring that having no children was their choice, but that in itself was just evidence that something was amiss, wasn't it?

'If an able-bodied adult can't find work at a decent company, then what? Cameraman and convenience store manager, that sort of work is for men who have skipped the rails of society. You know, I ran the factory for Kagami Press—'

'All right, that's enough!' Junko snapped. 'Is it so amazing that you were employed by a big company? Does receiving a promotion make you a great man? That's the only thing you're proud of, and it's meaningless now that you're retired. It's time to let go of all that.'

Junko looked at him defiantly. Takiji was at a loss for words. There were deep creases running from her nose to her mouth and a couple of discoloured patches on her cheek. Her skin was starting to sag, and crow's feet were beginning to assert their presence at the corners of her eyes. But in the midst of all that, her black eyes flickered with their old brilliance, unchanged. In the grip of these contradictory impressions, Takiji wondered: *Is this really the face of my wife? What happened to the sprightly young woman I knew?*

Not knowing what to make of Takiji's silence, Junko said, 'I'm sorry,' and bowed her head. 'I got a little carried away. I only want to take a little trip together with my friends. Shiba was just the icing on the cake, but if he weren't coming, I'd still want to go. I don't do this all the time, so just this once, hold your tongue and let me go.'

For the second time, Takiji could say nothing but 'Do as you like.'

The morning of the trip, Junko looked a little uneasy, but she made all the necessary arrangements with her usual determination and departed. Takiji looked down from his balcony as a minibus pulled up in the convenience-store car park, and the members of the association began to board. The ladies were all decked out in showy clothes and carefully made up, laughing gaily together as they surrounded Shiba. *The men in this building are all fools. Aren't they embarrassed that their wives are all losing their heads over this man who's young enough to be their son?* And to think that he was in the same boat!

As if he felt Takiji's eyes on him, Shiba glanced up as he was boarding the bus. Their eyes met.

'I'll take good care of your wife, so don't worry!' he called out pleasantly, beaming up at Takiji. The easy-going look on the manager's face infuriated him. The man had some nerve, joking about it like that.

'I'm not worried about anything at all!' Takiji called back, trying hard to mask his twitch of irritation with a semblance of a smile. If he raised his voice in anger now, he'd have lost the battle. Takiji stepped back inside, smile still plastered to his face. Back in the tidy living room, he sank down onto the sofa and closed his eyes. He remained in that position until the commotion downstairs had faded, and then, once all had returned to quiet, he stood up.

He went down to the Tenderness convenience store on the ground floor. A male clerk was attending to customers at the register, and a female clerk was busy restocking items on the dessert shelves. Takiji took a casual look around.

Takiji seldom visited convenience stores. It annoyed him that everything was sold at full price, and he also remembered reading an article in a magazine years ago, about how the food items in the boxed bento meals were full of additives. Aside from purchasing the occasional canned coffee drink, or maybe a pack of lozenges in order to be allowed to use the toilet, he never went into the places. He had always told Junko and Nanao to use supermarkets and discount stores instead, whenever they could, in order to save money. Convenience stores were for the lazy, he said. To those who lived their lives properly, they were of no use.

He purchased just the single can of coffee and moved to the dine-in space that Junko and her friends cleaned three times daily. Maybe there were members of the group who didn't participate in the trip, or the staff at the store had taken over while they were gone, because the place was as tidy as usual. Vases containing cosmos had been placed in three suitable locations.

'Hmmph.'

Takiji sniffed, taking a seat at the window counter. Nursing his coffee, he considered how he was going to spend the next three days. Ah! – perhaps he should get in touch with a few former colleagues and arrange a visit? It was just a few hours to Nagoya on the bullet train. He could suggest a drink that evening at a grill pub in the Higashi Sakura neighbourhood, downtown. That might interest a few of them. He was halfway out of his chair, but then sat down again. He had been to Nagoya about a month ago, for the funeral of an old mentor of his. There were a number of people who failed to show, even for an event like that, because they were sick in hospital or had settled into retirement. And the ones who did come had nothing to say about the deceased, they just droned on and on about their own physical infirmities and nursing situations with no sense of propriety. Everyone seemed to have become a bit tired and slow somehow, and just thinking of the impressive figures they had cut in their former lives set Takiji's teeth on edge. Even if he contacted the lot of them out of the blue like that, who would take the time? It was likely that not one of them would show up.

'I've been leading a dull life, haven't I?'

He said it quietly, out loud, and then thought to himself, *that's really the problem.* He had tried his best to be true to himself, but that clearly wasn't good enough. And what could he do about it now? His wife had left him, his daughter blamed him, and he had no friends around to know his feelings.

He felt a presence and turned. A boy had just entered through the side door from the store. Looking at the boy's sunburned face, Takiji let out a short bark of surprise. It was the boy he had seen the other day, through the coffee-shop window. Ah, that was it! He had recognised him because he had seen him so often before, here in the dine-in space. The boy was always here when Takiji went for his evening walk.

The boy directed a quick glance his way and their eyes met again, but it seemed that he didn't remember seeing Takiji before. He looked around the room and took a seat at one of the four-person tables. He removed a curry bento and a bottle of carbonated fruit juice from his bag, and started to eat.

A convenience store bento for breakfast, on a Saturday morning?

Takiji shook his head slightly. What on earth were the boy's parents doing? From what he could tell, the boy was probably still in elementary school. Weren't they concerned about letting their young child eat such a poor break- fast? And just the fact that he'd seen the boy's face often enough to remember it meant that he must be relying on convenience-store bento for most of his meals. A growing child should have meals made with love and care, and with much more nutritional value.

Takiji's thoughts had little effect on the boy. He finished his meal quickly, gathered up his rubbish and dumped it in the bin, then took a portable game console from his bag. He inserted a pair of earphones into his ears and began to play. Sneaking surreptitious glances at the boy's blank face, Takiji bit his lip in frustration. It was utterly deplorable. Convenience-store bento and video games, on such a beautiful autumn holiday morning! It just wasn't right.

There was a peal of laughter, and another group of boys on bicycles rolled into the car park. They parked their bikes in the rack and entered the shop. Soon after, they made their way into the dine-in space.

'Look! Isn't that Hikaru?' A large boy noticed the young man with the video game and spoke.

'Oh yeah, it's Hikaru.'

The three boys surrounded Hikaru at the four-person table. For a moment, Takiji was relieved that the boy's friends had arrived, until one of them smacked Hikaru on the head.

'Hikaru, what are you doing here?'

'If you have free time, you need to practise, practise, practise!'

Hikaru responded to the chorus of voices with a sullen look. 'Go away,' he said. 'It's just a sports day. *Practise, practise, practise* is dumb.'

'We want our class to win first place. How can it be dumb to practise?'

Listening to them talk, Takiji gleaned that the Sunday after next was the field day for the school the boys attended. Apparently, Hikaru's entire class had been staying late after school to train, but Hikaru hadn't joined them once. Takiji was looking at Hikaru in disapproval, thinking 'this is no good', when one of the boys piped up with a sneer in his voice.

'Your dad will probably be away for work again, anyhow. It's the same every year. He doesn't show up, and you have to have lunch with the teachers in the faculty lounge.'

'Huh, what? What are you talking about?' one of the other boys interjected.

'Hikaru's mum moved out,' said the boy with the sneer. 'His parents got divorced. His dad always misses special events because of work or something. My mum said he hasn't come once – not even on Parents Day.'

'Wow, seriously? Then what about the father–son three-legged race? Our class has to win all the races! My dad bought a new track jacket and he's really ready this year.'

'Maybe we could pair him up with some teacher? Like Mrs Noda from the infirmary?'

'No way! Mrs Noda's too old, isn't she? Can she run?'

'I want to win, but I'd really like to see that! Mrs Noda is even fatter than my mum.'

The boys burst into raucous laughter. *Whoa, that's too funny! I want a photo of that!*

As Takiji observed quietly from the sidelines, Hikaru's face became visibly red with anger. His hands, still holding his game console, started to tremble. Finally, he slammed it on the table and shouted, 'Shut up, all of you! It's none of your business! And it's not funny, so stop your stupid laughing!'

'What's up with you? Don't get so mad over nothing.' The boy sitting next to him slung his arm over Hikaru's shoulder, but Hikaru swatted him off violently. At the sound of the slap, the boys' expressions shifted.

'What the heck, Hikaru? That's messed up!'

'Hey there, sorry about that. That's our Hikaru for you,' Takiji stood up and called out loudly. The children, who had seemed like they were headed towards an explosive situation, paused, flustered by the sudden sound of an adult voice. They looked at Takiji, who smiled back at them.

'I'm going to attend field day this year. I'm older than all your parents, but I still know a trick or two, and I think we can win that – what is it? That three-legged race of yours.'

Hikaru gaped at him. Confirming this out of the corner of his eye, Takiji continued. 'I hope it'll be good weather on field day. I'm quite looking forward to it, too.'

'Oh, er, okay . . . you are?'

The boys gave him a wary look, then left, calling to Hikaru on their way out, 'Don't forget to practise!' Takiji watched them go, waving goodbye as they rode off on their bikes.

'Um, what . . .?' came a small voice. Hikaru was looking at him quizzically.

'Ah, sorry. I probably shouldn't have butted in.'

He had intended to keep his mouth shut and listen, but then he couldn't help but get involved. He scratched his head in embarrassment, and said, 'I just got so annoyed listening to them. So I made up that strange story. I shouldn't have.'

What was he thinking, getting so worked up over a children's quarrel? Hikaru's shoulders relaxed. 'Thank you,' he said. Takiji looked at him in surprise. The boy was smiling, ever so slightly.

'I was surprised, but those boys were totally shocked. It was funny to see all of their faces. Thank you.'

Hikaru took the game console from the table and stowed it in his bag. 'It'll be okay. I'll just tell them that Grandpa got sick and couldn't come.' He started to leave, but Takiji called out to him.

'Uh, wait a sec. Would it be really bad if I came? To the field day.'

Hikaru turned back towards him. Takiji looked at his round eyes.

'Are you sure I can't come?' he tried again. 'I'm retired, so I have lots of free time. To pretend to be your grandpa, see?'

'I don't need you to feel sorry for me or anything. I'm used to it,' said Hikaru.

'Well, bye.' The boy raised one hand lightly and left.

'You're a fool,' said Takiji to himself, watching the boy's bicycle leaving the car park. It should have been obvious to him that he'd be rejected. Was the boy supposed to take the ravings of a strange old man seriously? He should have just scolded them all for fighting.

Except, he thought, it wasn't pity that had caused him to call out to those boys. He was surprised to learn it was so painful for the child that his parents couldn't come to the school field day. Takiji, as Nanao was only too happy to remind him, had no real memory of actually attending any of her field days. On the other hand, he had a definite recollection of skipping one, in favour of a round or two of golf to entertain clients. Of course, Junko had been up early in the morning for their daughter's field day each year, making a picnic lunch for the event, and she would take the girl's grandparents as well. So at least his daughter never had the experience of eating lunch alone with the staff. But somehow, Hikaru's face and the face of his daughter in her youth seemed to overlap in his mind. Nanao might very well have had the same distraught look on her face as this boy, waiting for a father who never came . . .

Takiji tossed his empty can of coffee into the rubbish and returned to his apartment.

The following day, a little after noon, the situation changed. He went down to the ground floor to get a can of coffee, and who should be standing in front of the lift but Hikaru.

'Oh, good! I found you.' Hikaru smiled.

'Why?' Takiji asked.

'You looked sort of familiar, so I thought you might be from the building. I hung around here, thinking I might see you.'

Hikaru said this a little proudly, and then, 'So . . .' He looked away for a moment. 'Maybe you can come to field day with me after all?'

Takiji murmured in surprise. 'You changed your mind. Why?'

'They all came to my house this morning and wanted to practise together. They didn't believe me about yesterday. I tried to ignore them, but they were really bugging me.' Hikaru shrugged. 'Finally I told them not to worry about it, that we were doing a special secret training routine, just the two of us. So, um . . . if it's okay with you, I mean, I was wondering, could we?'

Hikaru looked up at Takiji nervously.

'Just the three-legged race would be enough. It's in the afternoon, so you'd only have to come for a little while then.'

'Might I come in the morning as well?' Takiji said, and Hikaru looked at him in surprise.

'I haven't been to a field day in ages. I wonder if you'd let me come to yours and enjoy it as your grandfather, just for that one day?'

'Um . . . you're sure you wouldn't mind?' Hikaru's cheeks blushed red. Looking at his face made Takiji very happy, somehow. *Someone is glad that I'll be there.* 'Good. Now, I have a favour to ask you. You've told your friends that we're doing some kind of special training together in secret, haven't you? Shall we practise a little together starting now?'

'Really? Yes! Let's do it!' Hikaru's voice was suddenly sounding a whole lot louder.

'Well, then, wait over there in the dine-in space for me, while I change into some gym clothes. And I'll need trainers for this.'

With light steps, Takiji returned to his room and dug around in the closet. When they'd moved here, they decided to declutter their lives, and he had ditched all his suits and golf clothing. But there was probably at least an old tracksuit around somewhere.

'Aha! Got it.'

He pulled out a tracksuit that hadn't seen the light of day for a long time, and put it on. He also stuffed an old necktie into his pocket to use as a tie for the three-legged race, and after wrestling for a while with the trainers, he returned to Hikaru.

Oimatsu Park was a quiet, peaceful place near the apartment building. With no shortage of free time on his hands, Takiji had wandered over to the library in the park once or twice, but this was the first time he'd come here for the purpose of exercise. He looked at it with fresh eyes. People were running or walking everywhere. A group of foreigners posed for a photo with an old man on a red cargo bike. He had seen the fellow around the neighbourhood more than once, and always wondered what his story was.

Takiji looked at him curiously for a moment, wondering if he might be some sort of local celebrity, but that wasn't important right now. He shook his head and shifted his attention to the boy.

First things first. Standing by the Manneken Pis fountain in the centre of the park, Takiji and Hikaru turned to each other, and made their introductions.

'Hikaru Minakata. Fifth grader at Moji Elementary School Number Two. Pleased to meet you.'

Takiji watched as the boy bowed his head in formal greeting. He seemed a little small for a fifth-grade student. His face was tanned from the sun and looked healthy. Takiji saw an intelligent gleam in the boy's eyes as they met his own.

'Takiji Ōtsuka. I'm going to be your grandfather, so would it be all right if I called you Hikaru?'

'Sure. And I guess I should call you Grandpa?'

'Of course.'

Nodding, Takiji repressed a smile. Grandpa. It had a nice ring to it. He had thought the day would never come that he would be addressed in that way.

'Well, Hikaru. Let's get started on our training, shall we? We can use this instead of the usual *hachimaki*.' He took out the necktie, and used it to bind the boy's skinny ankle to his own. He took an awkward pleasure in the childlike activity.

'Are you good at sports, Grandpa?'

'I used to be good, but now, well, I wonder . . .' He had given up golf, and hadn't done anything remotely resembling exercise in years. His belly had started to protrude and his blood sugar was high enough that he had started taking a little walk in the evenings.

'Well, in any case, let's give it a try and see, shall we? Today we'll just focus on our breathing.'

The two of them walked around the park grounds until the sun went down. As they walked, they talked about everything that came to mind. That Hikaru's father worked as a care manager at a nursing home. That the staff there was shorthanded, so everyone was always busy. And how that was why Hikaru often had to eat alone.

'I was making a fried egg, and I burned myself. So after that, my father said I shouldn't cook while I was alone.'

Hikaru still had the scar, like a pink snake on his right arm. 'The frying pan tipped over,' he said regretfully.

'And that's why the convenience-store bento?'

'My father says the dine-in space there is clean, and there are always grown-ups watching, so it's safe.'

'Hmm,' Takiji murmured. With all the store employees and apartment residents coming and going so frequently, that place would certainly be less dangerous for a child.

'Sometimes I get food to go, but when I eat by myself at home, somehow it doesn't taste so good.'

'That's very true.' Takiji nodded seriously. He knew well enough the empty feeling of eating alone.

But although Hikaru felt lonely spending time by himself, it seemed he didn't blame his father for that. When he spoke of his father, not even a hint of a shadow darkened his face.

'He takes care of a lot of elderly people, but he remembers everything about everyone so well, it's like there's a computer in his head. Like Mr Takigawa needs to have his food pureed, and Mrs Okita has a rubber allergy. People's lives depend on him, so he can't just do whatever and think it will be okay.'

Hikaru's father clearly believed in his work. And Hikaru could see that clearly in him. Takiji watched the boy's face, radiant with pride as he told his father's story. They were a good pair, this father and son.

Takiji knew it was an extremely difficult task to manage a full-time job, childcare and housework, all perfect and all at the same time. Like many others, he had lived his life entrusting everything other than his job to Junko. So it seemed obvious that there was much more to Hikaru's father than met the eye. Even so, he wanted to tell the man that his boy needed more care. Work was important, but the boy's field day came only once a year. He should be able to find at least enough time to show his face there.

He's probably completely unaware of this, Takiji thought. *You need to work and earn a living, or it's no way to raise a child.* An old phrase came to mind: 'A child must see his father's back, bent in hard work.' In the grip of such concerns, there was no space to consider a child's feelings. He had been that way himself. He had believed that earning money and leading a financially unencumbered life was the number-one priority. It would never have occurred to him to prioritise his daughter's field day over a day at work.

'Let's take first place in this three-legged race, shall we?' Takiji smiled at Hikaru. 'And try to top your class, too. Shall we do that? Then you'd really have something to tell your father.'

Hikaru gave him a shy smile. They had been working hard on their pacing for a while now, and sweat was running down the boy's temples. Takiji's tracksuit, too, was clinging to his back. His calves were throbbing and would probably be sore in a day or two.

He looked around. The sun had nearly set. The horizon was a blend of orange and purple, while far off in the opposite direction the sky was beginning to turn black. The night's first star was twinkling above them.

'Well now, it's getting dark. Shall we call it a day?'

'It's already evening? Hey, do you think maybe we can practise together again another time?'

'Of course. If it suits you, let's make a date to meet here late afternoon tomorrow.' Takiji was about to add 'Only if you really want to, that is' but before he could speak, the boy's face lit up. 'All right!' he said happily. 'That's okay? Then I'll come right after school.'

'Will you? Well, then.' Takiji felt a flush of emotion at the boy's response. 'Then it's a date. I'll be waiting for you.'

Takiji returned to his apartment suffused with a pleasant tiredness. Entering the deserted apartment, he felt a little of the old loneliness, but calling to mind Hikaru's happy face, he soon forgot all about it.

The following evening, Takiji was putting on his trainers in the front hall when Junko returned from her trip.

'Oh! Where are you going dressed like that?' Still holding her suitcase as well as a paper bag from a souvenir shop, she looked him up and down in surprise. She seemed perplexed to see him in the tracksuit, which was hardly part of his regular repertoire. She asked again: 'Is something going on?'

'Not particularly,' he replied. 'Just going out for a little bit.'

'A little bit where?'

'Anywhere, really. It doesn't matter,' he said with deliberate carelessness, leaving the apartment and stepping into the lift. When he exited on the ground floor, he noticed that a number of the ladies hadn't returned to their apartments yet and were still standing around in the lobby, talking amongst themselves in evident amusement.

'Oh! It's Mrs Ōtsuka's husband.' Mrs Nosé, the president of the Ladies' Association, noticed him and bowed slightly in greeting. Takiji didn't know what kind of games they had played on the trip, but she seemed tired. He gave her a polite smile.

'Welcome back. Did you enjoy the trip?'

'Yes, thanks. We had a good tour. We apologise to all the husbands for the inconvenience, but we're very grateful to them for sending us off so willingly.'

Mrs Nosé spoke deferentially and bowed her head, perhaps more politely than necessary, but Takiji waved her off, saying 'Please, don't mention it.' Perhaps Junko had told them that she had encountered objections from her husband. She had never been an indiscreet woman, but he wasn't sure about this new Junko. He hated to think that way, but it couldn't be helped.

'Well, I'm off for a walk,' he said. 'See you later.'

He left the lobby without dropping his smile. Still, a dark feeling was welling up inside him. It made him mad, and there was nothing he could do about it. For all the smiles and apologies, he thought he'd probably be angry when Junko returned from her trip, and sure enough, he was. Was this what Nanao meant when she said he kept her mother under lock and key? No, that wasn't the whole story. Junko had to share some of the blame. Her conduct may have been perfectly natural to herself and their daughter, but from Takiji's perspective, she had just suddenly begun to indulge her every whim, out of the blue, without the slightest explanation.

'Damn it.'

He had given up tobacco all of ten years ago, but at times like this he just wanted a smoke. He was thinking maybe he should just go have a beer at a pub somewhere, when he heard a voice. 'Grandpa!' He gave a start, and there was Hikaru, standing at the entrance to the park. He was wearing gym clothes and beaming from ear to ear.

'Hello! Have you been waiting?'

'Nope, I just got here! Thank you for coming!' the boy said, as Takiji drew closer. 'I don't have as much time on weekdays. Let's start our training quick.'

Takiji patted the boy on the head, and noticed he was already sweating. *He must have run all the way here*, he thought, and the emotional storm that had been raging inside him began to subside. *Let's forget about the problems at home, and spend some time with this child.* Takiji smiled.

After that, for days to come, he spent his evenings in Oimatsu Park, training with Hikaru for the three-legged race.

The training was intense. Takiji suffered from bad muscle cramps all over, but the pain in his legs was the worst. He covered them with compresses, but after his bath, exhaustion would overtake him and he'd barely manage to finish his dinner before crawling into bed. There wasn't even time for his evening drink. During the daytime, he would just sprawl on the sofa in a desperate attempt to recover his strength for the next training session. *I'm dead on my feet*, he thought. *That's the perfect description of it.* But when he was with Hikaru, he forgot his exhausted body completely. Besides, he didn't want to give up the training sessions. He had become too committed to helping the boy take first place.

It was hard to believe. Takiji lay on the sofa, eyes closed, wearing the tracksuit that had already become like a uniform to him. The idea that he'd be working himself half to death over a child's field day – and the child of a complete stranger, to boot! If his former self could only see him now, he'd be shocked beyond words.

'You know, dear, you've been acting funny lately.'

As he was chuckling to himself, he heard a voice and opened his eyes. Junko was seated at the dining table, giving him a dubious look.

'Oh. Are you home today?'

'I told you, today's my day off at the supermarket.'

'And the Ladies' Association?'

'They said it wasn't my turn.' Junko heaved a deep sigh. 'What's going on with you?' she asked listlessly. 'Are you still mad about my trip?'

'Huh? Oh that. No, I'd forgotten all about that.' When he was with Hikaru, his anger had just evaporated somehow. He wondered if he had attacked the training sessions with such fervour because it allowed him to let go of such fruitless burdens. 'I'm just doing what I want, the same way you're doing what you want.'

'Even so, it seems like you've changed somehow.'

'I could say the same about you.'

Junko sighed again, and an uncomfortable silence descended upon them. As the seconds ticked by, Takiji's frustration grew. He had been completely unable to understand Junko since they moved here. He was the one who wanted to ask what was going on with her.

'I'm going to take a little nap now,' he said. 'And you should do whatever you want, too, as always.'

Junko didn't reply. Takiji wondered if his remark had come off as sarcastic, but decided it was okay to leave things as they were. He closed his eyes again and fell asleep in spite of himself.

He awoke to the buzzing of his phone, which he had set as an alarm clock. He got up and did a few deep stretches. He looked around, but there was no sign of Junko in the room, or anywhere in the apartment. She seemed to have gone out.

'So, this is what it's come to,' Takiji said to himself, and laughed bitterly. He couldn't help but think that the old Junko wouldn't have left the house after a conversation like that. But maybe that was just his own self-centred emotions having their say.

Standing in the kitchen, he drank down a cup of cold barley tea, then headed to the front hall. He put on his trainers and hurried to Oimatsu Park, where Hikaru was waiting for him as always.

After their training sessions, Takiji had fallen into the habit of walking Hikaru back to the apartment building. He would return to his room, and the boy would buy a bento at Tenderness for dinner. It seemed that Hikaru had been extra hungry of late, so he was now buying two bento instead of one. When he heard that, Takiji wanted to invite the boy up to his apartment for dinner, but he felt that such a decision wasn't entirely up to him alone. Takiji's repertoire only included two items – fried rice and fried noodles – so he would have no choice but to ask Junko to prepare Hikaru's meal. Furthermore, he hadn't met the boy's father yet, or been properly introduced. The plan was to do that on the man's next day off.

'See you tomorrow, Grandpa.'

'Yes, see you soon.'

With that, he returned home to the silent apartment. The lights were off, and in the kitchen Takiji's glass was still sitting where he had left it.

'What? She's not home yet at this hour?'

She had said she didn't have work or volunteer duties, so what was she up to? Was she determined to make a fool out of him, staying out so late without contacting him? Well, for now he'd take a shower at least. But going to the bedroom to change, Takiji received a shock. There in the darkened room was Junko, lying in bed and crying out as if in the throes of a nightmare.

'Wh–what? You . . . were here?' He raised his voice involuntarily.

'Oh! It's you . . . yes, dear. I think I'm sick.' Junko's response was interrupted by a deep coughing fit. Her voice was so hoarse she sounded like a different person.

'But what happened? You weren't at all like that earlier today, were you?'

'I haven't been feeling so well since then.'

When he thought about it, she had seemed out of sorts, hadn't she? She was sighing a lot and had sounded distracted and listless. Takiji had thought she was just in a mood.

'Why didn't you tell me? I could have taken you to the hospital right then!'

'I thought I'd feel better if I got some sleep,' she said. 'But we're old now, aren't we? It isn't that easy.'

He turned on the light and looked at Junko's face. Perhaps she had a fever? Her cheeks were bright red.

'Okay, first things first. Let me take your temperature. Uh . . . where's the thermometer?'

'Not here. It disappeared somewhere when we moved . . .'

He wasn't sure what to do next. Takiji and Junko had both been blessed with strong constitutions, and neither of them had ever been bedridden. When Nanao got sick, Junko was always the one to care for her, so Takiji had no experience nursing anyone.

'Should I call for an ambulance?'

'What are you saying? It's not that serious. I just need to keep warm and sleep, and I'll be fine.'

Junko tried to laugh but dissolved into a violent coughing fit. Takiji became suddenly anxious that she would start to vomit. Weren't you supposed to cool the head of a feverish person? Maybe he could use ice cubes or something. But was there anything like that in the house?

'I need something to cool your head. What should I do?'

Junko just said, 'Down below.'

'Down below? Down below where?'

'They sell frozen bottles of water downstairs. I can put them under my arms . . .'

Bottles under her arms? Not on her head? He didn't understand, but Junko seemed to think it would be fine. In any case, Takiji grabbed his wallet and hurried downstairs to do as he was told.

He passed through the dine-in space on his way to the convenience store. Hikaru was still there, eating his bento dinner.

'Hey, Grandpa. What's going on?'

'Oh dear, well, when I returned to my apartment, my wife was in bed. She said she didn't feel well.'

Takiji explained he was looking for some kind of ice pack to cool her down, and Hikaru stood up. 'That's rough,' he said. He stuffed the remains of his bento into his mouth. 'I can help.'

'No, that's . . . it's okay.'

'I'm a really good nurse. Because when anything happens to my father, I take care of him.' Hikaru threw away his rubbish, and Takiji entered the side door of Tenderness with the boy at his heels. 'Does she have an appetite?'

'Hmm . . . I'm not sure. Now that you mention it, I don't know if she had lunch this afternoon . . . she may have left her toast this morning, too. It's possible she hasn't eaten anything.'

'You don't know?' Hikaru looked surprised.

'Sorry,' Takiji replied, scratching his head. He had never paid much attention to Junko's appetite.

'If you want an ice pack, she must have a fever, right?'

'Oh, I forgot – we don't have a thermometer, so I'll have to go to the pharmacy after this.'

The pharmacy was at least a ten-minute walk from the apartments, wasn't it? For a moment, Takiji thought it would probably be best just to go back to the apartment, but Hikaru broke in: 'They sell them,' he said. 'They have them here, I'm sure.'

Without hesitation, Hikaru led him straight to the household items. Takiji had never so much as glanced at the products here, since he didn't think it was economical. Lined up on the shelves were hot-water bottles, flasks, thermometers and the like.

'Oh! They have all this?'

When he looked more closely, there were all sorts of products – nappies, aprons, electrolyte solutions. Takiji was surprised, and wondered why. 'Probably because it's all older people upstairs,' Hikaru said. 'It makes life easier for them, doesn't it, Mr Manager?'

Hikaru raised his voice towards the dessert aisle. Shiba's head popped up. His hands were full of cakes, so apparently he had been restocking.

Shiba smiled gently and said, 'That's right. We serve the residents of the building, and we also have quite a few elderly customers among our regulars in general. We give careful consideration to our stock, so they won't run into trouble in a time of need. By the way, our stores in student neighborhoods carry a much wider selection of stationery – and desserts, too.'

Takiji nodded. It was undoubtedly convenient.

He put an ice pack and a thermometer in his basket, then added a few bottles of electrolyte beverages. He took a few bottles of frozen tea, too, as per Junko's instructions.

'She said she'd put them under her arms, but maybe she was just delirious from the fever?'

Takiji spoke quietly, almost to himself, but Hikaru spoke up. 'It's easy to bring down a fever that way,' he said. 'There are a lot of large blood vessels in the armpit.'

'Is that right?'

He was impressed that Hikaru had such information in his repertoire.

'Next is food,' said Hikaru. 'I recommend these.' He was holding a heat–and–serve bag of rice porridge.

'They have these, too?'

'Grandpa, why are you so surprised about everything?' Hiraku gave a little laugh.

Takiji was slightly embarrassed and shrugged. 'I guess I've never really made proper use of a convenience store. I'll admit, though, they're unexpectedly convenient. I'll have to change my thinking.'

When he first looked at the apartment, he remembered, the agent had mentioned how handy it was to have a convenience store downstairs. At the time he had snorted, and wondered exactly what was so convenient about having a shop right downstairs, with people coming and going at all hours, non–stop. At the very least, they'd have to put up with a terrible racket all the time, he'd thought.

In actuality, things turned out to be very different, and the building had decent security, so he didn't have to worry about strangers going in and out. In light of his current situation, he suddenly appreciated the value of this 'convenient' store the agent had touted.

'If you have these, you don't have to worry about meals,' said Hikaru. No matter how little he knew about cooking, he could at least heat up a bag of food. He took the porridge, whereupon Hikaru said, 'And this, too.' He looked. It was an egg custard. Apparently the boy had found it in the section with the bento boxes.

'Egg custard?'

'I'm telling you, I recommend it.' Hikaru grinned, as Takiji looked at him curiously.

Junko's fever climbed steadily as the night progressed. She started to shiver violently and complained of the cold, so he covered her with blankets and had her drink the electrolyte beverages as often as he could. He filled the hot-water bottle with ice, replacing it frequently, and when the ice box in the freezer was empty, he ran downstairs to purchase more.

'How is your wife doing?' Shiba asked with a look of concern. He seemed to be taking the night shift. Takiji replied that she was conscious, and he thought she would be okay. 'Let me know if there's anything that I can do,' Shiba said, his voice gentle but firm. 'I'm always here.'

The man that he had dismissed as so shallow and strange smiled at him. At least he had a certain trustworthy quality, Takiji thought, or maybe he just felt that way because he was so desperately out of his depth trying to care for his own wife.

'Thank you.' He bowed his head in acknowledgement and hurried home.

Dozing by Junko's side, he kept a careful watch over her. In the middle of the night, she broke out in a sudden sweat, and he mopped it up. When she told him she was hot, he wiped the back of her neck with a towel soaked in cold water. 'That feels good,' she said, smiling for the first time. 'That's much better. I may be past the peak now. I think the fever will start to go down soon, too.'

'How could you know that?' Takiji asked. But he heaved a sigh of relief when he saw that her pained expression had eased.

'Don't you remember when Nanao used to get sick?' Junko replied. 'I'd tell her that when she started to sweat it meant the bad germs had fled, and she'd soon be on the mend.' A little of the old firmness had returned to her voice.

'Maybe I do. Oh, wait, that's right. I thought that was some sort of superstition.'

'Hmm . . . If there's something you want to say, just say it.'

Junko seemed hot, so he opened the bedroom window a little. A slight breeze and some moonlight spilled around the edges of the heavy curtains that darkened the room. He spread the curtains a little more, and a milky glow flowed into the room. The gentle light touched Junko's face as she lay in the bed. Indeed, her face seemed calmer than before. As she had predicted, it looked like she was past the peak.

'You're not sleepy?' she asked him.

'I'm okay for now. Besides, my schedule happens to be wide open again tomorrow. It won't hurt anyone if I oversleep a little.'

Takiji spoke in a playful voice, and Junko smiled. Then she lowered her voice, and said 'Remember when Namie passed away?'

'Yes. That was very sad.'

Namie Toyota was a friend from Junko's school-days. Takiji had also come to know her quite well. She was smart and energetic, a born leader. She had a way with words, too, and had bested Takiji in verbal exchanges more times than he could count. She was a caring soul, and had even helped the two of them through some marital disputes. She had actively pursued a career at a time when the working world was still dominated by men, but for a woman like her it seemed natural.

Ever since she was young, Namie had always said that she was married to her work, but just before her sixtieth birthday, she married a man her own age. She said they decided to get together because they were both unwed and getting up there in years, but it was easy for all to see that they made a great pair. From then on, the two of them were going to spend the rest of their lives doing exactly what they wanted to do, together as a couple. They'd do their bucket list!

Namie, who had taken early retirement, related her many dreams to Takiji and his wife, and even showed them the notebook where she had collected them all. Touring the tombs of the royals in Egypt, viewing the northern lights in Finland, staying at an undersea hotel in Dubai, and so on. They wanted to make 'his and hers' beer steins, too, and challenge themselves to run a full marathon. But a month before Takiji and his wife moved to Mojikō, Namie died. She had cancer.

The cancer was found shortly after Namie was married, and she was hospitalised. After an endless series of surgeries and hospitalisations, most of Namie's dreams remained unfulfilled. When Takiji and his wife received the news and rushed off to the hospital, they found Namie lying in bed, weak and withered, with the exception of her eyes, which were still burning bright. 'You know, I couldn't do any of it. I had so much, but now, it's all for nothing.' In Namie's hand was the notebook with her list of unfulfilled dreams.

'When Namie passed away, I started wondering when I was going to die,' Junko said. 'No matter how you look at it, you have to admit we're pretty old. That's why we talked about this being our final home and moved here, but do you honestly think of your life as being so near its end?'

Takiji was at a loss for words. He was strong of body, and he hadn't once suffered a serious illness of any sort. Death and disease seemed like faraway things to him. But when he looked around him, it wasn't so easy to say. He had lost friends already, and colleagues were even now battling serious illness. There was the acquaintance at his mentor's funeral, too, with his narrative of all the troubles attending the onset of old age. But that had nothing to do with him. Or at least, he had managed to look the other way and avoid the subject.

'Since Namie passed away, I've become quite familiar with death. There's nothing wrong with me physically right now, but you never know when that could change, isn't that true? So I thought I'd try to write a list of my own – a list of dreams, like Namie did. Things I've always wanted to do but haven't done. Things I want to do before I die. Like going to work, like drinks with colleagues, like grumbling together with them about the job, even.'

Bit by bit, Junko unspooled her story. She wanted to live a new life in this new land they had found. 'The same

way dear Namíe was looking forward to her life after retirement, I was looking forward to my life after we moved. I
couldn't help but wonder what I'd do if I ended up like she
did, so I suppose I was just a little anxious to get started.'

'Why didn't you tell me?' Takiji asked.

Junko was silent for a little while. 'Nanao scolded me.
She said that I shouldn't talk as if I were preparing for my
own funeral. She said that Namie's death was pulling me
under. I wondered if she was right, and I never found the
right time to talk to you. It was really bad of me.'

Junko lapsed into silence. With a forlorn smile on her
face, bathed in moonlight, she seemed suddenly older.
Takiji looked down at the backs of his own wrinkled hands.
When had those large dark spots appeared? He passed his
hands over his cheeks, and the skin there was slack. *Ah,
that's right, isn't it? It's the same for me, too.* Both his legs
were throbbing and plastered with compresses.

'Have you done everything on your list?' he asked.

'Well . . .' Junko let out a sigh. 'At first, you know, I
was able to do everything I had thought of. I checked off
a lot of boxes. But lately . . . I don't know. I started to
wonder if I was doing the right thing.'

Junko continued. There were a lot of dreams on her
friend Namie's list that couldn't be done alone. They were
all things to be done together with her husband, Tetsuya.
When she remembered that, she started to think that she
might have made a mistake about what to do first.

Takiji looked at her quietly, waiting for her to continue,
and Junko nodded.

'I should have talked with you properly when we moved
here. I should have told you first about my list, instead
of Nanao.'

'I don't know. When we first moved here I was full of hope for my own second life. If you had talked to me about Namie's list back then, I might have just yelled at you not to talk about depressing things.'

Takiji was being honest. If Junko had told him she wanted to make a list like Namie's, he probably would have tried to put a stop to it and been harder on her than Nanao. He would have told her it was weird to go around imitating the deceased.

But now he listened instead, quietly taking in what his wife was saying. He was beginning to understand everything that had happened up to that moment, as if the tangled threads were at last coming free.

'I had a lot of fun on this last trip.'

'Isn't that what you wanted?'

'We all took hot sand baths, soaked in the open-air spa, and ate until we couldn't eat any more. Then we talked until we fell asleep.'

'Just like schoolgirls,' Takiji laughed. Junko laughed as well. But her smile quickly turned forlorn.

'It was tremendous fun. But . . . well, just as we were saying it was time for bed, Mrs Nosé told us all that she was stepping down from her post as president of the Ladies' Association. Her husband had to go on dialysis, she said.'

Takiji called up a mental image of Mrs Nosé's husband, the owner of their apartment. He was a stout man who reminded Takiji of Hotei, one of the Seven Lucky Gods and the patron saint of happiness.

'He'll have to go to the hospital twice a week. Until the trip, Mrs Nosé had relied on his kindness and did more or less as she pleased. She was always out and about, and at times, she'd leave him and be away for as much as half a month, she said.'

Mrs Nosé had thought the two of them could go anywhere at any time, Junko explained, but now they could go nowhere at all. Why had she let her time with him become an afterthought? She had wept quietly into her futon and told the group that this was her last trip with them, that from then on she wanted to spend more time together with her husband.

'When I heard that, you see, it really made me think. That maybe I should have talked more with you, and the two of us . . . the two of us should have made our bucket list together. That if I check off only my own items from the list, I might regret it someday.

'You see?' Junko looked at Takiji. 'That's why I seemed different. I'm sorry.'

'No . . . I was wrong, too. I know I've caused you all sorts of trouble up to now.' He bowed his head to her. 'That's how it came to this.' He knew himself that he could be a hard-headed and cranky old fool. 'I thought about what Nanao said to me over and over again. I wasn't doing it consciously – not at all – but now I think I was holding you back. Shackling you.'

'That's what I did to you.' At Junko's words, Takiji looked up.

'Husbands are raised by their wives,' she continued. 'So I was the one who trained you to be that way. A very long time ago, when I was still young, I thought it was great that you had such a strong sense of duty, and that you were so passionate about your work. I even wanted it to stay like that forever. When other people said that you were working too hard, I kept quiet. My husband can handle it, I told them.'

Junko coughed. When Takiji held out her drink for a sip, she slowly raised herself to a sitting position and took the bottle from him. 'Are you okay?' he asked, and she nodded. Holding the bottle in her hand, she took a deep breath, her shoulders relaxing as she exhaled.

'Year by year, your passion for your work grew, and soon you no longer seemed to notice your family. I started to think it was a weakness rather than a strong point. It's a selfish thing to admit, isn't it? That I was upset by the kind of person you were, when I was the one who had encouraged you to be that way.'

Was that what had happened? Takiji's thoughts travelled back to that time, so long ago. 'You love your work so much, I haven't a care in the world!' His wife had said that to him one day, a smile on her face, her belly big with child, and he swore to himself he'd work harder and harder.

'I guess I forgot about that, didn't I?' He was talking to himself, but Junko nodded.

'How many decades have we been together now?' she asked. 'Just as I raised you to be that way, there are parts of me somewhere that were created by you. Husbands and wives raise each other.'

Is that how it was? Is that how it is? Takiji thought about it. Junko's words lodged somewhere deep within him.

'"Raise each other" . . .? You always find the perfect way to describe these things, don't you?' He could never have come up with a phrase like that himself. When he expressed his admiration, a mischievous grin crept over Junko's face.

'Actually, I stole it from Mrs Nosé's husband. That's what he told her when she came crying to him for forgiveness. "I like you free, so I raised you that way. You have nothing to be sorry for. I did it."'

'Hey, that's a great love story, isn't it?'

'It is. When we heard it at the inn, we all made a great big fuss. We thought it was wonderful.'

The two of them laughed as if they had shared a private joke. Then Junko took another sip of her drink and lay down again.

'Dear, let's make a bucket list together, the two of us.'

'Okay. Yes, that would be good, I think.'

Takiji thought about what he would put on his own list of dreams. He wanted a hobby, most of all. Something he could really get lost in and, if possible, something he could do together with Junko. Also, he wanted to travel. He couldn't even remember the last time they went somewhere fun as a couple.

But the most important thing was probably to take first place at Hikaru's field day. And – that's right, he had almost forgotten – he needed to tell Junko that she had a temporary grandchild.

'Ah, Junko . . . Oh, is she asleep again?'

Junko had slipped into a peaceful sleep, her blanket rising and falling in a slow rhythm together with her breath. He put a gentle hand to her forehead to confirm that her temperature had returned to normal. Takiji closed the window and drew the curtains, then slipped into bed.

When Takiji awoke, Junko was still asleep in the bed next to him. Checking the bedside clock, he discovered that he had slept thirty minutes longer than usual. *Now I know I'm getting old*, he chuckled to himself. *In my younger days I could sleep until any time of the day*.

He got out of bed carefully, trying not to wake Junko, and left the bedroom.

He got dressed quickly and was at work in the kitchen when Junko appeared. She seemed a little unsteady, but her complexion was good. He asked her how she was doing. 'My throat still hurts a little, but I'm feeling much better.' She gave a little fist pump. 'Anyway, I'm sorry I overslept.'

'You probably don't have to work today, right? Maybe you should just sleep in.'

'There's no time. I have to cook.'

'Don't worry about it. I'll take care of that this morning,' said Takiji.

Her mouth fell open in surprise at his words. 'You? Cooking?'

'Uh-huh. But don't get your hopes up. I'm just going to try to do something with this rice porridge. You just sit.'

Junko brightened up a little. 'I'll just go wash my face, then,' she said, and disappeared into the bathroom. Takiji went back to work.

'Will it really taste all right?' Takiji murmured to himself uneasily, then quickly corrected himself: 'No, it'll be fine.' Hikaru had recommended it, hadn't he? The boy had said it was 'super good'.

'Ahh, washing my face was so refreshing . . . Oh! What a wonderful smell!'

Returning to the kitchen, Junko took a deep breath. Seeing her response, Takiji took heart.

'Well, it's ready. Let's eat.'

Takiji carried the clay pot from the stove to the dining table.

He had made an egg porridge. When he removed its lid, steam rose from the clay pot, carrying the rich aroma of the broth. 'Doesn't that look delicious!' Junko exclaimed. 'How did you make it, dear?'

'Well . . . we won't know if it's any good until we've tasted it.'

With a porcelain spoon, he ladled the porridge into a shallow bowl and passed it to Junko first. She had always been sensitive to temperature, so she blew on it for a while to cool it down, then inhaled a mouthful directly from the bowl.

'Ahh . . .!' she exclaimed. 'It's delicious. It's really delicious.'

'Oh. Really?'

Takiji filled his own bowl and took a sip. The rice had dissolved fully into the porridge, so that it was smooth and gentle, with the rich flavour of *dashi* broth. It would be soothing enough, even with Junko's sore throat.

'It's not bad, is it?'

'Not bad? It's really delicious. How did you make it? I didn't realise you knew how to make *dashi* and the like,' Junko said and Takiji puffed out his chest in pride.

'It's semi-homemade!'

'Eh?'

'I put a steamed egg custard from the convenience store into a heat-and-serve porridge. Isn't that what you'd call semi-homemade?'

He had stirred the porridge and egg custard together in the clay pot and heated them. Then he had added some chopped green onions, which they also sold at the store, for a finishing touch of colour.

'You can also do it in the microwave,' Hikaru had told him. 'When I make it for my father I use a microwave pot.' The boy had spoken with such confidence that he had tried it, and it was surprisingly good.

'I used to make fun of convenience stores, but this was actually quite convenient,' Takiji said earnestly, taking another sip of the porridge. 'The manager said he'd always be there if I needed anything. I liked that.'

Whenever he came, there would be someone there, ready to help. Just a few simple words, but they gave him such peace of mind.

'I'm glad you said that about Mr Shiba. He's truly a good person. Oh, now I see! You asked Mr Shiba about the porridge, didn't you? How to make it? This is the sort of thing he would think up.'

He looked at Junko and thought for a while before he answered. 'Actually, it was my grandson. And well, hmm . . . we could say he's your grandson as well.'

'What? What are you talking about?'

Takiji laughed as Junko looked at him in confusion, then began to explain the story of Hikaru from the beginning.

★

Hikaru's field day arrived comfortably, with perfect autumn weather. The sun was shining gently, and a crisp breeze was blowing. Takiji, sporting a new tracksuit, headed to the boy's elementary school together with Junko, her arms full of bento lunches for their picnic.

'Are you okay, dear? You didn't sleep much last night, did you?'

'I'm fine, I'm fine. Ready, willing and able!'

That morning he had risen early and gone for a run. His body felt exceptionally nimble, possibly because he had gone for a massage the previous day. He was in peak condition.

'I just wasn't sure what to do. I hope it's okay for us to go.'

The previous day, Hikaru's father, Akihiro, had called to say that he had been able to get away from work for the event.

A little before that, Takiji was finally able to go and meet Akihiro properly, and they had talked in some detail about everything. As Takiji had imagined from Hikaru's comments, Akihiro was serious and steady, and a kind father. Also as expected, he wasn't aware of his son's feelings regarding the field day. He had been dejected to hear about his son's loneliness, but somehow, it seemed, he had managed to get the day off.

Takiji had told him at the time that if the two of them could participate, father and son together, nothing would be better than that. And that he hoped they would enjoy the field day. But as he was about to hang up the phone, Akihiro had urged him to come. His son was dead set on taking first place in the three-legged race with Mr Ōtsuka, he said, and if he didn't come, there would be trouble.

'Did you tell me his actual grandparents had passed away?' Junko asked. 'If that's the case, maybe he'll let us stand in for them as a couple.' She was even more excited than Takiji about participating in something as far removed from their everyday lives as an elementary-school field day. When Takiji had opened his eyes that morning, she was already up and bustling around the kitchen, happily cooking for the event. Then he recalled that she had always made exquisite bento lunches for Nanao, who had adored them as a schoolgirl.

'Mr Ōtsuka!'

When they arrived at the school gates, which were clogged with a chaotic mass of parents and guardians, Akihiro was waiting for them. He ran up to Takiji and

Junko, bowing his head and saying, 'Thank you for what you have done.'

'No, no, it's the other way around. We're very grateful to you!'

'Grandpa! Grandma!'

At the sound of his voice, they looked and saw Hikaru running towards them. The sight of his ear-to-ear grin brought smiles to all of their faces.

'Listen, dear! Did you hear that? I'm Grandma!' Junko's cheeks flushed as Takiji nodded.

'Hikaru, today you're going to take first place with your grandfather!'

'We sure will! Let's do it! Hooray!' Hikaru lifted a fist into the air, and Takiji joined him. Looking up at his raised hand, he saw the blue sky, with not a cloud in sight.

It was the beginning of his second life.

Chapter Five

Advent Calendar Cookies
of Love and Longing

Kōsei Nakao didn't believe in love.

It might sound like an exaggeration, but it's true. He believed there was no such thing. Celebrity couples would talk about how destiny had brought them together, but then scarcely a year or two later they'd be tearing each other apart in a messy divorce. Meanwhile, just about every month one of his classmates would wail about how they had trusted this or that person, and how wrong they had been. Social media was swimming with cheap declarations of love and longing, and the most trivial, everyday exchange between some elderly couple would prompt an absurd flood of comments from people about how moving it all was.

'Being manipulated by something as elusive as love is just stupid,' Kōsei muttered to himself. He was watching television. Out of curiosity, he had tuned in to a romance reality show that the girls in his class had all been gushing over, but it left him cold. The show would end soon, one way or the other, and then a few years later each of the people on it would move on to different partners. He couldn't help but smile faintly at the thought.

'Don't be so cold-hearted, Kōsei. Why can't you show a little more empathy?' His mother, Mitsuri, spoke up from the kitchen. He thought she had been taking her bath, but she must have got out at some point.

Mitsuri was wearing her favourite Snoopy pyjamas and a pink terry-cloth turban, and holding a bottle of the home-made detox water that she'd been obsessed with lately. She pursed her lips. 'Although I always get too hyped watching this sort of thing, you know what I mean?'

Mitsuri turned forty this year, but even though she was getting up there in years, she dressed in loud, flashy clothes like a teenager – and what was with that 'hyped' business? Suddenly irritated, Kōsei turned off the television. It was a scene in which one of the girls was about to confess her love to someone.

'Hey, wait!' Mitsuri said loudly. 'That was the best part! Why are you switching it off?'

'It was boring as hell,' Kōsei snapped, then returned to his room upstairs. Next to Kōsei's room was his father Yasuo's study, and across the hall from that was his parents' bedroom. The door to the study was ajar, so Kōsei peered in. Yasuo was happily tending to his fishing gear. There was a DVD of a fishing show that his father liked playing on the small television there.

'You going fishing again?' Kōsei asked, and Yasuo, noticing his son, looked up, beaming.

'Well, winter is flounder season, of course, so I have to make sure you get some nice fried flounder for dinner, don't I?'

Yasuo was a hardcore fishing fan who had wanted to be a professional angler when he was young. His free days were given over entirely to fishing, and more often than not, his daily catch graced the dinner table. He cleaned and cooked the fish himself, so Mitsuri was delighted with her 'easy evenings', as she called them, but Kōsei wasn't as pleased. Meat was seldom seen in the house. He was on the verge of telling his father he would prefer fried chicken, but then gave up. It wouldn't make any difference, anyway.

'Don't you want to come with me?'

'I told you, I'm not interested in fishing.'

It was an exchange they'd had many times before, but Yasuo had been persistent lately. Apparently, the son of a fishing buddy – a sixth grader – had made his fishing debut the other day. Yasuo was the one to take the commemorative photo of the boy and his father, holding the fish they had caught, and he had mentioned that he was very envious. 'I want one of those too, Kōsei. Hey, what do you say? Let's go, shall we? Even if it's just the once.'

Sorry, but no thanks, Kōsei thought. He had hated his father's hobby ever since he was young. The man had ditched family outings over and over for various reasons but always something to do with fishing – tidal conditions were particularly good, say, or he got a last-minute call to go out with a buddy. Mitsuri would take Kōsei to Space World instead, or to some movie he had wanted to see, but he was always disappointed that they didn't go as a family – it felt somehow like the pleasure was incomplete. And when his father stood there afterwards, flaunting the fish he had just caught, asking if he had enjoyed himself, how could he even nod? He protested a few times, but Yasuo would just say, 'Sorry, sorry!' Eventually Kōsei gave up trying to detach his father from his rod and reel.

'Oh, it's already that late?' Yasuo looked up at the wall clock. 'Time for bed.'

Kōsei followed his father's gaze. It was just past 10 p.m.

Yasuo's life generally ran like clockwork. He woke at six every morning and made breakfast. Mostly the menu was miso soup and a Japanese omelette. Sometimes bacon and eggs. He would eat them with rice bran pickles that he bought at Tanga Market, a shopping arcade in the city centre, wash it all down with a cup of roasted *hōjicha* tea, and then he'd be out the door on his way to work. He came home around 7 p.m. and had his bath, one beer, and dinner. Then he'd watch fishing DVDs in his study, tend to his fishing tackle, and by 10 p.m. he was off to bed. It was a healthy enough way to spend his days, thought Kōsei, but on the other hand it was also exasperatingly boring. Aside from fishing, his father's life was completely lacking in sparkle.

'Well, I'm going to sleep. Good night.' Yasuo tidied up and withdrew to his bedroom. At just about the same time, the aroma of coffee wafted up from downstairs. Kōsei frowned reflexively. This was the start of his mother's 'Golden Time'.

His mother Mitsuri's day was disorderly in comparison with his father's. First of all, her wake-up time was hard to pin down. Yasuo would make breakfast for himself and leave for work, then Kōsei would wake up, eat his father's breakfast leftovers, and go to school. He and his father ate at the school cafeteria and company canteen, respectively, so no one had to make lunch, and Mitsuri's schedule followed her shifts at the convenience store. The daytime was devoted to household tasks and her job, before she returned home in the evening. She made dinner, and after the meal she took a bath and tidied up.

Starting at 10 p.m. it was Golden Time. Mitsuri would spread out her materials on the dining table and pass the time as she liked. Her bedtime varied according to the following day's schedule, but when she was 'in the zone' she sometimes disregarded schedules altogether and stayed up all night. Once Kōsei got up in the middle of the night to go to the toilet and heard a noise downstairs. He went down to see what was going on, and to his surprise, his mother was jumping around in such high spirits that he thought she was drunk.

Mitsuri's hobby was manga. She liked to read them and to draw them. Although she said that she preferred drawing to reading, there didn't seem to be much difference. When she was reading a manga that she particularly liked, she became – at least in her son's eyes – hopelessly weird. She mumbled to herself in an incoherent voice, saying things like 'Isn't that fantastic . . .' or 'Thank you very much.' And when it seemed like she was settling down and getting into the story, her eyes would suddenly fill with tears. When she was done reading, she would shout, 'I'm ready! Let's do it!' and start scribbling away frantically. So, if he had to guess, Kōsei would say that reading and writing were inseparable to his mother.

A lot of Mitsuri's favourite manga were romance-themed. Her bookshelves were full of volumes in all sorts of sub-genres, from true-love stories that make him squirm to romantic comedies – and then, he's not sure exactly what they were, but there was also a genre called 'Boys' Love' manga. In addition to all the physical books, his mother was really into online series as well.

And then, she also posted her own manga online.

It was a comedy called *The Phero-Manager's Indecent Diary*, whatever that meant, and it was always top-ranked on some website, he didn't remember the name. Once, when she made it to the very top of the list for the first time, she started jumping around for joy, then took him out for Korean barbecue to celebrate. He liked that, but he also thought that it would have been good if she had made that the logical stopping point and given up the whole manga thing.

It wasn't an appropriate obsession for a grown woman, Kōsei thought, let alone a mother with a son in high school. His friend Kozeki Daisuke's mother was into yoga – he heard she had become a certified instructor. He'd seen her a few times, and she was as slender and beautiful as a model. It wasn't that he wanted his mother to be exactly like her, but it had got to the point where he wanted to tell her 'Anything but manga!' It's a hobby you had to graduate from after middle school, surely.

He had only read Mitsuri's manga once, but honestly, he failed to see what was so interesting about it. It was the story of a convenience-store manager who was so overloaded with pheromones that all the people around him were at his mercy. The character was a mirror image of the store manager at Mitsuri's part-time job. There was definitely something funny about the guy, and when he looked at you, you got the feeling he was playing with your heart somehow, but other than that, he seemed normal. Kōsei didn't understand why everyone around the manager got so worked up in the manga, and in his opinion, Mitsuri was just exaggerating it.

When he'd said that to his mother, Mitsuri suppressed a laugh and said, 'Well, you're still a child, you know,' which annoyed him. So he told her flat out that her manga wasn't interesting and she brushed him off with 'Yes, yes,' which annoyed him even more. He wanted to tell her that at her age she should know better than to get carried away just because some people said a few nice things about her dull manga. And that she shouldn't be so eager to hang out on a site like that just to feed her ego. But she'd probably just brush that off, too, so he swallowed his words.

And also, why didn't his dad talk to her about it? She was his own wife! When she told him stories about the comments she received from high-school students, or how some girl in her twenties covered Mitsuri's manga on her blog, he shouldn't just smile and nod. He should tell her to chill out! He only thought of his fishing obsession to start with, and if she did the same and just followed her own interests, it could lead to trouble between the two of them.

About ten days earlier, Kōsei had started to think that something was going on with his mother. He tried to avoid her during her Golden Time, because it drove him crazy to see her like that, but when he needed something from the fridge, sometimes they ended up face to face. On the day it happened, he was studying for a test and had gone to make some coffee during a break, but Mitsuri was on the phone with someone. That was no big deal, she was always just getting worked up about something pointless, like 'Mr So-and-So is a treasure', or 'that scene was really intense', so he didn't really pay much attention. But this time, her tone of voice was somehow different: 'I was *thinking* about you, you know,' she said. And then, 'It's about time. I just wish you had come to me sooner.'

The way she was giggling felt different from usual. He strained his ears in vain to try to hear the voice of the person on the other end of the line. Then the kettle started to whistle. Hurriedly, he turned off the stove, but Mitsuri said, 'I'll call you again soon. Good luck.' And hung up.

'Oh no! Kōsei, how long have you been standing there?' Mitsuri pursed her lips.

'I just came down,' Kōsei replied. *Who was on the phone?* he wanted to ask, but somehow he couldn't do it. Watching Kōsei make coffee in silence, Mitsuri said, 'Do you want a cookie?' She handed him a star-shaped cookie that fitted perfectly in the palm of his hand. It was enclosed in a small, transparent bag and the number '2' was printed in the centre of the star. Before he could ask, Mitsuri said, 'We're giving one to each customer up until Christmas. It was Niseko's plan. I told you about our mysterious correspondent, didn't I? *The Tenderness Advent Calendar Cookie.* We're going to have one a day until December 25th. We had some extras today.'

'Not my thing,' Kōsei said, waving her off, and left the room.

After that, Mitsuri quietly called someone on the phone nearly every day. Sometimes she would stifle her laughter, or be sunk deep in a conversation, but when Kōsei entered the room, she would always end the call in a hurry. She seemed to feel guilty about something, or at least she was acting strangely. Kōsei became more and more suspicious. Could she possibly be having an affair?

★

The story was that Yasuo and Mitsuri fell madly in love and got married soon after. Two months after they met, they both realised they never wanted to be with anyone else and, ignoring their parents' protestations that they should wait a little longer to be sure, they made it official. Instead of staging a big wedding ceremony, they travelled around Asia for a month on an extended honeymoon. Even now, they had three volumes of photo albums on the living-room shelf, full of pictures from the trip.

When Kōsei was in kindergarten, he used to look at the photos of the happy young couple on their travels instead of the usual children's picture books. 'What's this one?' he would point and ask, and his parents would squint at the photo and tell him stories of their memories. *Oh, that one? Your father swallowed all the ice cubes in his juice. You see, the water they use to make ice in developing countries isn't very high quality, so you're not supposed to eat them. He got very sick to his stomach – it was terrible! They rushed him to the hospital and put him on intravenous fluids overnight.* Mitsuri would tell the story happily, and Yasuo would nod. *I had to take my IV to the toilet with me. But they had run out of paper!* It was much more interesting than any fairy tale.

His parents had always got along well together. Kōsei thought their relationship felt as natural and constant as his own name (which meant 'star'). Even now, it didn't seem like they were in a crisis. He had never seen the two of them argue or even raise their voices in anger. But at some point a distance had opened between them. They each had their own separate hobbies and their own pleasures. No one looked at the photo albums anymore. They just sat on the shelf.

'So that's why she's having the affair.'

They were on their way home from school. Kōsei was speaking with some difficulty because his mouth was full of a steamed pork bun. 'That's still unconfirmed,' his friend Kozeki said, laughing. 'Your mum doesn't seem like that type.'

'No, but they say when it comes to affairs, the innocent types are the ones who fall the hardest.'

'What are you talking about? You sound like you want your mum to have an affair!' He grinned and took a long drink from his bottle of warm green tea. When he exhaled, a long white trail appeared fleetingly in the frosty air and just as quickly disappeared. Holiday lights twinkled across the street.

With Christmas almost upon them, the area around Mojikō station was beautiful. The grand façades of the old buildings were lit up all year long, but during this season they were next-level and really captured the eye. When Kōsei was young, he used to badger his parents until they would take him to gaze at the night-time city streets, awash in a sea of tiny grains of light. But now his feelings about it were somewhat dampened, and he looked bleakly at the scene before him.

'It's not like that, but, well . . . what if she really is having an affair?' Kōsei stuffed the rest of the steamed bun into his mouth. It was the winter of his junior year in high school, and all his friends were excited about finding girlfriends to take on Christmas dates, so why did he have to be stuck worrying about this?

'Okay, but say your parents are having some issues. Why don't you just ignore them? You're old enough,' Kozeki said, stuffing the plastic tea bottle in a coat pocket. Kōsei felt a slight sense of shame at his words. Maybe he was being too emotional? He didn't want to come off as a mama's boy.

'W-well . . . I just don't like being lied to, that's all.'

He stuck his hands in his pockets and looked away. He was sorry he had brought it up. Kozeki was the most grown-up of all his friends. He was probably shocked that Kōsei was so dependent on his parents, not to mention the fact that he was being such a baby about it.

As they walked, Kōsei stole a quick glance at his friend. They had been buddies since elementary school. Although Kozeki was tall and physically fit, he said he wasn't the type to enjoy sports and instead had joined the 'Going Home' club. He was really into photography, and he was always reading magazines on the subject. He was good enough that he had won first prize in a newspaper photography contest when they were in middle school. Kōsei still remembered the prominently displayed photograph and interview, in which his friend had frowned, and said, 'I'm not particularly happy about this one.'

If I could just have a little more self-confidence, like Kozeki, maybe I wouldn't worry so much about these things. Deep in his pockets, Kōsei's hands clenched into fists.

In middle school, Kōsei had played basketball. His hero was the point guard in a basketball manga that he was reading, and he'd trained like mad to be just like him. Kōsei himself was short and kind of a weakling, to be honest, but he could do anything if he worked at it hard enough. Or so he thought.

As it turned out, he couldn't even get in the game, let alone the starting line-up. In his head, he could picture himself with the ball in his hands, dashing speedily this way and that, but on the real-life court, the coach was always yelling at him to run – run more, run faster. His teammates said not to worry about it, that he was the team mascot, but who'd be happy to hear that? He wanted to be the hero, not the mascot. When the final game of the season ended without a second of playtime for him, he decided he was done with basketball.

In high school, he too joined the 'Going Home' club. He had no interest in sports outside of basketball and declined invitations to join other teams. Track and volleyball left him cold. *Love is not the same as talent*, he thought, but knowing that didn't help him much.

When he gave up basketball, he started to feel like there was nothing that he could really call his own. Even if he didn't get in the game, or wear a uniform, he had still been on the team before, actually a part of it, and that was over now. It wasn't like he was going to die or anything, but still, he felt lonely somehow. It had been two years since he quit, and the loneliness seemed to have soaked into him so deeply that he could no longer say with confidence that he knew who he was.

After school, he would hang out with friends to kill time. At home, he'd play games on his phone, or watch television. His game scores kept getting higher, and he had heard the same old material from the same old television personalities so often he was fed up with them. But he wasn't interested in becoming an entertainer himself, and he never reached No 1 on the high score charts for the games. This kind of halfway life was just like it was with basketball – or actually, it was worse than that, because he cared about it way less than basketball. Was he really that shallow a person?

'Hey,' Kozeki said suddenly, pointing. 'Isn't that Misumi, from your class?' Kōsei looked over and saw his classmate Mifuyu Misumi, entering a familiar building.

'Oh, yeah. Maybe she has relatives there or something.'

Misumi had gone into the Golden Villa building. From the third floor up, the building apartments were reserved for seniors. The ground floor housed the convenience store (where his mother Mitsuri worked part-time) along with a dry-cleaner, and one empty storefront. On the first floor there was an osteopath's office, a dance studio, and some administrative offices. He couldn't think of any reason for Misumi to be there other than to visit a resident.

'I've seen her go in there before. She doesn't live here, does she?'

'That's an old folks' home! I'm pretty sure she doesn't.'

The two of them stopped and looked up at the building. Then a gust of winter wind hit them, and Kōsei shivered.

'It's cold. I should have got something hot to drink too.' The steamed bun hadn't warmed him up very much.

'Okay, Kozeki. Let's go!' Kōsei said with a little more urgency, and they hustled home.

It was Mitsuri who revealed later why Misumi was going into the Golden Villa building.

'A student from your school started part-time at our store. Her name was, let me see . . . I think it was Misumi?'

Kōsei was at the dinner table with his parents. He put down his miso soup.

'Misumi? Was it Mifuyu Misumi?'

'Right, that's the younger one's name. Her grandmother is on the fourth floor, you know, and apparently they're living together now. She said she was glad to have a zero-minute commute to work, and her grandmother is happy, too.'

'What's she living with her grandmother for?' asked Kōsei.

'I don't know,' Mitsuri responded. 'The manager said she was a nice, attentive kid.' She continued. 'We're always short-handed during the holiday season, so I'm sure it will be helpful. Hey, how well do you know her?'

'She's a classmate,' he said tersely, and Mitsuri let out an amused chuckle.

'Would you mind if I tell her that I'm your mother?'

'It's going to come out whether I mind or not, so it doesn't really matter.'

Kōsei bit into a cream croquette and thought about Misumi. She'd been in his class since tenth grade, but they hadn't spoken much to each other. She was short and seemed a little temperamental. He had a strong image of her sitting in the corner of the classroom, reading a bulky book. He also had the feeling someone, maybe his friend Kakita, had said that she was his type, but he didn't recall her looks with any detail. He didn't spend a lot of time staring into the faces of girls he barely knew.

'*It doesn't really matter.* Does that mean you're not interested?' Mitsuri said, trying to sound casual.

'I think it's fine,' Yasuo interjected. 'If it were a girl he liked, he'd probably do everything he could to stop you from talking to her. Isn't that right, Kōsei?'

'I don't know.'

There was no particular girl that Kōsei liked. When he looked at idols and models, he thought they were cute enough, obviously, and sometimes he was even a little jealous of the people that dated them. He vaguely imagined that someday he'd fall in love with someone, but it was like they were on the other side of the ocean, and there was no way to get across.

Once, at his middle-school graduation, a student on the girl's basketball team called him over and confessed, 'I really like you, Kōsei.'

She was a small forward on the girl's team, and her face had turned bright red. She had beautiful form when she was shooting, and sometimes she caught his eye during practice. She was cute and she was kind, and the rest of the team relied on her. It made him happy that a girl like that would even look at him, but she was a better player than he was, and he couldn't live with that. He turned her down. He said it was because he liked someone else, but he wanted to cry almost as soon as the words left his mouth, it was so petty of him. If she hadn't been a basketball player, he would have accepted her affection gladly. It was pathetic of him to have pushed her away just because she was better than he was. But he just couldn't handle it somehow.

He didn't see her again until the beginning of his first year in high school. She had gone to a different school, but he ran into her one day, walking down the street with some tall guy. They were holding hands. When she noticed Kōsei, she waved casually to him. *This is my boyfriend*, she said happily. *He's on the baseball team.* As she told him all about the boy, how he was working so hard to become a regular in the line-up, she looked so cute that Kōsei couldn't help but remember how much he'd loved to watch her. When he was cheering for his team from the bench, she would always tell him, 'You can get in there, too!' Nobody else ever said anything like that. She was the only one. Why hadn't he realised that earlier? Could he only see it now that she was with someone else? What a self-centred fool he was.

He didn't really understand what it meant to love someone. If he could be so callous, thinking only of how he looked to others, how could he properly love anyone? If love was as pure and beautiful an emotion as they said in all the manga and television dramas, then he felt like he was fated to spend eternity without it.

Then came the suspicions of his mother's affair. His parents still seemed to believe that love existed, even if any sparkle of romance was gone from their relationship. Still, it looked like his mother was having an affair. He didn't know what to believe anymore.

A few days later, Kōsei dropped by the Tenderness store where Mitsuri worked. His friend Kozeki accompanied him. Usually they frequented a different shop, but there was a photography magazine that Kozeki wanted, and it was only available there. According to Kōsei's mother, some of the building residents were photography enthusiasts. The magazine section was designed to reflect the building residents' interests, and it was surprisingly interesting, including everything from gardening to traditional dance, with weekly variety magazines and even picture books. Things you wouldn't even know where to look for in a regular bookshop – obscure publications on theatre appreciation, for instance – were piled up in stacks as if they were commonplace items.

Kōsei snagged a few things to take home as after-dinner snacks, and a bottled soft drink. Shiba, behind the checkout counter, noticed him and said hello, flashing him a smile.

'It's been a while. How are you?'

'Yeah, well . . .'

Kōsei observed the store manager as he spoke. He was just a normal 'heartthrob' type, he thought. The manager's older brother was the totally cool one, a junk collector with a shaggy beard. His name was Tsugi, Mitsuri had told him. Kōsei couldn't grow any sort of beard, but in a few years he'd probably be able to, and then he'd let it run wild, like Tsugi did.

'Oh, Misumi! This is Mitsuri's son.'

Shiba called out to one side, and a face peered out from behind the hot foods. Spying Kōsei, she said, 'Oh. Yeah, he might be in my class at school. I think.'

'What . . . are you serious?' In disbelief, Kōsei's voice went up a notch. What did she mean by that, when they were in the same space, face to face, every single day?

'We've never had a conversation before,' Misumi said, in an indifferent voice. 'I don't even think we've ever said hello. Nakao, you don't know me very well, either.'

Kōsei faltered for a moment, then said, 'That may be true, but . . .' He raised his voice. 'That's true, but still, we've been in the same class since tenth grade!'

'Really? Is that right?'

It seemed to make no difference to her one way or the other, and that bothered Kōsei. Maybe he didn't particularly stand out in class, but he wasn't invisible either. Didn't she see him at volleyball during intramural sports the other day? He had spiked the ball twice, evading blocks by actual members of the varsity team. He had helped his class win the championship and was even picked for MVP. But Misumi just squinted at him and tilted her head like his face was unfamiliar to her.

'Don't worry about it, Kōsei, I understand Misumi's eyesight isn't so good,' Shiba said, chuckling. 'Now she works here part-time, she can afford new contact lenses, right?'

'Yes, sir! I'm doing my best.'

Just because her eyes are bad, that doesn't mean we're strangers!
Kōsei was still sulking when Kozeki came over, magazine in hand, and asked him what was wrong. He jerked his finger in Misumi's direction. 'They said she's working here.'

'Who, Misumi?'

Kozeki looked over at her, and Misumi's eyes opened wide. 'Oh! Kozeki, right?'

'How do you know Kozeki, then?' Kōsei asked, aggrieved. 'He's not even in our class!'

'Because he's famous, obviously. Hey,' she turned and said to Kozeki, 'I thought that photo of yours was really awesome. It's incredible that a dog could make a face like that.'

She was talking about the photo that won the newspaper contest prize. It had captured a dog looking directly into the lens of the camera. It was Kozeki's write-up more than the photo itself that had left an impression on Kōsei, so he didn't remember the image in great detail. But after all these years, Misumi seemed to remember even the composition of the photo in detail. 'It was so adorable that when I looked at it my heart started to hurt.'

Kozeki coolly said, 'Right. Thanks.'

The boys paid for their items, Kōsei at Shiba's register and Kozeki with Misumi.

'Your mother is always very helpful, putting up with all my selfish demands about her shifts,' the manager said.

'Oh. Okay.'

'Oh, and here – have an advent calendar cookie.'

The cookie, with the number 13 on it, was cocoa-coloured, in the shape of a Christmas tree. He took one, thinking about what his mother had said about Niseko's plans, but then an angry voice cut in: 'Whatever! I don't care.' He looked over. Kozeki was glaring at Misumi. 'Leave me alone! I don't want to hear any more about it.'

'Oh . . . s-sorry,' she said.

Kōsei watched open-mouthed as Kozeki snatched his items roughly from Misumi's hands. Realising he was being watched, Kozeki said, 'Kōsei, I'm leaving!' and stalked out of the store.

'Kozeki! Wait!' Kōsei ran after him. 'What's the matter?'

'Nothing,' Kozeki replied curtly.

'It's not nothing! You never get this mad.'

Kozeki stopped suddenly and took a deep breath. Then he bowed his head slightly, and said, 'Sorry, I got a little annoyed.'

'Don't worry about it, but what happened?'

'Misumi was being a little pushy.' Kozeki had returned to his usual calm self. 'She wanted me to join the photography club, or something like that.'

'Aha.' Kōsei nodded in understanding. Since he'd won the prize, Kozeki hadn't taken any photographs. Kōsei had asked him about it just once, and all he would say was, 'I don't feel like it.' He still liked photography, he said, but he didn't feel like looking through the viewfinder any longer.

Kōsei understood that feeling completely. He still loved basketball, and he went wild watching NBA games, although he couldn't imagine holding the ball himself anymore, no matter what. If someone talked to him the same way about basketball, he'd probably get mad too, he thought, so he gave Kozeki a couple of gentle pats on the back. Kozeki smiled slightly and nodded.

'Anyway, that guy has an amazing power,' Kozeki said, as if he had just remembered, and then, half to himself, 'I just don't understand why he's working at that convenience store.'

'Who, Mr Shiba?' Kōsei asked. 'What kind of power? Is there something wrong with the convenience store?'

Kozeki laughed at the questions. 'You don't have enough experience points for that.'

'And you don't know what you're talking about!' Kōsei was certain that he was being mocked, although he wasn't sure exactly how. He huffed and puffed a little, and then realised Kozeki would just laugh at him all the more, so he quickly decided to let it go.

'My mum's always saying stuff about him, like he's got pheromones, or some kind of charm, but is that actually true? I don't think so. I don't feel anything like that around him.'

'That's why I said you don't have the experience points! But listen, that's not necessarily a bad thing,' Kozeki said, slipping the magazine into his bag. 'It's a little like the sense of smell, maybe. Some people have better noses than others. Take Tabuchi, for instance. He can tell right off the bat what perfume a girl is wearing, but to you and me it could be any perfume, or soap, or whatever – we don't have the faintest idea. But if we picked up some life experience by smelling a lot of different things, we'd probably start to figure it out, don't you think?'

'Sure, I guess.'

Tabuchi was in Kozeki's class. He was known as 'the demon king' among the boys and had maintained a long string of girlfriends stretching back as far as elementary school. He had the uncanny ability to recognise someone's scent just in passing, and all the girls doted on him. Of course, the fact that he had the sweet face of a model was probably a big factor in all that, but Kōsei thought the way he paid attention to small details was also important and watched him with some admiration.

'To a person with the right nose, Shiba's type gives off a strong smell. If Tabuchi met Shiba, he'd probably be impressed.'

'Hmm . . . so that's how it works?'

He had never really noticed a girl's scent, and to be honest he wasn't particularly interested in doing so right now, so no wonder he didn't seem to understand what made Shiba so great.

Satisfied, Kozeki let out a little chuckle. Somehow, his mood seemed to have improved. 'Kōsei, you're fine the way you are. Innocence is a virtue.'

'What the hell?'

'I'm giving you a compliment! Ah, but maybe that's it,' Kozeki says, as if he'd just realised something. 'Maybe Misumi's nose doesn't do that either. She was standing right next to Shiba, looking cool, calm and collected. She's like your mum – they aren't the types to get off on that smell.'

Hmm. Kōsei thought about the scene earlier. Misumi had seemed a little tense about something, probably because she wasn't used to the new job yet, but she didn't seem to have any special feeling towards Shiba.

'Isn't that normal?' Kōsei asked.

'Normal, hmm . . .' Kozeki looked up at the night sky and repeated the word, as if talking to himself. Normal was a strange word, wasn't it? Normal was actually different for everyone.

Kōsei looked briefly at Kozeki, his breath turning white in the cold air. He was a good guy, Kōsei thought. Although he would never say it out loud, he wanted to be more like him. Kozeki had a depth to him that Kōsei had never managed to achieve. They had been together since elementary school, and it felt like they had grown up in similar ways, although Kozeki had quickly outstripped him in height – and then, he was also better-looking. *I would choose Kozeki over Tabuchi, no contest.*

Mifuyu Misumi may have had bad eyesight, but she had a good eye.

Kōsei was impressed when he thought about how Misumi tried so hard to share her impressions of Kozeki's photograph with him. Kozeki was a calm, quiet guy who didn't stand out at school. When he won the photo contest, of course, everyone's eyes were on him, but that was years ago, and now even the people who went to the same junior high school had forgotten about it. It was amazing that Misumi remembered it so clearly, and on top of that, she even knew that he wasn't taking photos anymore. Maybe Misumi liked Kozeki?

'Kozeki, um . . . well, is there a girl you like?' Kōsei asked, with no particular reason in mind. Kozeki gave him a surprised look. 'That's an unusual question,' he said. *Yeah*, thought Kōsei. It was the first time he'd ever asked a question like this.

'Why are you randomly asking me that?'

'It's nothing, I was just thinking that if you had a girl-friend we wouldn't be able to walk home from school together like this, would we?'

Since they'd enrolled in high school, Kōsei had gone to school and home again with Kozeki nearly every day. Kozeki had a wealth of knowledge, and conversations with him were easy and fun. At times they were even exciting, and he was a good friend, Kōsei thought. Perhaps he imagined that if Kozeki were to find someone special, he might be left behind, and that made him lonely. When he thought about it, there was little chance that a girl would overlook a great guy like Kozeki.

'Actually, I don't know why I asked that.'

Kozeki let out a deep breath. 'Well, I don't really want a girlfriend.'

'Why not?' Kōsei was surprised at the definite assertion.

'I mean, I don't really know. I can't imagine having someone like that who's always at my side.'

'Oh, I get that! I'm the same.' Kōsei brightened up a little, and smiled. He felt that he and Kozeki had become just a little bit closer.

When he arrived at school the next day, Kōsei was informed that his class had been temporarily suspended. Apparently half the group was off sick with the flu. After complaining for a while with the rest of his classmates about how they should have been told sooner, Kōsei decided to go home.

'I wish they had cancelled our entire grade!' Kozeki complained. The number of cases in Kozeki's class had been under the limit, so he had school as usual. Kōsei boarded the train on his own, and soon arrived at Mojikō Station. But on his way out of the station house, Kōsei had a real shock. He couldn't believe his eyes.

There, walking down the street in front of the station, was his mother, and she was with a man he had never seen before.

The man seemed slightly younger than Mitsuri and was wearing subdued clothing – a black down jacket, jeans and black trainers. Mitsuri was wearing a long down jacket and, over it, her favourite crossbody bag. The two of them seemed friendly, but there was a certain distance between them. You could even say they had the feel of a new couple.

'I don't believe it.'

Was this the moment he had been dreading? His head spun as if oxygen wasn't getting to his brain. It felt like his legs might give out under him if he wasn't careful. What should he do? Should he run up to the two of them and demand to know the nature of their relationship? But then what if they apologised to him, or something like that? He wouldn't know what to say.

Oh, if only Kozeki were there! He would have told him what to do.

'What are you doing?'

He heard a voice and turned with a start. There was his classmate Misumi, in a peacoat with a scarf wrapped around her neck. She frowned. 'You're blocking the exit.' Then, 'Are you feeling sick?'

'No, it's not that, I . . .'

He didn't know what to say. He struggled for words, but Misumi said, 'Okay, whatever. Bye.' She tried to squeeze past him. Kōsei grabbed at her scarf and said 'Sorry! Can you just stay here for a minute? I can't figure out what to do.'

Kozeki wasn't there, and Kōsei needed someone right now. Someone to help him get through this. He couldn't handle it alone.

'What?' Misumi turned back to Kōsei. 'Has something happened?'

'Happened . . .? No, it's, uh, something I saw, or something that's going on, I guess.'

'I have no idea what you mean.' Misumi let out an exasperated sigh. Her manner was completely different from when she was speaking with Kozeki, which annoyed him momentarily, but he quickly reminded himself that this wasn't the time to be critical.

'Listen, okay? You know my mum, right?'

'Oh, Mitsuri, you mean?'

'Right, well, I caught her. Having an affair, I think. Just now.' Kōsei said, as if it were being wrung out of him.

'Eek!' Mitsuri let out a little shriek. 'What? Are you serious?'

'I'm serious . . . I think. What should I do?'

'Which way did they go? By car? On foot?' Misumi scanned the area as she spoke.

'On foot,' he said.

'Which way?' she repeated and took Kōsei's hand. He was surprised by the strength of her grip. 'Hey, I guess you can't do this alone.' She gave his hand a tug. 'I'll go with you. Come on.'

'Th-thanks.'

For the first time, Kōsei took a good look at Misumi's face. Cool, elegant eyes, a small nose. Her features were more beautiful than cute. Her earnest expression had something kind about it that gave Kōsei a slight feeling of relief.

'Um . . . they went that way.'

Misumi nodded and started walking, half a step ahead of Kōsei. Looking at their tightly clasped hands, he wondered how this could be happening to him. He meant the trouble with his mother, of course, but also he couldn't believe he was walking hand in hand like this with a classmate whose existence he had only the vaguest grasp of until just the other day. Or that she'd be taking care of him like this.

'Oh! There they are.'

Hearing his mother's voice, he quickly scanned the pavement ahead of him. He spotted the two from behind, talking as they walked. The man had a large paper bag in his hand and was wearing a bashful smile. Mitsuri, too, seemed to be enjoying herself. It was the same smile he had seen a hundred times at home, but somehow the sight of it directed at this man he had never seen before made him shudder.

And then the two of them, side by side, walked into the Premier Hotel Mojikō.

'A hotel . . .? No!'

So it was true. Kōsei almost collapsed on the spot, but Misumi said, 'Come on now, let's go.'

'Go and do what, at this point?' He felt like he might cry. He didn't want to see his mother in a place like this.

'We don't know for sure yet.' Misumi looked up at the hotel, which was modelled after a ship. 'If you're having an affair, you don't come to a place like this,' she said flatly. 'It's too public. You meet in an out-of-the-way place, not where you live.' Surprised by her decisive tone, Kōsei looked at her, and she smiled back reassuringly. His heart skipped a beat.

'I don't think Mitsuri is the type of person to have an affair. I've only known her for a short time, but I get her. So let's go.' Misumi gave a quick tug on Kōsei's arm.

He stood up reluctantly. 'I've got no choice,' he said, as if trying to convince himself. 'If this is how it is, I've got no choice. Affair or not, I have to see it through.'

'Yes, that's right. Let's go.' Misumi gave his arm another tug and the two of them entered the hotel.

Inside, the splendid lobby was awash with Christmas colours. Kōsei fidgeted awkwardly, feeling that two uniform-clad high-school students were a little out of place there, but Misumi paid no heed to the elegant surroundings. She simply dropped her voice and said, 'Over there.' Mitsuri and the man were heading straight for the staircase. Kōsei had thought they'd go to the front desk first, but Mitsuri said 'Come on!' and with her urging him on, they followed stealthily behind as the couple entered an Italian restaurant on the second floor.

'Huh. A restaurant?'

'Hmm. I wonder if we can get in without them noticing. Excuse me, can we sit anywhere we want? I'd like a quiet table, please.'

Misumi called out to the staff and entered the restaurant confidently. She took a seat at a table next to the wall, a small distance from the couple they were following.

'W-wait, Misumi.'

He hurried after her and with complete composure, Misumi said, 'Sit down now – quickly! Also, hold your head up. People will notice you if you act like you're sneaking around.'

'Oh . . . uh . . . okay.'

He sat as he was told, and Misumi took a careful look behind her.

'Mitsuri is facing the other way, so she can't see us. We're okay.' Misumi looked around. 'It's still a little early for lunch, but it's going to keep getting busier, and then I think we'll be much harder to spot.'

'Misumi, have you done this before?' Kōsei couldn't help but ask. He knew it wasn't his business, but she just seemed too sure of herself.

'Well, I have some experience . . . Ah, we'll have two of the pasta lunch specials, please. You have to choose a main course. I think I'll have the cod and turnip Alfredo. What will you have, Nakao?'

Kōsei took a menu from the waiter, who seemed to have appeared out of nowhere, and tried to order. 'Um, er . . . well, the peperoncino pasta?' Once the waiter had departed, he turned back to Misumi. 'Experience?' he asked.

'My mother *was* having an affair. Around this time last year, I was following her around all the time. I wanted to be sure, so I was gathering evidence.'

Misumi spoke casually, as if it were a matter of no importance whatsoever. She removed her scarf and coat and dropped both into a small basket that the waiter had placed next to the table for them.

'My mother only stayed in love hotels. She would never use a local hotel like this, where you never know who you're going to run into.'

'What?' asked Kōsei, flustered. 'Wait, why are you telling me all of this?'

It was too much for Kōsei, but then Misumi said, 'That's all over now, so don't worry about it. Besides, it's only fair, since you told me all this stuff about your family.'

'Huh? No, that's . . .' He didn't know how to respond. He rubbed his head in confusion.

'Your mother and mine are completely different people,' Misumi said. 'Maybe it's because Mitsuri has enough time for herself? She gives the impression that she's satisfied with her family, but also personally. People like that don't have affairs.'

Misumi put the cold glass of water to her lips briefly, then continued. 'A lot of people are unfulfilled in life,' she explained. 'The really pathetic ones look for love wherever they can find it, cheating and having affairs.'

Looking at that cold face, Kōsei thought about Misumi's past. He wondered what kind of sadness had to be buried there, that she would dismiss her mother as pathetic that way.

Before too long, food had arrived at both tables. Eating his pasta without tasting it, Kōsei peered at his mother. She seemed to be enjoying the conversation, but there was something a little awkward about her manner. Misumi was watching them the same way. 'I knew it. It's definitely different,' she said. 'Intimacy? They don't have anything like that.'

'But maybe it's because they just started seeing each other . . .'

'Hmm. I don't think so.'

When dessert and coffee arrived, there was a new development at Mitsuri's table. The man took a tablet out of his bag. The two of them put their faces close together to look at something on the screen. As their faces drew near, Kōsei let out an involuntary gasp – 'No!' Misumi instantly covered his mouth.

'Your voice is too loud!' she hissed in his ear. 'So far, they haven't done anything that's not normal.'

'Whoops. S-sorry.'

Her hand was touching his lips. Hastily he pulled back. Hiding his embarrassment, he returned to watching the pair at the other table and quickly settled himself down. The man was gazing at Mitsuri earnestly. Mitsuri seemed oblivious to this and just kept talking, her eyes fixed on the tablet. *What are you doing, Mum?*

'Oh! Someone's coming.'

Misumi briefly raised her voice and Kōsei looked over. A second man approached his mother's table and sat down heavily in an empty seat.

'What?! Tsugi?'

This time Kōsei's voice rose to full volume. The three people at the table instantly looked at him.

'Oh! Kōsei?' Mitsuri looked over in surprise, then smiled in satisfaction. 'It can't be! What, are you on a date?'

'D-don't be stupid!'

At Mitsuri's question, devoid of guilt or anxiety, Kōsei's voice got even louder. Heads at the surrounding tables all turned their way, and noticing the attention, Misumi scolded him: 'Shhh!!! Too loud!' He hastily shut his mouth, bobbing his head apologetically in all directions.

'S-sorry, Misumi.'

'Hello, aren't you Mitsuri's son?' said Tsugi. 'Why don't you join us?'

Tsugi beckoned them over, and at his invitation, Kōsei and Misumi switched tables. The man who had been eating across from Mitsuri moved over next to her, looking a little put out. Seemingly unconcerned, Mitsuri just giggled to herself, looking happily back and forth between Kōsei and Misumi.

'Now this is a surprise! I had no idea you and Misumi were so close. And shouldn't you both be in school? Are you looking for trouble, mister?' His mother put on a show of mock anger, but she couldn't hide her amusement.

Kōsei responded fiercely. 'This is about you, Mum! What are *you* doing here?'

Mitsuri said, 'Oh, right, right. I haven't introduced you! She gestured towards the man sitting next to her. 'This is my apprentice, Yoshirō Kiriyama.'

'Huh? Your apprentice?' Kōsei had no idea what she meant. He frowned in confusion.

'Mr Kiriyama draws manga, like I do,' Mitsuri said, with evident pride. 'He wanted to distribute his work more

broadly, so I'm coaching him on how to share it online.'
Kiriyama bowed his head in grateful acknowledgement.

The details emerged. It seemed that Kiriyama now lived
in Ōita, but he had originally been a regular at Tenderness,
and so he and Mitsuri had become acquainted. From the
time he was a child, he had wanted to be a manga artist,
but things hadn't gone so well for him. He thought he
should probably quit, but he couldn't bring himself to
give it up, and so had been fretting about how to find a
few readers for his work. At that time, Tsugi, who was
acquainted with both of them, had suggested he ask Mitsuri
for help. 'She's not a pro,' he said, 'but she draws manga,
and she's active online.'

'I didn't know the first thing about any of that,' said
Kiriyama. 'I had been really obsessed with drawing by
hand, so I didn't even know how to use a digital pen and
tablet. Ms Nakao was tutoring me every evening, and I was
learning, more or less, but still, there were a lot of things
that were hard to understand over the phone, so finally
she was kind enough to spare me some time in person.'

Speaking shyly, Kiriyama explained that he was friendly
not just with Tsugi, but also his brother Shiba, and that this
evening he would stay at Shiba's place. Then, to Kōsei's
complete surprise, Mitsuri added that her husband Yasuo
also knew of today's meeting.

'Mr Kiriyama said he really wanted to see my work
set-up, so we invited him over for dinner. Your father is
very excited to take him fishing!'

He had thought his father was just working as usual,
but it turned out he'd taken the day off to go fishing. To
the stunned Kōsei, who hadn't known any of this, she said
simply, 'I thought if I told you, you'd just make a face. I

figured you'd probably just say "Manga again, Mum?" So I decided not to mention it until the last minute. That's what you'd say, right?'

'That's . . . well, maybe.' With everyone's eyes on him, now, Kōsei looked down at the table.

'It seems you don't approve of your mother's activities, do you?' Kiriyama said gently. 'Personally, I think it's wonderful. That she didn't give up on the thing that she loved all her life, and that she can still take pleasure in it. That's incredible. And on top of that, other people love what she does. Have you read the comments on your mother's work? *I'm looking forward to the next instalment, I can't wait* – they go on forever! It's incredible that so many people depend on something that your mother drew. You could even call it a miracle.'

Kiriyama's passion grew as he spoke. Watching him, Kōsei had a funny feeling. It was the first time he had ever seen anyone praise his mother this way. Also, he had no idea that his mother had loved manga since she was a child. He knew she was a good artist, but he had never thought about why she started drawing manga. He'd always imagined it was something she had just sort of stumbled upon. So when had his mother started her manga work?

'Ms Mitsuri, you draw manga?' Misumi asked.

'That's right,' Mitsuri said, 'but for various reasons, I don't talk about it much. You won't tell anyone, will you?' She tapped a few times on the tablet and passed it to Misumi. 'This is it.'

'No way!' Misumi exclaimed. 'This is you? It's one of my favourites! I really love it. I follow all the updates.'

'Really, Misumi? You're serious?' asked Mitsuri.

'Wait! That can't mean that you-know-who is the Phero-Manager?'

'Yes! He's the one!'

'Aha! That's top secret, isn't it? Oh, wait – so, is Ayu also a real person, then? The puppy-dog hairdresser?'

'Haha, it's a secret!'

Misumi was getting so excited, she seemed like a different person. She grabbed Kōsei by the shoulder. 'Mitsuri is fulfilled,' she said. 'She's got it all!'

'I don't get it.'

'What? You really don't understand? Mitsuri's manga is super popular, but more than that, it's fun. If you read it, I think you'll have more respect for your mum. But also, I don't think you'll worry anymore.'

'I read it once, but I didn't really get it,' he confessed.

Misumi shook her finger at him. 'That's no good,' she said, frowning. 'You only read one episode. You gave up too soon! You have to read at least five.'

'Thank you,' said Mitsuri, and smiled as if Misumi understood her. Kiriyama sighed, looking a little envious, but said, 'That's nice, isn't it? Being able to meet a real fan like that is the best thing in the world.' Tsugi just watched and grinned.

What in the world? Kōsei thought to himself. *What was happening here?* But he was relieved that Mitsuri wasn't having an affair.

That evening, not only Kiriyama but Misumi, too, showed up at the Nakao household.

'Well, well! Is this Kōsei's girlfriend?'

Yasuo looked at Misumi happily, and in high spirits got busy in the kitchen preparing his daily catch. In the living room, Kiriyama, Misumi, and Mitsuri were in front of the computer, excited about something. Mitsuri seemed even happier than usual, and couldn't stop smiling.

'Hey, Dad. Did you know that Mum has always been into manga?' Kōsei was sitting at the kitchen counter, watching the three of them from afar.

'Yes, that I knew,' his father said. 'When we first met, she wanted to be a manga artist. But we got together, and then we got married, and soon enough, you came along. So she gave it up. She said she'd focus on raising you until you were bigger.'

'Why?' Kōsei asked, surprised. Was his father saying it was because of him that she quit? 'Well, obviously,' his father said in a slightly exasperated tone, 'it must have been because you were so adorable, don't you think? From the time you were born, you were a little sickly. Also, you didn't nurse well, you didn't sleep, and – well anyway, it was a lot of work. If she was going to bring you up properly, there would be no room for manga.'

Kōsei hadn't known any of that. Seeing his amazement, his father said, 'You started playing basketball late in elementary school, you know? From then on you got much stronger, and you fell in love with the sport. In middle school the love turned into real dedication, and from then on we didn't get to go out much as a family.' Yasuo looked a little nostalgic. He cut and trimmed the flounder in front of him with well-honed skill. It looked like he was going to deep-fry part of it and make a soup with the rest.

'Your first year of middle school, I invited you to come with us on our New Year's visit to the local shrine, but you had an important basketball practice that you wanted to do instead. Your mother told me then and there she thought it was time for her to start having some fun pursuing her own interests again.'

Kōsei said nothing, just watched his father work. It was true he had been obsessed with basketball, and had definitely put the team before everything else in his life.

'It's unexpectedly difficult to keep doing what you love,' Yasuo said. 'Look around you. Those who care enough to risk anything real for what they love are actually surprisingly few. First of all, it's very rare just to discover that you feel that way about anything. And when you do, the environment and circumstances you need to devote yourself to it are fairly hard to find. Maybe you also need talent, right? Most people get frustrated and think, *it's no good, I've gone as far as I can go*. Then they quit.'

Kōsei looked at the palm of his own hand. Since he had given up basketball, the skin on his hands had become much softer. Even though he had loved playing the game with a passion, he had let it go because he didn't have the talent. His parents hadn't said anything about it to him, but that was probably because they knew how difficult it would be for him to continue.

'Back then, I told your mother I'd quit fishing for a while, too, but she said it would be wrong for us both to give up the things we loved. Instead, she told me I had to support her without complaint when the time came for her to start doing manga again.'

'I'm lucky to be able to do what I want, as much as I want,' Yasuo said, putting half of the flounder into a pot. The broth that he had made of soy sauce and *dashi* stock was beginning to simmer. Kōsei took a deep breath, inhaling the pleasant aroma, and looked over at Mitsuri.

When his father went fishing, his mother never made a fuss about it. Eating fish for dinner night after night, she never protested. Was that her way of supporting his father's interests? And then, when his father went to bed at 10 p.m. sharp, that must have been a sign that he supported Mitsuri's activities as well.

'It makes me happy to see your mother happy,' Yasuo said earnestly. Kōsei looked at him, but Yasuo was gazing fondly at Mitsuri. The look in his eyes was no different from the times when they used to look at the photo albums together. Ah, there was still something unchanged between his father and mother. At that thought, a warm feeling spread through Kōsei's chest. And respect, too, for this couple who had held fast to the things that they loved. There must have been times when they were frustrated or fed up, but they'd found a way to stay happy.

I wonder what it will be like for me? Will I ever want to pick up a basketball again? Or will I find something new and fall in love with that? If I do, will the empty place inside me be filled, and my self-confidence return to me? That would be good, he thought.

Yasuo began to sprinkle potato starch on the remaining flounder. Watching his father's familiar movements, Kōsei asked, 'Next time you go fishing, will you take me?'

Yasuo looked up quickly. 'You'll go with me?' he asked, with a small quiver in his voice.

'Well, maybe once.'

'Yes? Well, that's very nice indeed.' He repeated this last several times, then started to hum a little tune.

After the meal was over, Misumi said, 'I have to go home, or my grandmother will start to worry.' Kiriyama had offered to take her back to the Golden Villa building, since he was staying there too, but he and Yasuo had got on so well that they were quite busy pouring each other drinks. Kiriyama made as if he would try to wind up the session, but Misumi just laughed and said, 'Don't worry, I can get home on my own.' She was getting herself ready to go when Kōsei stood up, saying, 'Well, in that case, I'll see you off myself.'

'Take her home properly,' Mitsuri said, watching them, and the two of them left the house.

'Look how beautiful the sky is,' said Misumi to Kōsei, who was shivering in the cold wind. He looked up at the clear winter sky spread out above him, stars twinkling. 'That's true, it is beautiful,' he said, and meant it. It had been a long time, he thought, since he had looked at the sky with this feeling.

'Thank you for today,' Kōsei said, 'I couldn't have done it without you.'

'I didn't do anything, really.' Misumi shrugged. 'Even if I had gone straight home and left you alone, Kiriyama was there, and he would have explained everything, you know? I can't take credit for it.'

'It's not like that,' Kōsei said firmly. And then, 'But I'm sorry.' He lowered his head. 'I made you tell me all that about your family.'

'You're a good kid, but it was my decision to tell you, wasn't it?' Misumi laughed as if she were teasing him.

Kōsei was bewildered by her composure. 'Oh, um . . . is that why you're living with your grandmother? Because of your mum's affair?'

'My parents got divorced because I uncovered the affair,' Misumi said in an uninterested voice. 'When I told my mother to stop having the affair, she just said, "So I guess you

223

caught me." She didn't seem ashamed or anything, just like "You caught me, so I guess I'll stop being your mother."'

'Huh? What did she mean?' Kōsei asked, surprised.

Misumi nodded. 'It's crazy, right? But it's true. My father must have half guessed that she was cheating on him, too. He told me it didn't make sense for us to continue as a family after that, so they were going to split up. And that he didn't think I could depend on them anymore. Then they both went away somewhere.'

Kōsei's legs stopped of their own accord. Not knowing what to say, he desperately searched for words, but Misumi just said 'Don't worry about it,' and kept walking. 'They both say they'll take care of my college tuition and stuff like that, and my grandmother is happy to have me living with her. It all worked out fine.'

'But . . . but, wasn't it lonely?' Kōsei asked. 'I know what you went through for your family.'

Just following his mother for the shortest time today had made his heart hurt like it might split in two. He had felt like he was going to cry at any moment the entire time, and had even considered running away. It was painful to imagine Misumi doing all that by herself – and then have her worst fears realised.

'You tried as hard as you could, didn't you? Even though you hoped you were wrong. That it wouldn't end with a broken home, or anything like that.' Kōsei's eyes grew hot. In response, Misumi shot him a cross look.

'Don't get all weepy on me, that stuff is all over now.'
'But . . .'

'I don't think about it all anymore,' Misumi said firmly. Kōsei was silenced by her show of strength. 'Really, I don't think about it.' She summoned a smile. 'Then tonight,' she continued, 'when I saw your family, I thought, yes, I knew it, there had definitely been something wrong with mine. The mood was different. It all just made so much sense that it was almost funny.'

Misumi slapped Kōsei lightly on the back and laughed out loud.

'Nakao, you're pretty popular among the girls in class, aren't you? Honestly, I didn't understand what they saw in you, but now I get it a little bit. It's this purity of yours, you know? '

'W-what are you talking about?'

Girls? Popular? Why did she have to bring all that up now? Kōsei turned a little red, and even though it was dark out, it seemed Misumi noticed.

'Aww, you're so cute!' she said, as if talking to a small animal.

'Okay, okay. So what kind of guy do you like, Misumi?'

'What? Oh, that would be Kozeki.' She answered so coolly that Kōsei was at a loss for words. Misumi wasn't the slightest bit embarrassed. 'He's nice, isn't he? Kozeki.'

'You like Kozeki?' he asked.

'Yup. I really like him.' Misumi nodded.

What now? This was totally confusing. Kōsei felt a flutter in his stomach and frowned. His head, which had been clear until just a moment ago, felt as if it had been cloaked in a dense fog.

He remembered feeling a little lonely yesterday, when he thought that Misumi might like Kozeki. That had just been because he didn't want to lose his friend. *All I did today was confirm that prediction, so why do I feel so upset?*

'Are you going to tell him?' Kōsei's voice was so weak he surprised even himself.

Misumi, who seemed not to notice, said, 'Yes, that's my plan. I want to get to know him better first. But that might be difficult. I made him angry the other day.'

'Oh, about the photo?'

'Yes. That photo gave me chills when I saw it. I couldn't believe there was a kid my age with that kind of sensibility. So I told him.'

Kōsei said 'Hmm . . .' under his breath. *She really liked Kozeki's photo*, he thought. The flutter in his stomach had turned into a weight that kept getting heavier.

'But I still don't know why he got so angry, you know?' Misumi mused. 'Maybe I should ask why, and then I could apologise?'

Misumi sighed. There was something appealing about that sigh, and Kōsei's heart skipped a beat in spite of itself. Wait – why was he getting so worked up?

'Oh, I see Tenderness!' Misumi said, as the lights of the store appeared in the distance. 'This is far enough.'

'No, it's fine. I'll walk you all the way there.' If he didn't take her to the lift, at least, what was the point in coming all this way? After all, he was a man, wasn't he? More or less.

He insisted, feeling a little flicker of something like pride. Misumi just said, 'Well, okay.' But then when they reached the car park, she gave a quick wave, said, 'Bye, thanks!' and ran off towards the building without looking back. With an empty feeling, Kōsei watched her go.

'Look who's here! Hello, Kōsei.' It was Shiba, peering out from the doorway of the store. 'You're alone? What happened to Kiriyama?'

'Oh . . . he's drinking with my dad. He may be a while.'

'Right, right. I'm still working, so that's fine. Are you coming in?' Shiba asked.

Kōsei nodded. He entered the store, and wandered the aisles aimlessly as he thought over what had just happened.

I wonder what Misumi likes about Kozeki? It must be that he's so grown-up. If he had heard her story, there's no way he would have responded as stupidly as I did. He would have said something to make her feel better.

'Damn.' Kōsei spoke out loud.

It's pathetic. I admire Kozeki so much he's like an idol to me, but the more I do, the smaller I feel. No, wait – why am I obsessing over Misumi like this? Didn't she say I was popular with all the girls in class? I should focus on how good I am . . . but then, didn't Misumi also say that she didn't get why they thought I was good?

'Oh, what's the point, anyway?'

He sagged, then sat down on the floor, right in the middle of an aisle. He rubbed his head with both hands and sighed

'Hey, loverboy! You're in the way.' He looked up to find Tsugi standing over him. 'I'm seeing a lot of you today, Mitsuri Junior.'

'It's Kōsei.' He stood up. 'Anyway, how about you, Tsugi? What are you doing here?'

'I told Yoshirō I'd have a drink with him,' Tsugi said. 'And I'm staying over at my brother's place, too. Snacks.'

Tsugi held up his basket in his hand. There were a variety of foods in it. Kōsei let him know, as well, that Kiriyama was likely to be coming late.

'That's fine,' Tsugi said. 'He really came to meet with your mother, so we're just piling on. But here's something much more important. Did you know that they've got new improved Korean barbecue short ribs in the frozen foods section? They're terrific. Delicious, and really thick cut, for starters!'

Tsugi lifted the package out of his basket with enthusiasm, and held it up for Kōsei, who ignored it and asked, 'By the way, what was that before? When you called me "loverboy".'

Tsugi was looking over at the frozen foods, apparently thinking about buying an extra package of short ribs for himself. He glanced back at Kōsei. 'Just calling it as I see it,' he said. 'I saw you and Misumi before, from inside the store. You like her, I think. Don't you?'

What? Me, like Misumi? His jaw dropped, but Tsugi just patted him on the shoulder. 'She's a nice, level-headed kid, isn't she? You've got good taste!' Kōsei could feel himself blushing as he thought about it. *Is that right? This is it? This is love?*

Completely embarrassed, Kōsei fled the store. A cold wind caressed his flushed face.

When he asked himself, he had to admit that what he was feeling seemed like love. But Misumi herself had told him straight out that she liked Kozeki, so what could he do? On top of that, he wasn't a better man than Kozeki in any way. If it was between the two of them, he'd have no chance.

Once his face had cooled completely, he stood still and just breathed in and out. His frosty breath quickly dissolved into the darkness and disappeared.

The suspension was lifted the following week, and classes resumed as normal.

Kōsei hadn't seen Kozeki for a while, so on the way to school, he reported that his mother hadn't been having an affair, after all.

'Well, that's good news, isn't it?' Kozeki grinned. 'Didn't I tell you it seemed unlikely?'

'Yup. It was all my own mistake, completely.' Scratching his head in embarrassment, Kōsei glanced at Kozeki. He had thought about his friend while they were away. He wondered how he would react if Misumi confessed her feelings to him. He might think she was interesting and give her the thumbs up, but on the other hand, he might turn her down because it was a hassle. He didn't even really know what Kozeki's type was in the first place, so it was hard for him to imagine.

'But how did you find out it wasn't an affair?' asked Kozeki.

'That's, well . . .'

Kōsei was about to say that he and Misumi had tailed his mother, but for some reason, he decided to hold his tongue. He wasn't sure why. He just didn't want to say it. So, as he explained, he left out the part about meeting Misumi.

'She brought the guy home! It turns out he's like her manga apprentice.'

It wasn't a lie. Still, he felt a little guilty about it. It was like he was hiding something, which didn't feel good. Like he owed an apology to Kozeki, who was listening intently to the story, with no way of knowing he was hiding anything.

'Interesting. So he was an instructor at a *juku*, and then became a manga artist? What kind of stuff does he do online?'

'For now, he said he's just going to upload the work he's already done. He showed me some of it, and it had a nice feel to it.'

It didn't follow any of the latest trends, and to be honest, it was a little, well, corny. But there was something pleasantly nostalgic about it that Kōsei liked. Still, the storyline was somewhat lacking, and he had the feeling that one of the episodes had been lifted from something he had seen somewhere before. His mother might have felt the same, because she had advised the guy to focus on the artwork and get someone else to write the story.

'He stayed here for around three days. I wasn't busy because school was out, so I hung out with him a lot, and he's the perfect teacher. When he explains things, he's super easy to understand. I want to try to meet with him before our final exams.'

Apparently, Kiriyama was a Japanese language instructor. He taught middle-school students, so he had a tremendous store of knowledge, as one might expect, and was clever at explaining things. When Kōsei had asked for help with an essay he had neglected, about the story 'Maihime' from his assigned reading, Kiriyama had been so dramatic and clear in his explanation of the main points of the story that Kōsei was actually moved and had no trouble writing the essay.

'I couldn't help saying it would be a real waste for him to give up teaching. Hey, Kozeki. You okay?'

Kozeki had suddenly fallen silent. Kōsei looked at him.

'That might work, don't you think?' his friend murmured pensively. 'Say he went through all the literary classics, first to last, and turned them into manga. And told you, just remember this or that part, like he's preparing you for college entrance exams? That sort of thing.'

'Oh!' Kōsei remembered a picture book from their elementary-school library, full of biographies of important historical figures. Back then he would read it to pass the time when it was raining too hard for them to play outdoors. It was pretty interesting – he had learned about Thomas Edison and Oda Nobunaga from that book. Maybe it could be something like that, but with Kiriyama's art, in his own teaching style.

'It could be good.'

And then, if you could read it easily on a smartphone, that would be even better. It made perfect sense, Kōsei thought, impressed. 'That'd be awesome,' he said to Kozeki. He was always coming up with things like that.

'Well, that kind of thing has been around forever. There are so many different works of that type available now, I just thought he'd at least want to start by focusing on his strengths.'

'I think that's really good advice. Hey, is it okay if I tell Kiriyama?'

'Sure, if you want. But even if he does them, there's no guarantee they'll be popular. It will depend on his adaptations.'

I'll contact Kiriyama later, Kōsei thought. 'Princess Yonaga and Mimio' would probably work really well in that format. He was grinning when he felt a pat on the back. He turned. Misumi was standing there.

'Morning, Nakao! Good morning, Kozeki!'

'G-good morning,' Kōsei stuttered, flustered.

Misumi overtook the two boys and just as quickly left them behind. Perhaps rushing to meet a friend, she waved and dashed into the station building.

'Misumi hardly ever says hello or anything like that,' Kozeki said with surprise. 'True,' Kōsei acknowledged. He thought she might have called out because of what had happened the other day, but in the back of his mind there was a voice telling him that she just wanted to speak with Kozeki.

'Kozeki, what do you think of Misumi?'

The question slipped out before he could think, and he instantly regretted it. He hadn't planned to ask, but now that he had, he needed to hear the answer. He looked at Kozeki, trying hard to hide his agitation, and the latter simply yawned, as if he hadn't a care in the world.

'Not interested.'

Although Kōsei had been seized by a great anxiety, he took pains to respond in a dull voice, as if he were stuck in class during a boring lesson, 'Oh. Yeah.'

A car passed by Kōsei, too close for comfort. 'Look out!' Kozeki exclaimed, yanking him by the arm. And then, after a moment, he said, 'To be honest, I don't like that type.'

'Oh? Um, Misumi, you mean?'

'Yeah. I hate when people force their feelings on someone that way.'

Kozeki said it so definitively that a small ache started somewhere in Kōsei's heart.

'Oh, that's . . . I might, um, like her . . . maybe, that is, I mean . . . Misumi.'

The words trickled out, drop by drop. Kozeki's eyes widened, but then he simply said, 'I see.'

Why? Why did I say that? Kōsei spent the rest of the day in agony. He shouldn't have said anything. Why had he opened his big mouth? To head off Kozeki? No, impossible – his friend had already said that he wasn't interested in her. Then why?

Sixth period would be over any minute now. Kōsei watched Misumi's back, diagonally in front of him. She'd probably be sad if she knew that Kozeki had said that she wasn't his type. Because even if she told him how she felt, she'd be rejected in the end. So, wait – maybe he was just trying to console her in his imagination? *I like you, even if he doesn't?* But what kind of consolation was that?

Kōsei was surprised to discover that his heartache hadn't subsided. The previous version of himself – the one who just a few days ago was snorting in derision at love and longing – had vanished from view, nowhere to be found.

Then, a few days later and surprisingly quickly, everything came to a head. Misumi confessed her feelings to Kozeki and was flatly rejected. Tabuchi told Kōsei about it. 'Misumi was crying like crazy in front of Mojikō Station, and everyone was saying that he must have been really harsh to make her cry like that.' Tabuchi seemed a little incensed. Tabuchi was invariably sweet to all the girls, and whether he broke up with them or vice versa, none of them ever had a bad word to say about him. This must have been hard for him to swallow.

'What?' Kōsei exclaimed. 'When was that?'

'Yesterday evening,' Tabuchi said. Yesterday, Kozeki had said that he was going to see his dentist in Kokura, so they had gone home separately. And today, Misumi hadn't come to school.

'You're friends with that guy, aren't you, Kōsei? Why don't you tell him he was out of line?'

It seemed that was all Tabuchi had to say, and after he finished, he returned to his own classroom. Kōsei started to stand up, then sat back down again. Kozeki had seemed his normal self this morning, and he hadn't mentioned anything about it. Why hadn't he told him?

Was it because I said I liked Misumi? Maybe he was just trying to be tactful. Although it would have been nice if he had said something. Because I knew about Misumi's feelings.

Kōsei turned to the girl sitting next to him and said, 'Sorry, I'm not feeling well. I'd better go home.' He started to pack up his things.

'Are you okay?' she asked, and he gave a perfunctory nod before leaving the classroom. To get to the cubbies where students kept their outdoor shoes, he had to pass by the neighbouring classroom. He tried to slip by quickly but Kozeki was in the hallway.

'You going home? Are you okay?'

'Oh, uh . . . yeah. I'm not feeling well. Sorry.'

He wanted to talk to Kozeki, or no, maybe he didn't. In the grip of emotions that he didn't fully understand, Kōsei ducked round his friend and left.

He went straight to the Golden Villa building. He had made it all the way to the lift before he realised he didn't know Misumi's room. He didn't even know what he'd say when he saw her. He was staring blankly into space when he heard a voice. 'Nakao?' He roused himself with a start. It was Misumi, a Tenderness shopping bag dangling from one hand. She was wearing black-rimmed glasses. So her eyes *were* actually bad, Kōsei thought to himself.

'What are you doing here?'

'Hey, um, I heard about yesterday, so . . .' he mumbled, and Misumi nodded as if she understood.

'You ditched school, didn't you?' she said. 'Mitsuri's shift is starting now, so let's take off.' She pointed outside.

The two of them started to walk and somehow found themselves headed towards the waterfront. Misumi broke the pork bun that she had bought into two pieces and gave half to Kōsei. They bit into the steaming hot buns. 'It seems that I liked him quite a bit,' Misumi said brightly, 'but the Kozeki that I liked was my own invention.'

'What do you mean?'

Misumi stuffed the remainder of the steamed bun into her mouth, swallowed, and then slowly began to speak.

'There was an ideal Kozeki, but he was just inside of me. I thought he looked at the world with a detached gaze and had the composure not to be manipulated by his own emotions. I thought he was strong. That he had a fearless, resolute spirit.'

'Why did you think that?'

'Have you seen Kozeki's photo? The one that won the award? It was titled *Fear*.'

Kōsei nodded. The other day he had dug up a copy of the newspaper with the photo, which their middle school had proudly distributed to all the students back then. He'd wanted to take a closer look at the photo that Misumi had described so passionately.

It was simple, in a manner of speaking. An old dog on its side lifted its head, gazing at the person on the far side of the lens.

'That was a photo of Kozeki's dog, just before it died. I could see it so clearly in its eyes – despair, and the fear of death. When I first saw it, I thought, *oh, even dogs are afraid of death*. Then later, I noticed how Kozeki had captured his own dog's fear so calmly. It gave me chills. *This person can see the world free of love and emotion*, I thought. That made a huge impact on me. Thanks to that photo, I was able to see my parents the way I needed to – detached from my own feelings.'

Misumi said it was hard for her to express how much that photo had meant to her. When she pressed the shutter button to capture her mother entering the love hotel with the other man, she was able to free herself from her emotions. She thought *oh, this is what they call 'perspective'* and she imagined that what Kozeki saw must be a more noble version of the same thing. It was only because she had Kozeki's photograph that she was able to achieve that kind of perspective.

Misumi and Kōsei made their way towards the Mojikō Retro Observatory. There, the top floor of a high-rise apartment building designed by a famous architect had been opened to the public as an observation platform. It overlooked all of the Mojikō Retro area, with the Kanmon Bridge spanning the straits off in the distance. Perhaps because it was a weekday, the place was nearly empty, so the two of them took the bench with the best view. Kōsei handed Misumi a can of hot milk tea that he had purchased en route and opened one of his own. The sweet steam tickled his nose.

'Yesterday evening I happened to see Kozeki alone,' Misumi said, 'so I just decided to talk to him. I wanted to ask him why he got so mad the other day, and then I also wanted him to know how I felt. But when I told him about it, the same way I told you just now, he got really angry.'

Misumi smiled sadly as she opened the tab on her can of tea with a little *pop*.

'He said, "I didn't take the picture like that!" I think he also said "Life and love are not that easy!" Or something like that.'

He had looked at her with contempt and spat out, 'You're the worst.'

'That really shocked me, and I'm afraid I ended up making a terrible scene. I was crying so much. I didn't understand why he had to say a thing like that, and more than anything,

I guess I just thought he'd understand how I felt. But those were just my own selfish ideas, weren't they?'

Misumi took a sip of tea and added, 'It was dumb of me. Although I shouldn't have got my hopes up.'

'Chiko was the dog they got as a companion for Kozeki when he was born,' Kōsei said in a subdued voice. 'She was like a little sister to him. He doted on her. The reason he first took up the camera was to take photos of her.'

From elementary school on, watching Kozeki take Chiko for her walk was an everyday occurrence. On rainy days, and snowy days as well, there was Kozeki, walking happily along with Chiko, stopping to take photos of the dog, the camera dangling from a strap around his neck.

Kozeki wasn't the one to send that photo to the newspaper, either. His mother thought it was so good that she submitted the photo on her own. When notice of the award came to the school and he learned what his mother had done, he was furious. He refused to accept the award, and nothing his teacher or the school principal could say would persuade him to change his mind.

'At the time I didn't know that Chiko had died,' Kōsei continued. 'So I thought it was strange he wouldn't accept the award. I told Kozeki I thought it was a good photo. But when I did, he yelled at me: "What the hell is good about it!"'

Looking at the copy of the photo, Kōsei thought back to his second year of middle school. He had just thought it was a 'good' photo. A normal, everyday photo. So he had told Kozeki so.

'I thought Chiko was just looking at Kozeki the way she always did. I told Kozeki: "I don't see anything in her eyes except your reflection."'

Then suddenly Kozeki's shoulders relaxed. After that, he agreed to accept the award. And he titled the photo *Fear*.

'Later I learned the photo was taken when Chiko was dying. I think the title was describing Kozeki's own feelings. I think he was afraid because this being who had been with him since he was born, who relied upon him and gazed at him always with trust in her eyes, was leaving the world. I'm sure Kozeki pressed the shutter because he didn't want to lose that, and was trying to hold on to it somehow.'

Kōsei sipped his tea and continued. 'I think that's why Kozeki got so mad when people called him cool-headed and things like that.'

Misumi toyed with her can of tea, then abruptly looked out through the window, off into the distance. 'He's definitely different from what I imagined. I had expected him to be less sentimental.'

'. . . I understand your feelings about Kozeki. I also understand what a big deal it is to have someone cool-headed with you in a hard situation. When you came along with me the other day it was a huge help. I'm glad you were there.'

Misumi returned her gaze to Kōsei, who continued.

'But, wouldn't it be different if I told you, "I think you're cool because you're strong and unsentimental"? If I said that's why I like you, wouldn't it bother you? I think that's why Kozeki got mad.'

Misumi looked at Kōsei for a while, then suddenly stood up, and quietly said, 'Nakao, you really like to talk about yourself, don't you?' She placed her half-empty can on her seat. 'Or are you just bragging about how much better you know Kozeki than I do? Well, you don't have to be such a jerk about it. Actually, it's really irritating.'

'Huh? Oh.'

'I'm leaving.' Misumi said. Before he could stop her, she had stepped into the lift and disappeared.

'What . . . why . . .?'

He didn't understand why Misumi was so mad. He stood up several times, only to sit down again immediately, uncertain if he should chase after her. Then he heard a low chuckle.

'Huh? Kozeki?' *What was going on?* Suddenly, Kozeki was standing there.

'You left school with such a grim look on your face, I was worried.' With an amused smile, Kozeki picked up the can that Misumi had left there. 'That's no good, leaving that there. I'll toss it later.'

Still holding the can, Kozeki sat down next to Kōsei. Then he said, 'Thank you.'

'W-what for?'

'I heard what you said to Misumi. And I realised that I never said thank you back then in eighth grade. Thank you for understanding that photograph.'

Kōsei had been half out of his seat, but hearing the serious tone of voice, he sat down once again. 'What?' He drank some more of his tea. 'It's not something to thank me for. Chiko's photo just looked that way, that's all.'

'That's all, you say. But you're the only one who understood,' Kozeki said earnestly. 'You're the only one who understands, so you're the only one who doesn't ask me about it. That's a great gift.'

Now it was Kozeki's turn to look out through the window. A gap that wasn't there before opened in the heavy winter clouds, and a small patch of blue sky became visible.

'When Chiko was dying, I was really scared. So scared I didn't know what to do. I wondered what would happen if this clear-eyed creature disappeared from the world, and then I pressed the button. As you said, I just wanted to hold on to her. All I could think about was how to keep her with me.'

Kozeki's hand was clenched around the can of tea, his fingertips white.

'When Chiko's photo came out in public, lots of people said I was cold. I couldn't understand it. I started to wonder if I was a terrible person, peering through my camera when this life that was so important to me was vanishing. Also, I wondered if it made Chiko sad that I was taking this photo for myself. After that, I couldn't carry the camera around any longer.'

It was the first time he had heard this confession from Kozeki. But strangely it didn't feel new at all. It felt like something that he had always seen, if only vaguely, veiled in mist, which had now emerged clearly, revealing its true form at last.

And then he felt a twinge of remorse. He had thought Kozeki was so grown-up, but the two of them had worried and suffered in similar ways. He believed he understood, so he never talked to him about it, but that only meant those cares were piling up inside his friend somewhere. He should have helped let them out somehow. *I was asking for Kozeki's advice on every little thing,* he thought, *so if I had thought about it just a little I would have understood.*

'I'm not really the only one who understands you. Besides, it's not like I was keeping my mouth shut on purpose, I just didn't know how to ask. That's not such a brilliant reason.'

Kozeki chuckled. 'It's good enough,' he said. 'That's why I feel comfortable around you.' The gentle tone in his voice made Kōsei happy. *I guess I must have been of some help to him, somehow.*

'I suppose that's why I respond so angrily when someone tries to push their own impressions on me that way. Like Misumi. I'm sorry about that, by the way – you really liked her, didn't you?'

He had almost forgotten – Misumi had called him irritating. It was too late to do anything about it now, but it made Kōsei a little sad. Still, it was clear Misumi liked Kozeki anyway, so there was nothing he could do about it.

'I'm okay,' he said. 'It's no big deal. Maybe there's still a chance for us to become closer someday. Besides, for now . . . it's okay. It would be nice to find someone who likes the same photos as me, and for the same reasons.'

Kōsei thought of the photo albums in his living room, and his parents, looking at them with a shared smile on their faces. *I want someone who can do that with me, for a long, long time.*

'Right. Me too, I think.' Kozeki suddenly grinned. Then he stood up, and said 'Why don't we get some ramen? My treat.'

'Seriously? Why?'

'It doesn't matter. If it's a problem, you can pay for yourself.'

'Hey, wait! I accept. I'm hungry. Please!'

Kōsei stood up in a hurry, and Kozeki laughed out loud. 'I like you, that's for sure.'

The advent cookies for '24' were in the shape of pink hearts.

'What are you staring at?'

Kōsei was looking at the cookie he had been handed when an arm reached out from behind the checkout counter and snatched it away. When it was returned to him, it had been broken ruthlessly in half.

'That's mean! Why do you keep doing that?' He put the cookie in his pocket. These cookie attacks were getting on his nerves, but when he said so to Misumi, who was behind the checkout counter, she averted her gaze coldly.

'I suppose I'm annoyed for some reason. Why are you two here?'

It was Christmas Eve. Kōsei had come to Tenderness to do some shopping with Kozeki, and Misumi was there, working. It was a little awkward meeting her at the register. Winter break had started that day, and the two boys were going to celebrate by playing video games all night. A big role-playing game had been released three days earlier, and they were hoping to clear all the levels in record time, but somehow he got the feeling that Misumi didn't want to hear about all that.

Misumi, who was wearing a Santa hat, scowled the whole time they were there and seemed to be in a bad mood.

'Did I do something wrong?'

'Oh, be quiet,' she growled, 'you're getting on my nerves.' Kōsei felt a slight pain in his chest. He didn't feel he had done anything to deserve this.

'Kōsei, if you've paid, let's go!'

Kozeki didn't so much as glance at Misumi and that only seemed to make her angrier. She glared at him, but Kozeki didn't seem to notice.

'Now, now! Is this a fight?'

The voice belonged to Tsugi. When Misumi realised who it was, a broad smile spread across her face.

'Welcome Mr Tsugi! It's Christmas Eve – shouldn't you be spending it with your girlfriend?'

'Ain't got nobody.' Tsugi shrugged his shoulders casually, and Misumi's face lit up.

'That can't be true! But if you really don't, I nominate myself.'

'No thanks. I'm not into younger women.'

What? Kōsei thought in surprise. *Is she after him now?* Tsugi turned to him. 'Kōsei, you're flying solo, too, aren't you?' Kōsei gestured towards Kozeki, and Tsugi laughed. He slung his arm over the boy's shoulder. 'In that case, let's get something to eat!'

'Are you free? Then you two should join me. I'll call Mitsuri.'

'Really? Are you kidding?'

It was Kōsei's first time hanging out with Tsugi, so he was excited. He was really curious to know what kind of person he was. He glanced at Kozeki, who nodded silently. 'Yes, please. We'd love to go,' he said, but feeling a little funny. He stole a glance at Misumi, who was glaring at him as if she could shoot poison darts from her eyes.

'Nakao, you really make me mad.'

A poison dart sank deep into his chest. But still, he was happy to be hanging out with Tsugi.

'See you, Misumi. Merry Christmas!' Kōsei smiled at Misumi, but she stuck out her tongue at him with some intensity.

'Right. Let's go!' They followed Tsugi out of the store. Something cold brushed Kōsei's cheek, and he looked up. Snowflakes were drifting down on them.

'Wow. A white Christmas!'

'And I'm hanging out with high-school boys. Not very sexy, is it?' Tsugi let loose with a hearty laugh. 'I guess you got dumped. Well, there are plenty of fish in the sea.'

'Uh huh. You got me. You must have been in love a few times, too, haven't you, Tsugi?'

Kōsei was still looking up at the night sky as he asked, but there was no reply. Tsugi's laughter had ceased. Kōsei looked over at him curiously and Tsugi, too, was gazing upwards into the night. His eyes were gentle and sad in a way that Kōsei had never seen before.

'Not me. Not anymore.'

Tsugi's sigh left a long, white trail that melted into the night sky. Kōsei wondered what could have happened to him. He wanted to ask, but couldn't. He returned his gaze to the heavens, and said nothing.

Until recently, I thought that love and longing didn't exist. But love existed long before I was born, and longing was there in me, too. It was there in Misumi, and love and longing were definitely there in Tsugi. The world is overflowing with it. And maybe one day, I'll know love. I'll pine for love, and lose it, I'll laugh and cry over it, and maybe like my parents did, I'll find a way to keep it. Even if that's still far off in my future.

'Tsugi, love is pretty awesome, isn't it?'

Tsugi laughed heartily. 'If you say so, high-school boy. Ask Santa, and maybe he'll bring you some!'

The wind blew, and Kōsei shivered. Involuntarily, he put his hand in his pocket and touched his heart.

Chapter Six

A Christmas Caprice

It was 8:45 a.m. Mitsuri Nakao's shift started at 9, and when she opened the door to the staff room, the scent of roses was so strong she almost choked.

'A richness of roses!' she blurted out, and looked around. Two huge bouquets had been left there, so big they barely fitted on the table. The roses in both were a deep crimson colour, but the petals of one were streaked with figures of gold. Thinking they were artificial, Mitsuri took a closer look, but they were actual roses, with letters impressed in gold leaf on the petals:

Mon Chéri

There were easily thirty roses in the bouquet, and on the petals of each, the same thing was written, in tiny, delicate letters. *Love is a heavy burden*, thought Mitsuri, and let out a sharp laugh.

'Those look really expensive, don't they? I'm sure it's something about love, but what does it mean?'

'It's French. Apparently it means *my darling*,' said Muraoka, a college student who worked part-time at the store. He had arrived earlier, and spoke without looking up from his phone, but he must have noticed the gold lettering as well.

He lifted his head for a moment and scanned the room, then grimaced. 'I mean, he's really popular, isn't he? You-know-who.'

Muraoka had started at Tenderness almost a year ago, but he wasn't a big fan of Shiba. It's not that he disliked him, he said, but when they got too close to each other, his nose would itch and he'd be unable to stop sneezing. He never made a big deal about it, just said it was probably his allergies, but Shiba always seemed a little lonely around him, being treated like pollen.

'I still don't understand what's so great about the store manager,' he said earnestly, 'but sometimes I get the feeling I'm in the minority.' Mitsuri, too, took a quick look around. The staff room, which was not particularly large, was piled high with gifts of all sorts. Large stuffed animals, gift bags from well-known stores, boxes tied round with brightly coloured ribbons. They were all for Shiba, the store manager, courtesy of his legion of fans, who weren't about to miss the opportunity to shower him with love during the holiday season.

'I mean, wasn't he working his shift until nine p.m. last night? Why didn't he take some of this stuff home with him?'

At Muraoka's words, the smile disappeared from Mitsuri's face. 'He took yesterday's lot home already . . .!'

Yesterday was Christmas Eve, and Mitsuri had been on duty from morning to sundown, but even now, thinking about it gave her heartburn. The store was jam-packed with Christmas sale items, and then on top of that, gifts addressed to Shiba kept arriving one after another, in quick succession. A crowd of people had queued up in front of the register where Shiba was stationed, so that the whole situation began to resemble a celebrity autograph session at a convention.

'I'm very happy that we can all be together on Christmas Eve,' Shiba said with a calm smile, and the store erupted in joyful shrieks. One by one, the customers stepped forward to present their gifts, fidgeting while the store manager would frown as if troubled and say something like, 'Of course, your patronage at the store makes me happy enough.' Mitsuri, who was busy scanning barcodes for rice bowls and energy drinks, could hardly keep track of where she was or what she was doing. Who in their right mind would expect to hear someone shouting 'Time at the front is limited to two minutes per person!' in a place like this? And their celebrity icon, well, it was just a convenience store, and he was just its manager.

The queue on Shiba's side of the counter went on forever, so he couldn't step away from the register, even for a minute. Shiba's fans purchased products in large quantities, probably because it meant they got to be close to him for a few seconds longer, so restocking the shelves – which were emptying at an abnormally fast pace – was added to the workload of the staff. Hirose, another part-timer who had come in yesterday, had said, with bloodshot eyes, 'This is just too much! Let's set up a tent for the manager in the car park and they can do what they want with him.' But even while Mitsuri was doing her best to restrain Hirose from making good on his suggestion, the shelves continued to empty.

Mitsuri shuddered involuntarily as she flashed back to yesterday's disastrous spectacle, then said to Muraoka, 'All I know is that the manager's already made two trips home to clear out the gifts. So all these must have arrived after he went off duty.'

'What? Are you kidding me? Well, his place must be a real sight to see by now, don't you think?'

Muraoka grimaced again, and Mitsuri nodded in response. There were surely enough gifts up there for him to open a small shop of his own.

'The manager ought to take on a new line of work. If he really applied himself he could transform Mojikō's economy. We could be bigger than Hakata!'

Muraoka picked up a small package that was near at hand as he spoke, while Mitsuri laughed at his words.

'I know how you feel,' she said, 'but you know, even if he has the ability, he doesn't have the desire.'

Mitsuri had felt much the same as Muraoka at first, but as she spent more time with Shiba and got to know him better, her thinking changed. She came to understand that Shiba loved the convenience store with all his heart. He observed all of his customers carefully and had a thorough knowledge of the regulars. Even in the midst of yesterday's insanity with the gifts, he'd addressed each and every person in the queue by name.

Shiba did his job with more care and precision than any of the area managers, or even the supervisors from head office. It was said that the number of customers had grown explosively since Shiba became manager, and now the Golden Villa branch boasted the top sales ranking for all of Fukuoka prefecture. He was in the store so often that customers speculated that he lived there, and his enthusiasm for sales events and other store activities was unparalleled.

It got to the point where it seemed as though Shiba was even devoting his personal time to the store, but he always seemed to be enjoying himself. 'I like to spend time in the shop,' he'd say. He took great pleasure in seeing all the joys and sorrows of his customers' lives, he said, and his happiest moment ever was surely the day he learned that two regular customers were to be wed. Apparently, the couple had met in the dine-in space, and one thing led to another. When the two of them had come to Shiba to let him know their plans, his cheeks had turned bright red and he said, 'Thank you!' almost as if they had confessed their love for him instead of for each other. 'It's an honour to be a part of such joy in someone's life. And I couldn't be more delighted that it happened at this store. I wish you every happiness!'

Shiba saw the two of them off, beaming from ear to ear, and Mitsuri could see that although the man might seem outwardly suspect, he had a true love for the convenience store, and that made her happy. No matter what anyone around him might say, the man had found his life's work.

'The manager is off duty today, right? It's Christmas, so he's got to be seeing his special someone,' Muraoka said, setting the box down next to the roses while Mitsuri pulled her uniform jacket out of the locker.

'I wonder if such a person exists,' Mitsuri said. She tilted her head. 'I've been working here for quite a few years now, and I haven't heard anything like that. Although I see him together with people in suspicious circumstances all the time.'

Over the years, Mitsuri had encountered Shiba out one-on-one with all sorts of people in various places around town. No matter the companion, the air was always thick with significance. Each time, Mitsuri would be certain she'd finally caught him at the crucial moment, but then when he'd see her, he wouldn't seem flustered at all – he'd just flash an innocent smile and say, 'Nice to see you! Keep up the good work.' He never showed the slightest sign of nerves or a guilty conscience, so Mitsuri would feel as if she were the one with the overactive imagination, and could never bring herself to ask about the relationship between him and whomever. She always swore she'd ask the next time, but she'd never caught him with the same person twice.

'Are they all one-night stands?'

'No, I couldn't say that. I really don't know.'

Shiba was single, after all, and had the right to love anyone he pleased. In fact, Mitsuri hoped he did. It just meant more material for her.

'But I don't think he has a special someone. If he did, we'd have heard about it by now from the Golden Villa Ladies' Association.'

Shiba's fan club, which managed the dine-in space, was a group of lively and battle-tested older women. Shōhei had told her that there were 'unofficial' members of the club in addition to the building residents and that their network extended throughout Mojikō. Even if she took his story with a grain of salt, she couldn't overlook the possibility that Shiba's actual favourite was among these.

'Normal people might have fan clubs in manga, but it's not something you see particularly often in real life. Also,

I don't know much about his private life outside the store, so I'm curious, you know.'

'Oh? Muraoka, are you falling under the manager's spell?'

'I'm just interested in the ecology of rare species,' Muraoka said nonchalantly. 'How about you?' Mitsuri laughed. How could she not be? Although they had been working together all these years, Shiba was still an enigma wrapped in a riddle to her, and she couldn't see where it all started or ended.

'I've made it my life's work to know everything about the manager. But if I had the chance to learn everything about him all at once, that might be boring.'

The Phero-Manager's Indecent Diary that Mitsuri had started drawing, modelled after Shiba, was still receiving a lot of attention online. She had also started writing a spin-off called *The Rough and Ready Life of Big Brother Furball*, which was already becoming surprisingly popular. The possibility flitted through her mind that she was making the Shiba brothers her life's work, rather than just the manager.

'Right. It's time for us to get out there.'

She gave herself a last quick once-over in the mirror, and then, with Muraoka in tow, she left the staff room and entered the store. Instantly, Takagi, who was working the checkout counter, came running over, begging for help.

'Mitsuri! It's an emergency!'

Takagi was a 'freeter' – one of the growing number of young freelancers in Japan who had opted out of the career-track lifestyle. He was a gentle soul with a laid-back attitude, and because he had worn a pink aloha shirt to his interview, his colleagues called him 'Ukulele'. He sounded agitated, which was rare for him.

'Are you okay?' asked Mitsuri. 'What happened?'

'Someone's here asking for the manager, but . . .'

'That happens a lot. Did you say he's taking the day off?'

'See, that's the thing . . .'

Ukulele's cheeks turned pink. It was the first time Mitsuri had seen him act bashful this way, and she had no idea why. She gave him a curious look, and said 'What is it?'

'Um . . . well, actually, it's a really beautiful girl.'

Muraoka, who was standing right behind Mitsuri, said, 'Coming from Ukulele, that's a new one.'

Mitsuri sighed quietly. At this point she had seen people of all shapes and sizes come to the store with Shiba as their exclusive object, including drop-dead gorgeous women and matinee-idol men. It seemed the troublemaker this time was a woman.

'And? You told her the manager was away, didn't you?'

'I . . . I told her. She said she'd wait until he came back, over there.' Ukulele pointed to the dine-in space.

Normally he'd just get the name of the girl and contact the manager for further instructions. Did he like her that much? Mitsuri said, 'Ukulele, why don't you and Muraoka cover the registers for now, and I'll go check on her.' Leaving the two young men, she headed to the dine-in space.

The room was quiet. Typically, there would be a handful of customers, and Shōhei as well would usually be present, but right now there was just the one girl, sitting by herself in a seat at the very end of the counter. She was facing away, so Mitsuri couldn't get a look at the girl's face, but her lovely straight black hair caught Mitsuri's eye.

'Ah, excuse me? I gather you're waiting for the manager.' Mitsuri addressed her, and the girl slowly turned. When Mitsuri saw her face, she took a small involuntary breath.

Wow. The girl was gorgeous.

She was like a fine-featured, life-size porcelain doll. Large eyes framed by lush eyelashes above a delicate, slightly upturned nose. Skin as pale as Snow White, with peach-coloured cheeks and cherry-red lips. Mitsuri thought she seemed about the same age as her son Kōsei, who was in high school.

Her bright white fluffy coat and tailored tweed dress heightened the porcelain doll effect. Her legs, too, were slender and white below the hem of her dress.

No wonder Ukulele had been so flustered.

'Could you call Mitsuhiko Shiba for me? As soon as possible, please.'

The girl's voice was sweet, too – as clear as a bell, although her eyebrows were knitted in what seemed to be an ill-humoured frown. Her every word and gesture were captivating. *She can't possibly be a living creature of the same sex as me*, thought Mitsuri. While Mitsuri looked at her in fascination, the girl repeated, with some irritation, 'Mitsuhiko Shiba?' Slightly taken aback, Mitsuri hastily said, 'The manager is taking the day off today.'

'I heard that. But I don't have a mobile phone, and there don't seem to be any payphones in the area, so please could you contact him for me? I tried asking the person earlier but he didn't seem to be listening.'

'Ah, that's what happened,' said Mitsuri. 'I'm very sorry. Well, I'll try to reach him, so would you mind waiting just a little while longer?'

The girl nodded, and Mitsuri returned to the shop in a hurry. She turned to Ukulele, who was standing behind the register, still looking nervous, and said, 'Sorry – the girl is an honest-to-god beauty.'

'Are you serious?' Muraoka piped up giddily. Mitsuri grabbed the handset for the store phone and crouched down behind the counter. She hastily dialled Shiba, but she couldn't connect. She tried several times more, but each time she heard the same automated message: 'The client you are trying to reach may be out of the signal area . . .'

'Now? At a time like this!'

No matter how many times she tried, she couldn't get through. She also tried the landline at Shiba's apartment, but there was no answer there either, so he had to be out somewhere.

Mitsuri returned to the dine-in space wondering what to do, but when she got there, she found the girl slumped over the countertop.

'I'm sorry for keeping you . . . hello?'

Perhaps the girl was annoyed because it had taken so long? Mitsuri approached her, but something seemed off. Curious, she reached over and touched the back of the girl's outstretched hand. It was as cold as ice. She put her hand to the back of the girl's neck, and it was the opposite. She was burning up.

'Are you sick?'

It was just like when her son Kōsei had a fever. Mitsuri lifted her head to look at her face, and the girl's breath was ragged. There was no mistaking it – the red in her cheeks signalled a fever.

'Come with me.'

Mitsuri took the unsteady girl by the hand and led her to the staff room. She was shivering slightly – maybe she had a chill? – so Mitsuri raised the temperature in the room. She draped her own coat over the girl's shoulders, and sat her in a chair. The dazed girl looked up at Mitsuri, her eyes cloudy with fever, and said, 'Mitsuhiko Shiba . . .'

'I'm so sorry. For some reason I can't reach him. But the more important question is do you live near here? We should have someone from your family come get you.'

Her self-assurance evaporated, the girl sagged against the table. Without rising, she shook her head slightly.

'My home . . . it's in Miyazaki.'

'What? You came all the way from there!?' Miyazaki was nearly on the opposite side of the island of Kyūshū. 'What can we do? Listen, you need to tell me what you want with the manager.'

'To see him, that's all,' she said, in a thoroughly forlorn voice. Perhaps she had come all this way holding back her illness? Or had the journey somehow pushed her beyond the limits of what she could endure?

'Excuse me, Mitsuri? What's going on?'

Ukulele stuck his head nervously in the door, and when he saw the girl looking so sickly he let out a pitiful moan. 'Oh no . . .! W-what happened to her?'

'She didn't seem well, as you can see, so I brought her in here for now. Forgive me, but would you mind taking my shift for the moment?'

'N-no, of course not.' Ukulele returned to the shop as asked.

'Well, I can't let you spend the night here, you know.'

'The Whatever Guy. Call him, please.' A faint voice. The girl had lifted her head slightly from the table. 'Maybe Tsugi will be home . . .'

'Tsugi? You know Tsugi? How . . .?'

'I'm . . . their sister.'

Their sister. The words bounced around in Mitsuri's head, taking a while to settle. Their sister. Their sister? Their *sister!*

I deserve an award for not screaming out loud right now, Mitsuri thought. Impossible! This doll of a girl, the little sister of those two?

'Oh! Okay, well, so you . . . you're Jewel?'

When she said the name she had been told earlier, the girl – Jewel – laughed a little.

'I guess my brothers mentioned me?'

She giggled sheepishly. Her face didn't resemble either of her brothers, but she was so beautiful that Mitsuri felt it had to be her. Any sister to those two had to be – well, something like this.

Damn! Mitsuri couldn't help but wonder at what sort of creatures the remaining two brothers must be. Her curiosity was mounting, but she restrained herself.

'I understand. I'll contact him immediately.'

She was still holding the store phone, so she dialled Tsugi's mobile number. But she couldn't connect to his phone, either. She just kept getting the same robotic 'out of range' message that she had heard when she tried Shiba.

'What? I don't get it. What could have happened to him?'

And it was an actual emergency! Resisting the urge to slam the phone down, Mitsuri shifted her attention to Jewel. A strand of hair cascaded down the girl's fever-flushed cheeks, and it seemed that at any moment she might fade away like a dream.

'First things first. I have to do something for this child.'

Mitsuri set the phone on the table and thought for a moment. She certainly couldn't leave the girl here in this state. Maybe it would be best for her to duck out of work now and take the girl home with her? No, when she had left the house earlier today, Kōsei was hanging around with several of his friends. It wouldn't be right to bring a sick girl home in the midst of all those hormonal teens – let alone such a pretty one. Hmm . . . was her only option to text Kōsei and ask him to leave the house? While Mitsuri was considering this, the doorbell for the staff room sounded. She opened the door. Several members of the Golden Villa Ladies' Association were standing there.

'We came because our Mitsuhiko asked us to collect the rest of his holiday gifts. He said that they were piling up here and becoming a nuisance to the staff, so he wants us to put them in the Ladies' Association meeting room for now.'

There was a common room on the third floor of the Golden Villa building, and it seemed that the ladies of the building were using it as a meeting room. Mitsuri had never set foot in the space, but the Ladies' Association clearly considered it their headquarters.

Mitsuri quickly scanned the group. Among them, she noticed the face of Mrs Sakuma, a retired nurse. She bowed to her and said, 'I have a small favour to ask. The manager's sister has come to visit him, but I can't seem to reach him. What's more, she seems to be unwell . . .'

Their faces transformed instantly. 'May I step inside for a moment?' Mrs Sakuma asked and then entered, the rest of the group filing in behind her.

'Well, well, well,' the woman clucked, 'What a darling dear you are! Of course our Mitsuhiko would have such an adorable little sister. So then, are you not feeling well? Let me take a good look at you. How long have you been feeling this way?'

After giving Jewel a quick examination, Mrs Sakuma turned to Mrs Kanagawa, another association member. 'Can you get your car? Let's take her to Dr Sakaida.

'I think it's probably just a cold, but since it's flu season, let's be on the safe side. Mrs Ōtsuka, will you go up to the meeting room and arrange the sofa, so the girl can sleep when she returns? I think a girl her size will be comfortable there. Mrs Misumi, I think the two of us should be able to get her as far as the car. Let's get to it!'

'Forgive the imposition, Mrs Sakuma. This is a tremendous help.' Mitsuri bowed her head in thanks, and Mrs Sakuma smiled. 'She's the sister of our dear Mitsuhiko, isn't she?' she replied. 'You know how grateful we all are to him. There's no way to repay his kindness, but we'd do anything for him.'

Mrs Misumi, standing on the other side of Mrs Sakuma, nodded in sincere agreement.

'When we're done at the hospital, I'll come back here to buy ice and something for her to drink. I'll let you know how she's doing at that point, so you can stay and run the store as usual, okay?'

'Yes, ma'am!'

Mitsuri went outside with Mrs Sakuma and the others, helped to put Jewel in Mrs Kanagawa's car, and returned to the store. Perhaps sensing the strange shift in the atmosphere, several customers looked worried. She returned to the checkout counter. 'I'm sorry for leaving you two alone on the job,' she said.

'Forget about that,' Ukulele said, 'but is the girl okay?' His voice was a notch higher than usual. 'Is she sick? Beautiful girls are always getting sick.'

'And while we're on the subject, what does she have to do with the store manager?' Unlike Ukulele, who was a study in sincerity, Muraoka adopted a more casual attitude. Mitsuri addressed them both. 'She's the manager's younger sister. She may have put herself through too much stress, coming to visit him when she wasn't well. Mrs Sakuma said it's probably just a cold, but her fever was awfully high, so that's a concern.'

Mitsuri let out a sigh and looked out the window towards the car park for a quiet moment, and then bedlam erupted in the store. It was almost as if an armed robbery were in progress.

'Wh-wh-what? The manager – the manager's sister? A beauty?'

'You don't say? He has family? I thought he was all alone in the world!'

'Wait, wait – I wasn't really looking when they came out! I want to see her! I want to see!'

'Excuse me! Did someone say the manager's sister is coming?'

'Mr Shiba has a beautiful, sick sister? No!!! Perish the thought!'

The occupants of the store surged in unison towards the checkout counter, surrounding Mitsuri. 'Now I've really done it,' she said ruefully, looking at the clamouring, hysterical crowd. She'd spoken carelessly.

'When I asked the manager if he had a family, he whispered, "Take some time to get to know me." Now must be the time!'

This last comment came from a friend of Muraoka, cheeks blushing red. Mitsuri didn't know how long he'd been in the store, but he'd been coming to do his shopping there nearly every day lately. Muraoka overheard and gasped in shock. 'Not you, too! What are you saying! You like the manager . . .?'

'Think before you speak!' his friend snapped. 'I'm not so crude that I'd look at him that way. He's a noble soul!'

Muraoka was speechless. A woman standing nearby blurted out, 'How can you be such a fool?'

'I knew that he had a sister! He has an older brother, too. So there are three of them.'

'That's right, you're way off base! There's also a dog that's like a member of the family. His name is Silver, and they're inseparable, I know for a fact.'

'Hey! Hey! Enough about the siblings, I know his grand-mother's name! She's called Hatsune, which means *first song*. Lovely, isn't it?'

'Her name has nothing to do with anything right now!'

This is utter chaos, Mitsuri thought. They're behaving just like my son Kōsei used to do. In elementary school, when he got really intent on a card game, he'd make the same faces. "Haha! My card beats them all!"

'Hey there, excuse me!' Takiji Ōtsuka appeared, appar-ently sent down by Mrs Ōtsuka. 'They said Shiba's sister was ill? That's rough. My wife told me to buy ice and frozen water bottles and leave them in the meeting room?'

Another woman, who had been waving around a gift card, called out, 'What? What? The manager's sister is returning?' She was holding a gift bag from a famous local confectionery, most likely another gift for Shiba. Mitsuri felt cold sweat running down her back. She had made a terrible mistake. She had completely forgotten what a high percentage of Shiba fans would be in the store today.

'Listen, Mr Ōtsuka, um, that is . . .' Mitsuri tried to send him a silent signal with her eyes to say only what was necessary. But he didn't catch on. He recoiled a little from the woman, who was now clutching his sleeve, but responded, 'Yes, that's correct.' Hearing that, the woman decided for some reason to give a triumphant fist pump. Then she thrust the bag towards Mitsuri, and said in a wheedling voice, 'Will you give this to the little sister to eat? It's a fruit tart from the manager's favourite shop. I'm certain his sister would enjoy it as well.'

'No, no, no!' another customer interjected. 'You can't give a tart to a child with a cold! That's nothing but trouble. Excuse me, but I've just purchased all these fruit jellies, why don't you give those to the girl instead. And if you don't mind, why don't I help care for her?' She raised her shopping basket, crammed with the store's entire stock of fruit jellies.

The fruit tart woman snapped at her. 'Don't be ridiculous! If the manager finds a strange woman hovering around his treasured little sister, he's just going to be offended. Isn't trying to lure him in with convenience-store jellies a little bit crude?'

'What? Mr Shiba loves Tenderness sweets, so I think he'll be delighted, not offended.'

'You think so? Or will he just marvel at what a dull, unimaginative woman you are?'

While the two were bickering, more customers were joining in with comments. 'What? The manager's sister?' 'A catastrophe!' The situation was getting out of control, and Mitsuri was starting to feel dizzy. What should she do . . .?

★

Mitsuri spent the rest of the morning trying desperately to deal with the distraught patrons – that is to say, Shiba's fans – and left it to Ukulele, who had completely missed any chance he might have had to go home, to try to contact Shiba and Tsugi.

'I felt like I might die . . .' By the time she had finally restored order, Mitsuri was more exhausted than ever. She had steeled herself for a difficult shift yesterday, on Christmas Eve, but today she had been caught completely off guard. Both Muraoka and his colleague Kido, a young woman who had the afternoon shift, had a hollow look about them.

'Even New Year's Eve won't be as bad as this . . .!' The make-up on Kido's normally perfectly styled face was smeared, and half missing in places. Muraoka nodded silently. Normally the two of them would have worked each other up into a chorus of complaints, but he no longer seemed to have the energy. One possible reason for that was the hard time his friend had given him about Shiba: 'You must be blind if you can't see how wonderful the manager is. If you're going to be a useless ass, who needs you?'

'Anyway, I hope the manager's little sister will be okay,' Kido said.

'Ah. Mrs Ōtsuka's husband dropped by a little while ago and said it was just a bad cold. They gave her fluids at the Sakaida Clinic, and now she's dozing in the Ladies' Association meeting room.'

'Oh, really? That's good.'

'Apparently the Ladies' Association members are looking after her.'

The ladies were all experts, trained over long years of caring for children and grandchildren, so Jewel had nothing to worry about.

'But where would the manager have gone?'

'You know, there have been times in the past when I couldn't reach him.'

The three of them were puzzling together over the question when Ukulele came galloping out of the staff room with the phone handset. 'I found him!'

'The manager said he was with the Whatever Guy, and now they're coming here. He said his little sister left to come here without telling their parents, and everyone was looking high and low for her. Mitsuri, he wants to talk to you.'

He handed her the phone, and Mitsuri hastened back into the staff room. 'Hello?' she said, and in a voice lacking his usual composure Shiba said, 'I'm so sorry for all the trouble! Takagi gave me the basics, but I gather it was a rough day for everyone?'

'It's all settled down now. But what in the world happened to you?'

According to Shiba, his parents had noticed Jewel's absence that morning. At around the same time, he and his brother Tsugi had left together for their home in Miyazaki, bearing Christmas presents for their sister.

'You couldn't reach us because our home is up in the mountains here in Miyazaki, so there's no cell signal. We didn't have any idea that Jewel was going to Mojikō, so we had just been searching the area here. Then my brother just blurted out, *I have a funny feeling she's in Mojikō . . .*'

'Of course. His magic sixth sense, right . . .?'

She heard a sigh from Shiba on the other end of the line. And Tsugi grumbling, 'Why'd she have to come all the way to Mojikō?

'Mitsuri, did Jewel say anything to you about it?

'No, even if she had wanted to, she wasn't in any condition to talk. My shift ends at three p.m. today, so I'll go look in on her then.' It would be wrong to make the Golden Villa Ladies' Association do all the work.

'Thank you,' Shiba said, 'that's a great help.' He thought he'd arrive in the evening and would have to rely on her until then.

Mitsuri finished her shift, and when her work was done, she went up to the meeting room. Ukulele hovered around as if he wanted to join her, but at the last minute, he just handed her an armful of bottled electrolyte and energy drinks, saying, 'Give her these. It might scare her to have a strange man around.' Mitsuri was just thinking how impressed she was by his thoughtfulness when he added, in all seriousness, 'Can you make sure she's really his sister? If she's his girlfriend, I might not be able to work anymore due to the shock.' His face was so solemn that Mitsuri just nodded silently and didn't make a single joke about the fact that he seemed to have fallen in love.

'How is Jewel doing?'

The meeting room was larger and more well-equipped than Mitsuri had imagined. There was a kitchen with a large refrigerator and an induction stove, a fancy leather reception set, and the furnishings in general were of such quality as to make the room look more like the office of the president of a small company.

The roses from that morning had been arranged in a large vase and were on display in the centre of a coffee table. Mrs Sakuma and Mrs Nosé, the association's former president, were relaxing on opposite sides of the table, having a leisurely coffee.

'Oh! she's not here?' Mitsuri asked. There was no sign of the girl.

'She's next door,' Mrs Nosé replied. It seemed that the adjoining room had been converted into a screening room, with a full-size screen and projector. Mrs Nosé explained that there was also a large sofa there, so the ladies could watch movies in comfort, and Jewel was sleeping on the sofa.

'Don't worry, there's a heater and humidifier in there, so the temperature and everything is just right for her.'

'Sorry to put you through so much trouble. Thank you for everything.' Mitsuri bowed her head in thanks, but she was still taking in the surroundings, impressed. Right next to where the two ladies were sitting, as if it were the most natural thing in the world, there were a number of life-sized panel portraits of a smiling Shiba. Were they custom-made . . .?

Mitsuri had never been a huge fan of people in real life. Her passions had always run towards the two-dimensional, and when she was young, the walls of her room were plastered with illustrated figures. Her mother would say, 'Whenever I go in your room, I always get a creepy feeling, like I'm being watched.' Mitsuri was always a little frustrated that nobody understood how cool it was.

I'm sorry, Mother, now I finally know how you felt! Mitsuri thought.

To someone who wasn't a member of the Shiba fan club, the way his eyes followed you around the room was quite unsettling. He was a good-looking man and one of her favourite subjects, but she still found it disturbing.

'You must be tired, Mitsuri. Please, have a seat.' Mrs Nosé stood up, and with easy motions, made Mitsuri a coffee. Mrs Sakuma gestured towards the sofa, and when Mitsuri sat, offered her an assortment of cookies and chocolates.

'Oh, Mrs Sakuma! There's also some cake in the fridge – will you put some out for Mitsuri?'

'Yes, of course! Mitsuri dear, are you hungry? We have a chilled Bavarian cream, too.'

'Um, that's okay . . .'

Of course, Mrs Nosé and Mrs Sakuma were perfectly suited to this space. It seemed natural to them that there were giant photos of Shiba. Once again Mitsuri felt the depth of his fan club's love for him.

'Well, anyway, I wanted to let you know that you were all a huge help today. You really saved us. Also, I just spoke with the manager, and he's on his way here now. He said to be sure to share his gratitude.'

Mitsuri explained that the brothers had gone home to deliver Christmas gifts to their sister, only to find that she had swapped places with them. Mrs Nosé and Mrs Sakuma nodded in satisfaction.

'He thinks of his sister, of course! Isn't that just like our Mitsuhiko?'

'I just knew it would be something like that!'

Mitsuri was drawn into conversation with the ladies. Mostly, they subjected her to a series of complaints about people lurking around the building trying to find out if this was where Shiba lived – the Ladies' Association would lay down their lives to protect their Mitsuhiko's privacy, of course, but people kept coming, no matter what they did, drawn to his charm like moths to the flame. It was clearly because he was such a fine and virtuous man, but it caused a lot of trouble.

After the topic had been more or less exhausted, the ladies seemed to subside. 'I should go home and get dinner ready.' 'And my husband's dialysis treatment should be over by now, I'd better go pick him up.' Making their respective excuses, the two of them departed.

'Ah, just amazing, as always . . .'

They were all about the same age as Mitsuri's mother, but the Golden Villa ladies had a certain formidable quality. When she asked them about it, a chorus of voices in reply claimed they were getting stronger every day thanks to Shiba's presence. *I ought to start a Shiba Health System,* Mitsuri thought. *A revolutionary new system where one simply drinks a cup of tea with Shiba and is thereby rejuvenated. Wouldn't that be something! I really want to do that.*

Mitsuri washed the coffee cups and dishes, amusing herself with such idle thoughts, when there was a faint noise, and the door to the next room opened. Jewel's face quietly emerged.

'Oh! You're up? How are you feeling?'

'Um . . . a lot better, I think.'

'You had a very high fever, so rest a little while longer. Do you want something to drink? There are also fruit jellies and ice pops.'

'Uh . . . mm. If you have an energy drink, I could have that.'

'We do! You go lie down, and I'll bring you one.'

Carrying one of the drinks that Ukulele had given her, Mitsuri entered the back room. There was an expensive-looking sofa and table, and fancy name-brand hi-fi speakers were installed in the corners and ceiling of the room. This would surely be a great place to sit back and watch a movie. But of course, all the walls were heavily decorated with portraits and photos of Shiba, so it would be difficult to focus on the film, thought Mitsuri with a wry smile.

'It's incredible isn't it, this room?'

Jewel, who was reclining on the ivory sofa, nodded and looked around the room.

'It really is incredible. The people from before – they said they were Mitsu's fan club?'

'Right, right, the fan club. They can be a little intense.'

Mitsuri thought she'd surely be surprised, but Jewel just said, 'It's always the same. It was like that when he was in high school, but I just realised it still happens now.'

Mitsuri gasped in disbelief.

'His high-school fan club had very strict rules. For example, each member could only write Mitsu two letters per month. And you had to write your member number on the letter. That sort of thing. We still get lots of New Year's cards with numbers.'

Jewel giggled, but Mitsuri was astonished. A high-school student with a fan club . . .? So had the whole charm thing started in his teens? She wished she could have been there to see it.

'Oh, that's right,' Mitsuri said with a start, 'I almost forgot your drink. Take this for now, but drink it slowly.'

She handed a bottle to Jewel, who had settled herself snugly back into the sofa again. She was as lovely as Snow White or Sleeping Beauty. When she lifted the bottle to drink, her slender throat was exposed, and that too was beautiful. If her brother had a high-school fan club, it wouldn't be much of a stretch to imagine that this girl had one of her own, Mitsuri thought.

'Oh, speaking of home . . .' Mitsuri remembered to ask, 'They said you came all the way here without telling your parents or brothers?' Jewel suddenly became very still.

'The manager said he and Tsugi went home to bring you their Christmas presents. If you had only told them, you wouldn't have missed each other.'

'What, really?' Jewel lowered the plastic bottle. 'They came home for me?'

'Why didn't you tell anyone? It must have been a hard trip, all the way from Miyazaki to here.'

'My friend was going to a concert in Hakata, so she said her parents could drive me that far.'

'Hmm. Still, why not tell someone? You know I'm not angry or anything, right? I just have a kid who's about the same age as you, so I'm curious. He's in eleventh grade.'

Mitsuri smiled as she said this, and Jewel murmured, 'One below me.' She thought for a few moments, and then asked, 'Um, your child. Does he have a plan for his future?'

'Who, Kōsei? Not at all!'

Mitsuri chuckled, picturing her son lost in the video game with his friends when she was leaving earlier, but then she saw the earnest look on Jewel's face, and added more seriously, 'Our son still doesn't know what he wants to do.'

'He doesn't? But he'll have to think about it at some point soon, won't he? Like a year from now, for instance.'

'Well, perhaps. But I don't think you can really set a deadline for that kind of thing, can you? I mean, he might discover it when he's in college, or else after he graduates when he starts working. Look at me. I'm doing exactly what I want to do, but I've only really felt that way for a few years now. If that's how it is for me, it wouldn't be very fair to tell my own child that he has to make up his mind immediately, right at this moment, now, would it?'

Mitsuri laughed, then added to Jewel, who was giving her a doubtful look, 'Of course it would worry me to see him stumbling blindly through life, searching for fulfilment. At some point he'll have to set aside his dreams and learn to live life as a mature, independent human being. But I believe there will come a time when he has a clear sense of what he wants to do. Or that's my hope, anyway.'

Jewel looked down at the bottle she had clasped between her hands. 'Mothers all say the same things,' she murmured in a small voice. 'My parents said that, too. But I don't have the slightest idea. My brothers all found what they wanted to do and left. But I can't. I'm worried I'll spend the rest of my life this way, living with my parents, chopping firewood . . .'

Mitsuri knew all about the vague anxieties of youth. She had been listening with sympathy to Jewel – but had she heard the last part correctly? Now, in this day and age, had she really said she was chopping firewood?

'It's not that I don't like life in the mountains. My parents love it, too. But I also really want to see what it's like to live in the city, with electricity and everything, so I don't know what to do.'

What was this! Mitsuri had heard that their house was set far back into the mountains of Miyazaki, but was it really that primitive there? She had a feeling this would be the wrong time to verify that with Jewel.

'Anyway, I wanted to talk to my brothers about it. The oldest one and the youngest one are overseas, so I thought I'd visit the two here in Mojikō.'

'Yes, yes, I see.'

Mitsuri had said she was going to make the Shiba brothers her life's work, but now their story was moving at such a breakneck speed that she couldn't keep up! What to do? Now was the time to act like an adult and offer Jewel some sage advice, but it was too much. Mitsuri had to restrain herself from asking the girl to break it into instalments.

'Well, I think I understand, more or less. Your brothers will be back soon, so you can take your time and ask them for advice. That will be good. And of course, I'll talk to them, too.'

Jewel gave a smile of relief, and Mitsuri smiled back at her.

Shiba and Tsugi returned after sundown.

'Sorry! And thank you, Mitsuri.'

With a brotherly protectiveness that Mitsuri hadn't seen before, the two turned their stern attention to Jewel, who was reclining on the sofa.

'Listen, now. We were at our wit's end searching for you.'

'I'm sorry . . .' Jewel hung her head and the two of them both sighed.

'Do you know how worried we were? This had better not happen again,' said Tsugi.

'I won't do it again,' Jewel said with resolve. 'I under-stand that I caused a lot of trouble for everyone.'

Shiba's expression softened. 'Well, obviously, you had your reasons, right? And we'll talk about all of that, but, uh – why is Mr Kiriyama here?'

At some point, Kiriyama seemed to have joined the four of them in the meeting room. 'Clearly, I've come at a difficult time. Forgive me.' He bowed his head in apology. 'A friend gave me some delicious duck meat, and I thought I'd bring it here, to thank you all for everything you've done for me.'

Kiriyama had come on the train from Ōita with a large cooler bag. At this point, he had stayed at Shiba's place so often it had become a regular part of their friendship, so Mitsuri didn't think it would be a problem and had let him in.

'Hey hey, Yoshirō!' Tsugi said gleefully. 'You remembered that duck was my favourite, didn't you?'

Kiriyama smiled affably. 'I brought a lot of green onions and grilled tofu, too. We can make a duck hotpot. I asked your sister, and apparently she likes duck, too. Also, I think the green onions might be good for her cold.'

'Ah, that reminds me,' Shiba said. 'How are you doing, Jewel? Your colour seems good.'

The trip to the clinic and the medication seemed to have helped. Jewel's fever had dissipated completely. She had a lingering cough, but according to Mrs Sakuma it wouldn't be a problem, as long as the room stayed humid and the girl continued to rest.

'Good, good. But deepest thanks to all of you. I'm in your debt, really.'

'Manager, the fridge is about to burst, it's so full,' Mitsuri piped up. 'Somehow the news got out that your little sister was convalescing here, and it spread like wildfire. We received piles of sympathy gifts on top of the Christmas gifts, and we're getting a little snowed under.'

It wasn't just the women in the Golden Villa apartments, but also the building's men and a number of other area residents who all joined forces and put together a care package. Fruits and jellies, puddings and more. It was far too much to fit in the one fridge, so extra items had been temporarily distributed to the households of the Ladies' Association members.

'Is that so? I guess it was a lot of trouble for everyone, wasn't it? Now, what's this?'

Shiba had noticed a plate sitting on the sofa end-table.

On the plate was a cookie shaped like a bear wearing a Santa Claus hat. The bear was adorable, carefully coloured with sugar icing, and a mischievous expression on its face. 'That one's cute,' Shiba said, 'Which store did it come from?'

'It's handmade,' Mitsuri replied. 'You see, there's this girl who comes to buy sweets on Tuesday evenings.'

'Ah, you mean Azusa?' Tsugi said.

'Right. She said that a friend of hers who had moved to Nagasaki had come to visit. So apparently the two of them made cookies.'

The girls had brought one to the store for the manager and Tsugi, but when they learned that Jewel was here they said they wanted her to have it instead.

'It was so cute I couldn't eat it. So I was just looking at it.'

'Wow. She did say she wanted to be the Tenderness pâtissière. It's impressive.'

The two brothers peered at the cookie in the dish, all gentle smiles. Watching them, Jewel said, 'My brothers are awesome.' You could tell she meant it with all her heart. 'When everyone here found out I was their younger sister, they all took such good care of me. They said they were so grateful to my brothers, they wanted to do all these things for me. It made me really happy. That everyone likes you both so much.'

Jewel sighed.

'You found what you loved and left home, and now everyone loves you, too. Obviously, you're both awesome. I can't do that. I can't do anything.'

At the sound of that lonely voice, her two brothers exchanged glances. Then they sat down next to her, softly stroking her head.

'Mother was telling us you've been worrying about your life to come,' said Tsugi. 'I'm sorry we arrived late.'

'Worrying a little is okay,' Shiba added. 'It's even important, as long as you don't get too discouraged. We've both lost our bearings many times along the way, and here we are.'

'Really? But I don't have the slightest idea what I want next. What should I do?'

Mitsuri glanced at Kiriyama, and the two of them quietly returned to the main meeting room. Jewel deserved some time alone with her brothers.

'Still, it's a wonder that their sister is that cute,' Kiriyama said, sinking into the sofa with a sigh. 'Isn't that in itself an exceptional quality?'

Mitsuri sat down opposite him and nodded. That kind of beauty was certainly an asset. 'I feel as though if I don't create a storyline right now, I'm going to explode. You know what I mean? How much valuable information do you think I've acquired, just in this one day? Both Phero-Manager and Big Brother Furball are in desperate need of updates.'

'Ha ha! I'm looking forward to them.'

'Right, shall we make some coffee? The story of those three will be a long one.'

Mrs Nosé had told her to help herself to anything in the room, so Mitsuri brewed coffee for herself and Kiriyama, and they slowly drank it together. When her absent-minded gaze happened to meet the gaze of one of the panel-portrait Shibas, Mitsuri gave a wry smile. 'The love is so thick in this room you'd think a stalker or someone had built it, wouldn't you? It makes me wonder if they watch video slideshows of the store manager in the projection room next door.'

'They might. Mr Shiba seems to be fairly comfortable in front of the camera.'

'Maybe we should develop a line of products to sell at the store. Shiba keychains?'

'Oh, I think those would sell. You should do Tsugi, too. He's also fairly popular.' Kiriyama chuckled to himself as if he had just remembered something, and Mitsuri looked at him questioningly.

'Sometimes Tsugi lets me stay at his place, too,' he said. 'It feels like a secret men's hideout, with all sorts of people coming and going. I was there recently, and in the middle of the night, a guy comes in. He's a professional chef, and he's carrying wine and a huge hunk of dry-aged beef. Tsugi was out cold, snoring, but the guy just starts cooking in the kitchen on his own, without asking anyone. As if it were his own kitchen. Then he goes over to Tsugi, who's still sleeping, shakes him awake, and says "Eat while it's hot!" He gave me some, too, and it was really delicious. But I still haven't the faintest idea who he was.'

'Wait, Kiriyama,' cried Mitsuri, 'Don't tell me all that now! It's too much – I don't want to miss any of it, but I can't possibly process any more material at the moment.' Jewel's entrance on the scene today had been so spectacular, she felt she needed to stick to the essentials.

Kiriyama looked around the room. 'They're interesting people, aren't they?' he said to Mitsuri. Piles of gifts had been placed here and there throughout the room, and a faint fragrance still emanated from the roses in front of them. Inspecting the gold lettering on the flowers, Kiriyama continued. 'They're loved and needed by all these people. It's hard to put into words, but they have a strange charm.'

Kiriyama paused. 'I'm so lucky to have met them,' he said sincerely. Mitsuri looked at his kind face and felt a heartwarming glow spread through her. Then suddenly she realised something.

Starting with Kiriyama, the lives of almost all the people surrounding the brothers had run through the convenience store, which was where they had met. Some were regulars, others just passing through. There was something special there – what Shiba had called 'joys and sorrows'. Perhaps that was what bound them all together. Mitsuri too, had met them the same way – through the convenience store – and thinking about that, she was deeply moved.

'Oh. Are these the presents for Jewel from the two of them?' Kiriyama had noticed a couple of parcels lying on the floor next to the couch and lifted one up.

'Hm? Oh, they might be. They weren't there before.'

'Oh, this one's from the manager. Here, take a look.'

A card had been inserted under a broad ribbon, and they could see 'From Mitsuhiko' written in Shiba's beautiful, flowing hand. What had Shiba got for his little sister? Mitsuri wanted to know, and as usual, the curious devil on her shoulder was getting the better of her.

'Aha, so that means this one must be from Tsugi. And what would he give to a teenage girl? Hmm . . .'

Mitsuri picked up the second package, and was rendered speechless by what she saw.

The second card, nearly illegible, read: 'From Nihiko.'

'H . . . hey, Kiriyama. Can you read this?

'Huh? What's that? Oh, um . . . Nise . . . ko? Niseko?'

In Tsugi's rough scrawl, the 'hi' (ヒ) in his nickname 'Nihiko' was indistinguishable from the 'se' (セ) in 'Niseko'. And the latter was a name she knew all too well.

'Impossible!' Mitsuri said slowly in wonder. 'Could the mysterious counsellor Niseko be . . .?'

'Sorry, sorry, you two! it's time for some duck hotpot!' The door to the screening room swung violently open, and Tsugi emerged, howling pitifully, 'I'm so hungry! With all the commotion over our vanishing Jewel, I haven't eaten since this morning. Let's have a duck hotpot. A duck hotpot! Mitsuri, will you join us?'

'What? But, Jewel's condition . . .?' asked Kiriyama.

'They say green onions help you heal. Anyway, that one, she gets sick at the drop of a hat. She's susceptible to cold, so she needs a *haramaki* to wrap her tummy, but she takes it off when she goes outside so it doesn't cramp her style. She did the same thing this time, and – ouch!'

A cushion came flying through the air – thrown by Jewel, no doubt – and struck Tsugi with a thump on the side of his head. Then a voice yelled loudly, 'Don't say that, Tsugi, you dummy!'

'Huh? I guess she's feeling stronger. Well, I'd like to thank everyone, one by one, but first, let's all have a nice duck hotpot. Mitsuri, will you call Kōsei?'

Epilogue

I like the time just before the end of the night shift. The morning sun appears in the spaces between buildings, gentle but steady, tinting the sky red-violet. When I gaze out at the view from inside the store, I feel like I'm crossing the threshold from the old day to the new one.

I like seeing the faces of my customers, too, during that interval between days. Whether they're heading off to work, or home to sleep, there's a soft, undefined look to those faces as they emerge from the night. It feels like there's something delicate and precious behind them, that you can just barely glimpse.

'Hard day today? Get some rest.'

'Good morning! Welcome to Tenderness!'

The young man buying a can of beer and a few snacks looks tired, perhaps because he's coming off a late shift at work, like me. I speak gently to him, so as not to rile him up before he goes to sleep.

The woman with her hair curled slightly too tight is probably hoping it will keep until evening, so I serve her briskly and add a little extra sweetness to my voice to bolster her for the long workday ahead of her.

'Thank you. Please take care.'

I bag the items, the customers pay the bill, and I hand them their goods. Then I say a final few heartfelt words. They say the finishing touch in cooking is always love, and I believe the same thing is true for serving customers. I always try to remember to smile with love at the person standing before me.

I was seeing off a few customers after serving them, when I heard a sullen voice behind me. 'Try not to overdo it this morning, sir. It's unnecessary.'

I turned around. Hirose, a part-time worker here, was scowling at me.

'Oh? What was that? Unnecessary?'

'I say it every morning, don't I?' he retorted. 'If you keep this up, they'll have the police after you.'

Hirose is in his third year of college. He's a good kid who works hard during his shifts and does whatever anyone asks, but he's always a little cool with me. He says that I overdo it with the customers, that I lay on the charm too thick.

'You know I don't do it on purpose,' I say.

'Let's just go over your actions step by step, shall we? You hand over the change with both hands, you take the customer's hand in your own, you smile and whisper, "Good night, sweet dreams." Whoops! Did you catch it? Anything extra there?'

Hirose prances around, twisting his body this way and that, concluding by licking his lips lasciviously and shooting me a come-hither look.

'That's terrible.'

'Exactly. It's terrible.'

'That's not how I smile. You make me look like a serial killer!'

It's a terrible impersonation. It feels like a small dagger in my chest, so I gently place my hand there.

'You're not a serial killer, sir, you're a heartbreaker! That guy who was in here before, his face was bright red when he walked out of here. You think he'll have a restful night's sleep in that state? And that woman who looked like she worked in a fancy office – did you know she's only made up perfect like that on days when you have a shift? When you're off duty, she leaves off the make-up and puts her hair in a ponytail. Also, she skips the green juice and goes for a Red Viper energy drink instead.'

Hirose is usually quiet, except when he's complaining about me. Then he has a lot to say. He can be critical that way, but I don't think there's anything wrong with my customer service, so there's not much I can do about it. There's a whole world of convenience stores out there, but our customers choose to patronise this one. Our store helps them get ready to begin or end the day. I can't tell you how happy and grateful that makes me. I'm just expressing my gratitude with all the love that I can give.

'I don't know what to say about the Red Viper drink, but it's not good if that gentleman can't sleep at the end of his shift. I'll try to speak to him with a little more compassion.'

Hirose's shoulders sag, and he says, 'Argh . . .! You just don't get it! Listen, I think it would be good if the customer service were more impersonal. Convenience store clerks don't need to show personality. It's the kind of place where people just drop in by chance.'

Hirose was on the baseball team when he was in high school. He doesn't play anymore now, but he still keeps his hair cropped in a buzz cut. It's cute and gives him a very mischievous look. I'd never say that to him, though, because it would make him mad. His cheeks puff up like a child when he's angry, and I can't help but laugh.

'I think it's good for convenience-store clerks to have personality. And as far as I'm concerned, I want the place to be as comfortable as possible, precisely because it's a place where people just drop by,' I reply.

'Sir, you still don't understand,' he said. 'See, you lay on all this charm and flattery for no good reason, and then our store is swamped with customers who act like stalkers. Did you know my friends at school call this shop the Convenience Cabaret? They say you can get all the pleasures of a host club at the cost of a convenience store!'

'Huh! Well, that's the first time I've heard that name. But with so many cute . . . er, handsome staff like you working here, it stands to reason, don't you think?' I smile at him.

'This is not about me! It's all your doing. Please try to understand!'

Hirose is rubbing his head in agitation when the door chimes its melody to signal the arrival of a customer. A bearded man in a light green coverall ambles in. 'Welcome!' I call out, and our eyes meet. His hairy face broadens into a knowing smile. He probably thinks he's being discreet about it, but he keeps waving at me.

'That guy, he's definitely one of your stalkers! He's here all the time.'

Hirose says this quietly, without dropping his perfect customer-service smile. I just laugh.

Then, as if led by the man in the coveralls, customers start to trickle in, one by one. Just a little while longer until the night shift is over. To each customer, I give a fond farewell:

'Thank you! Please come again soon.'

And to you, for choosing Tenderness – all my love.